URGENT
STATE

OONA —
ENJOY THE JOURNEY.

[signature]

Acknowledgement

Who could be more important in this endeavor?

To my father on his 100th birthday!

URGENT STATE

••• ——— •••

One Route to Saving our Species

Larry Pratt

SMP Press   Lacey, WA. 98509

Publisher's Cataloging-in-Publication Data

Names: Pratt, Larry L., 1946- author.
Title: Urgent State : one route to saving our species / Larry Pratt.
Description: Lacey, WA : SMP Press, 2019. |
    Series : Urgent series ; book 1 | Summary:
    Presents a near future look at the possible
    outcomes of today's political, social, and
    financial divides, and a roadmap for accom-
    plishing the goal of saving our species.
Identifiers: LCCN 2018914258 | ISBN9780996385534(pbk.)
                | ISBN 9780996385541 (ebook)
Subjects: LCSH: Climate change mitigation -Fiction.
    | Economics -- Fiction. | Education -- Fiction.
    | Technology -- Fiction. | BISAC: FICTION /
    Science Fiction / General.
Classification: LCC PS3616.R38 U7 (print)
                | LCC PS3616.R38 (ebook) | DDC 813--dc23
LC record available at https://lccn.loc.gov/2018914258

Printed by Bookmasters :   www.bookmasters.com

Questions regarding the content, or ordering of this book should be addressed to:
    SMP Press   or: *urgentbooknotes@gmail.com*
    PO Box 3852
    Lacey, WA 98509-3852

Urgent State

Introduction

The general election of 2016 was a turning point for the world press. Generations of readers have, with few exceptions, been informed of important issues and scientific advances via the respectable media. Reliance on the press is no longer advisable.

Although not entirely of their own choosing, the reporters must follow and share stories about the chaotic leadership in many countries, particularly the United States. The chaos, the smoke 'n mirrors, ultimately compromises the credibility of the daily announcements. In addition, the news that is viewed as bad by the citizenry, is an anxiety producing product. It has been all too easy to mindlessly consume this irritating programming waiting for the salve, the happy stories we used to receive. The comfort will not be coming any time soon.

While watching this process change the behavior of my lovely wife it became obvious that the long-range view, and truly large problems, were being pushed under the literary table. The truth was still inconvenient, but not even referred to in the mainstream media. Do we have the luxury of putting those issues on hold while we chase the political wanna-be's around the small arenas of half-truths, total falsehoods, and unabashed corruption?

Our family discussion resulted in my pursuing this exercise in speculative fiction. My better-half invests her time in local politics and more pleasurable short-term pursuits. I thank her for the support in this endeavor. I also thank the reader for the continued feeding of my imagination.

URGENT STATE

ONE

● ━ ━ ●● ━ ━ ●● ● ━ ● ●

"I call it the largest massacre in history. To refer to an extinction event bestows on it an other than man-made honor. We now know man is the cause. Our scientists have proven that we face a factual issue. Massacre is the most accurate description." As usual, Stephen was succinct in presenting his position. His two friends would have ample time to reply.

The three people sitting around the oak table were very ordinary looking. The fact that the hand-rubbed table was trimmed and inlaid with exotic wood did speak to some expense. The fact that they were seated inside an executive jet spoke volumes. Their combined wealth exceeded that of most countries.

These American businesspeople were the primary executives in their foundations. They were responsible for giving away more money than the next dozen of their peers. Active philanthropists earn a great degree of public celebrity. Every person in the airplane cabin was so well known that they were often identified by only their first names: indicative of rock-star celebrity status.

The car-full of assistants that normally followed all

1

three was pared down to one aide each, and those individuals were camped outside the airplane, yet inside the hanger doors. The pilots of the three planes that brought the philanthropists to this meeting knew enough to vacate their aircraft, also staying out of sight of the general public.

The sleek jet hosting the meeting had been configured to comfortably sleep six, although only the three leaders would be spending at least one night. They had previously concluded that their busy schedules would be interrupted for as long as was necessary and that they would not be bringing their spouses.

They all knew that each of these meetings was getting longer. More conversation yet, still, the upmost of confidentiality. It was quite unusual for no one to know exactly where these executives had landed but secrecy was mandatory. Instructions had been given to office staff in various cities around the country that personal business had called them away for a couple days.

The pilots had been vetted and sworn to secrecy. They would sleep on one of the other planes as would the aides. The host jet was isolated not only from view but from electronic surveillance. The complete set of avionics had been turned off lest the equipment brought along for the purpose of jamming of all radio frequencies cause some damage to the aircraft's built-in electronics. No one was to listen to this conversation. This was a very private meeting, the subject of which was highly controversial.

Sustainability was the issue. Not the day-to-day definition that the usual active environmentalists talked about. Not recycling or clean energy or coal trains. This third annual meeting was a follow-up on their discussions about our ability as a species to sustain ourselves on this planet. Global survival might be a better term.

Originally, the concept had been simple. The rate at which man was undoing the very conditions that provided for human life was criminal. Regardless of which scientists published data or who interpreted and reported on those facts, the conclusions were the same. At some point in time, if left unchecked, we could not live on our earth. One of our future generations would be the last.

What that generation inherited in the form of wealth or knowledge would be moot. There would be no reason to transact business and no reason to try to educate others. An unimaginable chaos would be the order of the day and not enough room (or reason) for prisons: let alone schools, offices, churches etc.

In order to slow down that gradual degradation and give humanity a chance to correct a few things, something needed to be done. Yet it was obvious that nothing could be achieved in time, through normal channels. The process of allowing democracy to help us was no longer viable: too slow. Big money had such a hold on the lawmakers that the dollar had the loudest voice at the table, and bigger profits were the total conversation.

Never mind that all logic revealed an end in sight. Business was in an autopilot mode and no mere mortal would change that: at least no visible mortal. It was for this reason that the meeting in the jet was held with maximum secrecy. The course of action chosen by this team was to be invisible, working within the confines of the law whenever possible. The three wealthy executives agreed on the understanding that the earth needed more time. Making it happen was another matter.

Whether they admit it or not, all ultra-wealthy people contribute more than their fare share to climate change. Environmental degradation is a by-product of big-business and the rich own hundreds of businesses. This fact presented a moral dilemma for the executives. The prominent conundrum though, was in the field of law. They were about to organize an endeavor that, if successful, will build success on a foundation of the rather flimsy adherence to many laws.

Their first meeting had been short. What started as a conversation over concerns on the large end of the scale, evolved into a philosophical debate. Each lived and worked in the United States. Yet all agreed that this country had not been acting like a democracy lately, Too many important decisions, whether made by the Supreme Court or the White House, were leaning far right.

Steven and friends had all studied the history of politics. During their talks they had recited chapter & verse of the rise and fall of political parties during that short history. However, the current situation was unique.

There had been a systematic weakening of the checks and balances built into the democratic process. The process was gradual. It had taken two decades and numerous presidential election swings to affect substantial change. One small decision by a committee, or a bit more gerrymandering led farther to the right. That patient approach had paid off: the popular vote in the national election did not dictate the winner.

Too many congressional elections were also not decided fairly. More legislation that degraded basic government came with each victory of this insidious game-plan. Still, the philanthropists were hesitant to try to use their wealth to help level the playing field. Pouring more money into the cauldron only results in a bigger pot of witches-brew.

They elected to not disturb the forces already at work on local and national issues. The adversarial political parties had such secure foundations, that moving their thinking, yet alone their game-plan, would require significant time. Money notwithstanding, the group needed to address the larger concerns, the more world-wide in scope. They also wanted to hurry.

At last year's meeting, they were brainstorming a list of 10 items which was soon was prioritized down to six. Survival of our species is actually one large complex problem: too large and too complex. Understanding and talking about such an issue is simplified by first looking at manageable parts of the whole   Each delegate was assigned two sub-topics to study for a year. The executives had compared notes on the six topics, and given a brief summary of their research. They again prioritized each and then dove into the realm of possibilities. Even with their extreme wealth they did admit the difficulty, and expense, needed in order to affect change within any one area. The undertaking began to look like a chess game.

* Climate Change   * Genocide
* Deforestation   * Income Inequality
* Demise of Democracy   * Water Issues

In alpha order these half-dozen issues were all large. In varying degrees, the importance ranged from the end of our way-of-life, to the end of our lives. Where to start to address this puzzle: that was the question. It was obvious that our climate, humanity, environment and governance were all interconnected. Because of the timing, and complexity, they agreed that each topic be treated as an independent, problem. From that perspective, more than one project may appear doable.

The easiest item on the list, they again agreed, was the demise of democracy. Business influence in law and rule-making was, after all, something these influential people understood. Naturally, there would not be a frontal attack on the system as it is, but rather a slow invisible encroachment from the fringes. To accomplish this, they needed to mobilize the people: the masses.

There were millions of average citizens out there waiting for a little guidance. Most were aware that they were being led (more like kicked) down some path that just was not right for them. Sure, business got richer but where was the worker's share? They used to have a middle class that worked to get ahead, got ahead, and retired to a rocking chair while the kids filled the vacant spot on the manufacturing floor. Where did it go?

Some of these changes needed to be undone. Privatization of public services had been quietly implemented. Just as quietly the philanthropists intended to change these services back. They had begun at the state level. During the previous few months, these three executives had met with the governors of five states. Those politicians represented one-fifth of the nation's population. Two additional governors had been approached but decided they could not join the others. To lead would place these young politicians in a very vulnerable position. It was too early to risk the office.

Each participating state was now in the throes of declaring a State of Emergency and each was about to undergo a serious fiscal reorganization to fund and solve their financial shortfall of education. It had been quite a sales job to convince the state leaders of the need to announce a declaration of emergency.

Usual congressional timing and decision making would just take too long. The freedom delivered through emergency declarations would be invaluable and the only speedy option. The fact that this freedom was gained on the shoulders of education would provide them more support from the majority of the public. The parents knew their public schools and would help carry the message. Those adults not familiar with today's education system would be shocked at the stories confirming:
-- Overcrowded classrooms
-- Less creative curriculum
-- Active shooter drills
-- Students who overdose
-- Repetitive high-stakes testing
-- Feeding and clothing students

On the front page, the public support would drown out all political condemnation. During this confusion, and inside numerous closed-door sessions, government staff would finalize the majority of legal work required to sustain this attack. The philanthropists knew that a national state of emergency was on the horizon. Those forces expected to be marshaled against the state's emergencies would be drastically impacted by the President's message to the nation.

The United States will be taking the first steps on the issues of income inequality and climate change. Only a select few should be aware of these actions, or the expected direction of seemingly tangential forces. The few were highly placed, or highly influential. Many of them were at this briefing on the jet.

One of these chosen few was a woman named Marina Whitehorse. A native American who had served the foundation funded by one of the philanthropists for many years. Her position had been upper management, but just below board level. Not a complete unknown, but a far cry from a public figure. She was included in this group and wholeheartedly agreed with the mission.

Because of her affinity for the planet, she had been closely following the erosion of the environment and our way of life. She read the reports and saw the impact of future sea level rise and species extinction. Deforestation was a problem faced by her ancestors and the future impacts loomed large in her mind. Her vision of the unforeseen consequences of man's actions was acute and she was very alarmed at what she saw.

As Marina thought through the steps this bold plan would require, she thought of seven future generations: just as her native tradition demands. There was no guarantee we had seven generations left. "The response to this massive attack on our land must be bold and earnest", she thought. Her corner office at the foundation headquarters was the ideal location from which to start this mission.

When Marina was growing up on the reservation she sat with her parents and the elders whenever she wanted. The open discussions about politics and leadership resonated with her at a very early age. She met the subjects of these conversations and learned the lessons the adults had been teaching. These attributes helped smooth the path into adulthood.

In her wanderings throughout the various nations within the United States, she became acquainted with most leaders and more politicians. Foundation business presented opportunity for further people watching. She had observed that too many leaders had been insulated by their social status. These were not the visionaries required for the task at hand. Her experience with this personality type had taught her to expect help, but from a distance.

She was looking for a more hands-on type. An individual not frightened by a little culture clash yet capable of meeting with the wealthy. Her thoughts traveled to the BIA and its upper management. Marina knew that agency had one employee dedicated to his work at the Bureau of Indian Affairs and honorable in his intentions.

Her intention was to steal him.

TWO

— •• • ••• — — — — — •

It is not unheard of for a governor to declare a State of Emergency. Often times a weather episode, such as a hurricane or blizzard, creates an interruption in the normal operations of the state and its citizens resulting in an emergency declaration. All states have amended their laws to allow for such an action. The top executive may even call out the National Guard in that state to help in restoring order or providing manpower for other emergencies.

Such a decree of emergency was the subject of the phone calls that morning, but no natural disaster had occurred. The group of five governors had been contacted, one at a time, about a private consultation. Each knew the identity of the major philanthropist that had initiated the call and each politician knew enough to respond positively to such major donors. A meeting was scheduled: a very private meeting naturally.

It was difficult, but not impossible, for a state leader to drop out of sight for an afternoon. Senior staff members had been trained not to ask too many questions. Those inside the upper echelon needed what is commonly referred to as deniability: what they didn't know wouldn't hurt them. What was not known to any one staff person, was that four other top state officials were also scheduling such meetings.

In order to not compromise any of these politicians, they were met with individually, at different locations: all airports. It took a week to coordinate schedules with these five. Security was tight, and the conversations were confidential. Each governor had blocked out more time than was needed to talk business. This resulted in a brief cocktail hour during which the executives talked sports, international issues, finance, the usual small-talk topics, then business.

As soon as each meeting ended and in the secure confines of their limousines, the governors each placed a call to his or her respective Attorney General. On the quiet, they needed to get a complete understanding of the laws surrounding a State of Emergency.

Perhaps the rules could be used as written, perhaps they needed some creative interpretation. The governor wanted confirmation that the soon to be declared financial emergency would stand. This was the beginning of a trend towards independence from the Wall Street congress. This was touchy business.

During the middle of the second decade of the 2000's there were many states that were in financial crisis. The nation was slowly recovering from a serious recession (almost a depression) and the unemployment numbers were not rosy. In fact, these statistics were being calculated without regard to those that were no longer looking for work. Hence, the unemployment numbers were also wrong.

Through a series of laws and unfunded mandates and with the help of some high-powered lobbying, the federal government was sharing less and less revenue with the states. One of the services hit hardest by the dwindling of resources was education. It is easier to trim a few percentage points from education than other departments, because of how funding is controlled in various budgets. This applies to both the state and federal budget – it is less complicated to take it from the schools.

Within each state, the public-school districts and smaller political sub-divisions receive money for education as the budget allows. The charter and/or constitution of 50 different states describe 50 different obligations the lawmakers have with respect to providing an education for their citizens. Interestingly, many states have language in their founding documents that clearly provides for a quality education for all citizens.

Possibly those framing the documents mentioned children as opposed to citizens, and possibly the intent was to include immigrants too. Regardless, the founding fathers wanted their people to be educated. Fast forward to the 21st century and many states have trimmed the budget for education so much that the quality of public education that the students receive is in question.

One closely watched indicator of educational health within the states, is the support for higher education. Virtually all primary and secondary public education is free to the citizen. However, the students pay to go to college. The amount paid to receive this higher education depends on the financial support the government gives a particular college or university.

The tuition paid to the university by the student represents the cost of the education that is not paid by the state. There is no profit motive in operating a state institution. The responsibility of the administration is to set prices that just cover the costs. What the legislature does not pay for, the student does. This simple equation makes it easy to analyze the effectiveness of education funding: what does tuition cover?

In 1990, 25% of higher education costs of state supported schools in the United States was paid for by tuition. In 2018 it was 50% - half. Averages notwithstanding, in 2018 there were 25 states in which the tuition paid for at least half of the cost of college. The students paid more than the government. In those cases, how does one define a state system? Has public education been underfunded to a similar degree in those cases?

More than one state has been sued (successfully) for this inferior, mandated service. The results have been court decisions demanding better funding for public education. Not just lower court decisions, but declarations from the State Supreme Courts to fix this issue which was in clear violation of the State Constitution. The recent financial crisis had caused these cases to sit idle. By declaring a State of Emergency, the governor may be able to impose an emergency tax, or rearrange some internal funding, and dedicate the new funds to education.

Within the charter documents of most states is language stipulating that the legislature must approve all appropriations. The normal change to any budget item, therefore, is quite time-consuming. The legal staffs at the disposal of the chosen governors were wrestling with a different set of laws. The big question asked whether the governor was within his/her rights to redirect appropriated funds to budget areas found to be funded in violation of the constitution.

To tax those of low wealth would not generate the revenue needed. The emergency tax would be paid by those that made the most money. A tax based on a simple percentage of gross income, paid by both individuals and corporations. The emergency declaration would call for little, if any, loop-hole tax avoidance. The need to get funds to every classroom in the state should outweigh any sweet deal worked out through the lobbying process. Furthermore, in writing the laws and the rules, there would be only closed-door sessions.

An emergency regulation needed to be written and implemented as quickly as possible. The traditional lobbying process does not lend itself to those rapid, or equitable, ends. The leaders in the budgeting office would form a committee consisting of willing participants from both parties. Then everyone would retire to an expense-free retreat and emerge with a workable plan.

No outside influence would be allowed. Only personal phone calls permitted and with minimum contact at that. Attention would be paid to the allocation of this new income and putting it to use creating new and more jobs. As an example, the new rules should provide for a gathering of like-minded educators from within the state to design any and all state-wide tests. Any K-12 proficiency tests would be made by state personnel.

Likewise, the GRE: graduate records exam. No state money would be spent for any student to take any test not made, administered and graded within the state. To confirm their independence from federal regulations, these educator/politicians would also mandate that schools supported by this new money follow new curriculum guidelines. There had been a current of religious, non-diverse, anti-Semitic philosophy that was gathering power in various education circles. All progressive educators predicted problems. All progressive educators would exclude any such leanings from the new education rules.

Each of the five states had unique circumstances. Infrastructure and fixing potholes are bigger priorities in the North, while water quality and supply can be a serious issue in the West. The top politicians began to gather their top people. Every budget item would be discussed. The governors would find the money.

The leaders in one state were investigating the financial impact of introducing a freeze on all corporate tax relief arrangements. To attract large businesses to relocate, it is not uncommon for states to arrange for tax relief for a few years. In certain economic situations, this accumulated deficit can become substantial. An emergency declaration might allow the state to reintroduce taxes on such companies.

The governors knew that pushback from any change

would be time consuming. The reaction to the emergency itself would be ongoing, and expensive. All legal avenues needed to be discussed. All decisions would require language easily understood by the public.

It was obvious that a detailed course of action was the only way to accomplish what they deemed necessary in the short time they knew they had. The governors were getting geared for a huge fight.

THREE

In the history of modern politics, the President has had a place to retreat. Only recently such places as Hyannis Port, Kennebunkport, Walker's Point, Camp David have been often mentioned in the news. While there, the inhabitants are under less scrutiny from the media and certainly less formality than when inside the White House. Such is the case with Gibson County, Tennessee.

The President has family history there. His people have a long tenure in Tennessee. A much longer residential tradition than the duration of the liberal political ideals they now support. No one remembered if the family had ever owned slaves. Everyone remembered that Sean Crockett was second generation turncoat. Yet the family was still well-loved here. The now-liberal President is also well-known, having worked his way up from senator.

The Crockett family is not truly wealthy but does own a lot of land in the Tennessee hills. Some of the more interesting features of these holdings are underground. Mines and caves dot the area and all Crockett kids, as they grew up, learned where the most wondrous adventures took place. Today they call it spelunking, or cave exploration. To a youngster it is another planet, an alien world. One particular advantage in such surroundings is isolation.

When the flashlight is switched off, there is not only a lack of visibility but total silence. While only a mile or so away as the crow flies, a passing train cannot be heard when the listener is inside a tunnel. The Crystal Mine was no exception.

Decades ago some enterprising miners had leased the land from the Crockett family and tried their hand at harvesting crystals. While trespassing one day they had stumbled upon this supposed mother lode and tried to negotiate their way into fame and fortune. It had never been profitable, and that effort had lasted only a few years.

The explorers had found investors, started digging and even laid some tracks to carry the riches. However, the money ran out before any real profit was made and they beat a hasty retreat from the heavily wooded hills of Tennessee. Since then all local children have played and dreamed inside that two-mile shaft and labyrinth of offshoot tunnels. Soon there would be a different group in there.

The philanthropist had arrived by helicopter and under the radar, just as the President's Marine One helicopter had when it approached the compound from the other direction. The private chopper carefully set down in a well-marked, small clearing in the forest. Two passengers disembarked and walked over to a waiting train that consisted of one enclosed car behind the small donkey engine. A mile away, an entourage slipped out of the big Marine bird and briskly stepped over to the President's summer retreat. At that moment only four people knew of the two groups.

The little electric powered engine pulled the lone train car at not more than two miles per hour. It was all about gearing, just like a ride at an amusement park. The philanthropist operated the train as written in the e-mail instructions received from the President, negotiating the one-mile trip into the tunnel. It took 15 minutes.

In that same span of time the President had said his hellos to the staff at the family home, had a schedule chat with his office and told the first lady that he was going for a stroll. Even in Gibson County he couldn't be alone, which is why he convinced the Secret Service to let him walk with his most trusted aide, Mark Madison. Mark was shorter than the Secret Service required but was more than physically fit. He could pass any physical and/or security exam the government would give him if he wanted to be an agent. He didn't, and they knew it. He was the Presidents man - period.

Fifteen minutes of easy walking bought them to a clearing. They noticed the visitor's helicopter, the entrance to a tunnel and a small shed. Mark had been there before. He headed over to the door of the rundown shack. Behind this door was a fancy electric golf cart – fully charged by the modern battery management station at the rear of the shed. They unplugged the gleaming cart and climbed in.

"Will you let me drive this time?" asked the President.

"All right, sir." said Madison. Off they drove, deep into the tunnel. The lights from the train car were obvious after they rounded the second turn of the dog leg. The headlights on the golf cart were seen at the same time by those on the train. Introductions were made at the base of the two-step stairway and the two aides sat in the golf cart and drove back to the first bend. From there they could see the entrance to the tunnel. They sat in silence – watching.

The President, in great shape due to his exercise routine, hopped up the stairs, took the controls and drove the quiet, electric train off onto one of the short sidings. This snaked them around two more gradual turns. When they stopped, they were completely out of sight and ear-shot of any human. Since it was early afternoon, they agreed on a short whiskey and got to work.

"Mister President, the reason . . ."

"Please, call me Sean." he interrupted.

"Very well, Sean. Please call me Henry. To continue – I want to thank you for agreeing to this meeting and assure you that the courtesy of giving you the story I am about to relate extends only to you. To confirm, my two partners, their aides and you are the only individuals on the planet that know this information.

You are an honorable man but more importantly, you care deeply about this country and its citizens. We are going to trust you, ask for your help, and do what we can to provide our unborn offspring a life. Politics and business aside, our sole agenda in this endeavor is to postpone the end of humanity. It's that simple."

The President was speechless. He had anticipated that the richest man on the continent wanted to meet with him to discuss some business deal, or an international trade scheme, as had happened in the past. But an end-of-time issue – who knew.

"You have my undivided attention for as long as it takes." President Crockett said.

"Our first meeting will be short in order to not arouse suspicion." was the reply. "But we will certainly meet again, and in more comfortable surroundings."

"Not an issue", he said "security is the issue. Please continue."

"We have already set in motion the unimaginable action of a governor out west declaring a State of Emergency. In fact, five of them will make such declarations within a short period of time. These will all be due to the fiscal crises these locations are under as a result of court decisions on unfunded education: the basic right of their constituents. Without normal legislative, sloth-like, might I say, processes, these leaders will form committees to write emergency tax laws that are fair yet thorough. Naturally, there will be nasty resistance from the conservatives."

"An understatement." Sean said.

Henry continued, "Part of these laws will result in more revenue. Other aspects will deal with responsibilities, such as ordering that only state employees compose all education exams in the state. Also, in the arena of job growth, provisions that favor employee-owned businesses when awarding state contracts. We even plan on language that encourages a state-owned financial institution.

"The five states in question are: California, Illinois, New York, Pennsylvania and North Carolina. Collectively they represent about 30% of the nation's population. Before these taxes can kick in and help, the shortfall will be big news. Each of these states will be declaring a crisis in education.

"At this point, you will have an opportunity, if you choose to use it, to also declare a national emergency, also in education and help these states. Your battle will be a public brouhaha, with a lot of talk about where the United States can come up with some money to help. The conservative controlled budget and appropriate committees are certain to gloat that they have you over the proverbial barrel.

"With a majority of the federal budget consisting of fixed, long-term line-items, where can you find the funds for your emergency? We suggest that you attack the problem through the defense department. Our accounting team has run the numbers and determined that if you audit the Department of Defense you will find the money. Pick a team of your own after the emergency is declared and make the unimaginable happen. Physically send them out there to follow the money. Finally do a real audit.

"If you need to, hide this audit within your declaration that all departments will be audited. Some loose change might surface in various locations, but the big dollars are in the Department of Defense. Since these are emergency conditions, there will be no lobbying, no special agendas (except yours) and no foot-dragging. Your people will find the money they need and at the same time discover the value of all the equipment left overseas. As you know, we have millions of tons of equipment that we never brought home. You will finally have an accurate lost/surplus inventory within the defense department report.

"As a bonus, you will get a valuation on the steel and the worth of the electronics and arms. Bring it all home and then we can implement the next phase of our plan. We will buy it from you."

Sean Crockett stood up. He liked to walk while thinking, and this idea was worth thinking about. His forefathers had been true conservatives. They were turning over in their graves because he was seriously thinking about this. But, he thought, the founding fathers had to be seriously thinking too.

This could help restore some of the balance their democracy used to have. Lately, business had too much influence on the running of the country and it had to stop, or at least slow down. The path the United States was on was unsustainable, but no one seemed able to change that course. Business only knew profits, and the rules and laws written with only a profit motive did not help all citizens. In fact, many had the opposite effect.

How could we continue to relax environmental regulations that had been passed after we learned the truth the hard way? Our world's food supply was threatened because the engineered crops we were using (and selling to the under-developed world) was not seed, only food. Nations were spending more and more of the dwindling budget to buy planting seed because the crop would not yield it. Poor neighbor relations, but business had no conscience.

It seemed to him the business community was like that alien species he saw in the movies once. They went to a planet, conquered it, and used up all the resources.

Then left and went to another planet leaving just death in their wake. What would happen when business had used up all the resources on our continent? Capitalism was already worming its way deep into China. India had billions of potential consumers. Africa was growing up. Then what? All under the threat, no – time bomb, of climate change.

It had recently been reported that a study commissioned by a big oil company in 1988 had concluded that the greenhouse gas effect on our planet would cause severe global warming. That study concluded, "However, the potential impacts are sufficiently serious for research to be directed more to the analysis of policy and energy options than to studies of what we will be facing exactly".

Crockett did not recall big oil emphasizing research in energy options. His primary recollection was that they buried this study and these rich companies paid for more scientific studies until they found one that announced results that downplayed global warming.

"Please continue" – he headed over to the small bar and grabbed the whiskey bottle.

"Thank you. I think the end of this drink will wrap up our first chat. OK – our next steps will take place after you leave office. Don't count on being elected again, but also don't worry about gainful employment. That's all I will say about that at this time.

"Deep in the heart of numerous labs we, that is our country, have researchers working on some great projects. The one of most interest right now to us is in the arena of super-conductivity. The art of moving electricity without losing much as it travels along the wire. As of today, one of the big limiting factors in sending our electricity supply all over the nation is that the farther it travels the greater the losses. We build lots of power plants where we can and route the miles of wires to the consumer. As you know, most of our power plants are dirty, coal-fired and old.

"It won't be announced for some time, but the first version of super-conductivity is in test mode at DARPA: the NASA controlled Defense Advanced Research Projects Agency. We, that is my group, are quietly funding it and when ready the technology will be ours. In anticipation of that great advancement, we will be building, in Wyoming, the largest power generation station on the planet. Modern storage capacity combined with wind and solar technology will enable us to cleanly deliver a massive amount of energy.

"Before too long we will be able to deliver electricity anywhere with minimal losses, thereby allowing this country to close the dirtiest power plants. It will no longer be necessary to keep erecting more power generating capacity near the population centers. The usual loss of jobs that comes with any plant closing will not be a problem. We will offer to relocate all employees to Wyoming and ask that they help us with this breakthrough technology

"Our dream is to have this new complex not only generate clean power but grab some carbon dioxide as it goes by and put it to good use. This is too technical to get into now, in fact I'm not sure I even understand it. However, we feel pretty strongly that without reducing the levels of green-house gasses we can't buy much time. We are going to throw everything we have at this.

"Our intention is to salvage and experiment with leftover military armament. We will make the steel with which to build the power plant that makes the electricity that travels through the wires on the towers we made. Call it a self-contained project - sort of a closed loop."

The President rose again: "All right, knowing that this is not a truly altruistic arrangement, what's in it for you?"

"Strangely enough Mister President, Sean, it is measured altruism. My group is prepared to spend a massive amount of money in an attempt to stay alive. If, and that's a big if, the human race survives the next 30 or 40 years we will own the super-conductivity technology and can sell it to the rest of the world. Those arrangements might put some money back in our pockets. If we don't survive, that money wouldn't do anyone any good in the end. Why not get it working?"

Still on his feet, glass empty, Crockett extended his arm. They shook hands. Neither said another word – there was no need. The President drove the donkey engine back to where the aides were waiting. The philanthropist waited until the little train was out of sight and then proceeded to drive the golf cart out of the Crystal Mine.

Initial conversation over.

"That went better than expected" Henry said to no one in particular.

FOUR

— • — — — — — ••• • — •• •

In a non-descript office out west, one member of the foundation's research team had been called upstairs. When Brian Knight returned to his desk, he summoned his assistant Kathryn to advise that he was being given a special assignment. Brian began cleaning out his desk. She moved into his former, vacant office the next day.

It was not unusual for the folks upstairs to send personnel into the field to gather data for a potential project. Philanthropy requires some hands-on visits to accurately evaluate the grant requests. Therefore, Brian's departure did not cause any immediate concern. Little did anyone know that he would never return.

In an effort to clean out his desk, Brian had nearly neglected the next step: to find a place to live, and work. His superiors had suggested a few options, at the north end of the county. Downtown Seattle was congested and not a great place from which to jet around. Brian knew he would be doing some traveling by private plane.

He looked at a few apartments and settled on an older farm house near the town of Snohomish. There was a small airfield nearby, and the Snohomish River ran through the quaint downtown. After unpacking a few necessities, he had a chance meeting with his neighbors. The husband had a little commute to get to his job at Boeing in Everett. She was teaching third grade at one of the local schools. Rural Snohomish was an open area. Not wide-open, but with as much land devoted to agriculture as housing. The nearest structure was across the street yet there were houses on both sides of him, each with a sizeable side yard. For security purposes, two dog runs would be ideal, but he only noticed one small poodle in the yard to the east. This was close enough. This breed was noisy and would sound-off at strangers. One morning he noticed hot air balloons quietly passing overhead, high enough to clear the tall fir and cedar trees. Brian told himself that he would feel comfortable living in this neighborhood.

In this part of the Northwest, the large employers attracted quite a few software types (Boeing Computer, Adobe and Microsoft) and a large group of blue-collar workers (US Navy, Boeing construction, forest products). Brian was clean-cut with a white smile and whiter skin, just like a mid-30's nerd but without glasses. He was stocky, a bit pale and in shape. Yes, he could pass for average in these energetic surroundings.

The foundation gave him three days to unpack, and then sent in their security team. His computers were set up, unobtrusive satellite antennas were installed, and the living space was outfitted with both jamming and eaves-dropping devices. He now had the fastest and most secure location in the town; maybe in the county. He was responsible for the only sub-rosa operation of the largest non-profit foundation on United States soil. It was time to get organized.

The elections in the year 2004 were the first held after the Citizens United decision. That was the Supreme Court ruling that foolishly says corporations are entitled to contribute to campaigns just like real people. Afterwards, the money just flooded into the conservative coffers. One highly financed election was the governor's race in Wisconsin.

After the votes had been counted, the newly elected governor in that state set about to disband, if not altogether eliminate, organized labor. There was an uproar. Many unions sent members to the capitol steps. Teachers camped out overnight more than once. It got so messy that members of the Democratic Party left the state house and crossed the state-line. They were absent and prevented a quorum.

In the midst of this turmoil, it came to the public's attention that the officers of a local bank in downtown Milwaukee were major contributors to the governor's conservative cause. Certain firefighters that were picketing the capitol got wind of this. Those that realized they had money in that bank set about to withdraw it. There was such a run on the bank that the concerned management closed the doors early.

This incident was not heavily reported by the media in general, and quickly forgotten, but not by everybody. Brian Knight had always been aware that the power of the average citizen was in the numbers. It's just that rarely did they ever band together. This time the firefighters chose to act against a successful system. For years these conservative officials had been weakening public programs and not truthfully explaining those actions to that public. Now the public was paying attention.

Brian observed that the firefighters tapped into this new awareness when they created the run on that Milwaukie bank. He felt this was healthy dissidence and decided to investigate those creative members. The tentative plan was a little complicated but, considering the morale and *esprit du corps* of the firefighters, he felt he could fulfill his mission.

One additional positive on the firefighter's balance sheet is their self-determination: their work ethic. Brian would never forget the train accident in Washington State and the immediate, successful response by numerous agencies to extricate and treat the victims.

According to one news report, in 2017 an Amtrak passenger train jumped the tracks because of excessive speed. The accident occurred within one mile of three different jurisdictions: two counties and one military base. The first responders on the scene arrived to discover numerous injuries that demanded immediate attention, but no command network. Different radio frequencies and command structures, particularly between civilian and military systems, caused severe communication problems.

Within one hour, without leadership, the three separate fire departments had transported all the injured to treatment centers. Some traveled north to hospitals, others south to hospitals, and a few to the nearby military installation. Before too long a command structure was established which enabled relatives to locate their family members. However, the important decisions had been made by the first folks on the scene, and without leadership.

To Brian, that concern for the public, that instant problem solving was what he needed on this project. He started working out the plan. First, though, to run it by those that signed his paycheck. He was met not only with enthusiasm, but a promise to fund a sweeter deal if need be and: did he think it time to hire some help?

Also, he knew that in order to sound like he knew what he was talking about he had better know what he was taking about. Where were the firefighters? What and who are politics in Wisconsin? It was time to do his homework and then get help.

One quick search and he had more information than he could ever grasp about Midwest politics. The conservative values and actions of recent individuals made this area a prime target for Brian. He turned to his laptop. "I think we will start in Wisconsin" he typed.

In a few minutes the reply arrived: "I'll get you a plane and send in an assistant."

The serious searching continued. The database for the local union revealed names of not only active firefighters, but retired members as well. With a handful of recently retired prospects, Brian was researching security and credit information when he noticed one husband/wife team that seemed particularly well put together. Both retired within the past two years at a young age, but the kids were not at home. The couple appeared to be done with middle age toys and on the verge of more community involvement. They had withdrawn their money from the evil bank. He decided to meet the Fosters, Jeff and Eleanor.

Before he left town, he wanted to make sure they were home. Research revealed that Jeff was at an annual firefighter's meeting and his wife went along. Perfect. Brian confirmed the jet was standing by and messaged the pilot to file a flight plan for Las Vegas – the location of the convention, and to get him a clean, non-descript room away from the Las Vegas strip.

The plane was still in the hanger as Brian parked his car. The pilot greeted him at the base of the stairs.

"Mr. Knight – I booked two rooms."

"What?" replied Brian as he entered the aircraft. He immediately understood when he saw her. As the door closed the pilot announced that there were about to roll and asked them to fasten their seat belts. He sat in a front-facing seat next to her and held out his hand.

"Brian Knight."

"I know – Brittany Odom, your assistant."

Oh, he thought, someone really wanted me to get some help.

It took over two hours to reach their destination. During that time, they learned a bit about each other, he more about her. She had been with the foundation for just shy of ten years and had lately been through a personal, bad time. The soon to be ex had left her with nothing (no money - no children) and the office talk was that she needed a long vacation.

The truth was that her superior had taken her into his confidence about an upcoming project that would be unlike anything she could imagine. Her qualifications were more than adequate, but the reason she was being given this opportunity was because of her honesty and work ethic. She would be asked to exercise extremes in both areas, and she would find more than financial reward.

"So, I'm on this plane, no questions asked, and going who knows where with some strange man -no offense- for who knows how long."

"Mrs. Odom ..."

"Miss Odom. I am using my maiden name again."

"Brittany. You are on your way to Las Vegas with me to meet an unsuspecting couple that I am hoping we can add to our team. We will have time for me to explain what that team is and does. Right now, we need to organize a few things. Until I boarded this jet, I had no idea I had an assistant."

She opened her laptop. Brian got on the phone. By the time they touched down she had an office 20 minutes from his place and an entire identity as an Odom. He had the hotel location and room number of the Fosters, and a schedule of the convention.

The hotel bar merged with a large sitting area on the upper level. After one of the afternoon sessions, the Fosters sat with other union representatives in that warm lounge enjoying a cool post-lecture beer. A uniformed security team approached.

"I'm sorry Mister Foster." said the male guard, "We have a security issue that requires your presence. We must ask that you and your wife please come with us. Excuse the intrusion, folks. This should take no more than ten minutes."

All pretense was dropped when the four of them reached the hotel room. Proper introductions were made, and they decided to move this discussion to the special room hotel security had assigned them.

As arranged, Brian Knight again visited security and returned the borrowed uniforms, but the return of the Fosters to the lounge was a non-issue. After two hours Brittany Odom, Jeff Foster and Ellie Foster knew the direction of the next path of their lives.

FIVE

Tom Lacey was a former employee of the Bureau of Indian Affairs. His departure was due to politics – he had not liked the way the bureau was led, and it became increasingly more difficult to keep quiet. The last day at the office was three weeks ago.

After a hard morning of job hunting, he returned to his apartment in Washington, D.C. and found a middle-aged woman sitting in his easy chair. Being recently divorced, Lacey only had one easy chair, so it was hard to not immediately notice its occupant. She introduced herself as Marina Whitehorse. He decided to not give voice to his indignation. Tom let her speak.

"I have been sent by the government and the nations of Wyoming to offer you the opportunity of a lifetime. In a nutshell, the Defense Department is going to help build a massive solar and wind generation station on the edge of the Wind River Reservation. We need your talents. I realize how unusual this brief conversation is, but we cannot discuss any more in this open setting. This is important enough for us to need to move future conversations to a secure location."

Without second thoughts, Lacey was quite interested. There was no doubt he would enjoy being in the company of this woman again, but the questions about compensation, chain of command, moving expenses, etc. needed to be answered.

It was agreed that they would meet again in two days, with the understanding that this meeting might lead them into confidential territory. It might also be long. She confirmed that 9 AM would be a convenient pick-up time, and excused herself.

With one day to spare, he decided to do some research and prepare for his meeting. The iMac on his dining room table was plugged into secure servers through the BIA. In reality, his former employer had cancelled his computer access, e-mail accounts and everything electronic he previously enjoyed. The fact that he was virtually the top techie genius they had hired must have slipped someone's mind. Agencies behave like that, and lose institutional memory.

It didn't take long to access the bureau's investigative center which was linked with most other similar data centers, since everyone was concerned about sharing information and terrorist identification. A few more clicks and he was on the defense departments projects page. Nothing.

Curious now, an in-depth search of the Indian affairs personnel chart revealed nothing about a Marina Whitehorse, or any Marina for that matter, other than a boating center on Boysen Reservoir in the Wyoming she mentioned. So, who was she?

The Wind River Indian Reservation is in central Wyoming. This is a massive expanse of prairie, home to the Shoshone and Arapahoe nations. Running along the edge of the reservation is the Bighorn River to the east. Shoshone National Forest lies to the west. The reservation is virtually bisected by the Wind River.

In siting the power generation station, the government had decided to involve Native Americans and the Bureau of Indian Affairs. He had been to that nation - the territory was massive.

To build a station capable of delivering power across a wide area would require thousands of acres of prairie: --Wyoming.

To support the technology, and the humans, would require a nearby water source: --Big Horn River or Wind River.

To soften the blow to the political conservatives of their not being involved from day one would require the Native Americans: --achieved.

The state of the art in alternative power generation at this time was sporadic power delivery when the sun was shining and/or the wind was blowing. At other times, nothing was being contributed to the electricity grid. But the art was changing.

Researchers had been exploring various ways to store energy in order to release it during those doldrums. Batteries were not practical for a variety of reasons, but thermal storage was becoming interesting to those that were serious.

This process requires heating a special liquid to temperatures hotter than boiling water and later releasing that temperature to actually boil water, make steam, and turn turbines. The excessive heat is generated by reflecting the sunlight into a tower filled with the magic liquid. Power generated by the wind turbines would circulate the excessively hot fluid through a massive holding tank. The turbines would provide power to the community that would be developed around the generation station.

A project of this magnitude would involve quite a bit of manpower, both skilled and unskilled labor. Initial Indian talent would be helpful in locating appropriate areas for centers of interest. Ritual and sacred sites notwithstanding, local knowledge would be of significance by making sure the site was safe from the elements. The construction site should be nestled within the land. The blades of the wind turbine need to be turned by the prevailing breeze.

Marina Whitehorse was aware of many of the aspects of this project and was about to share some of this information. Tom Lacey's ride in the black Lincoln with smoked windows took him out of Georgetown, out of Washington, and up the Interstate into Rockville, Maryland. Along the way he tried to take stock of Marina Whitehorse. No wedding ring, mid 40's, a bit too much weight, perfect teeth, not much tan, beginning bags beneath the eyes; conclusion: too much time working.

The limo stopped behind a non-descript, two-story motel. The units on the ground floor had back doors. He and Whitehorse entered one. The driver stayed in the car.

"There aren't so many eyes and ears out here." she said. "Have a chair. Care for some coffee?"

The pot was hot, and he sat in one of the two chairs next to a square table obviously made with phony wood. He noticed the lap-top on the table and the screen nearby for projecting images from the computer.

"Black." he said, then waited.

"First of all," she started, "you need to know that what I am about to share with you goes beyond Washington. You and I realize the suspicion that is omnipresent here. We know about surveillance and electronic eavesdropping. What you do not know is that I represent a project that most of Washington is unaware of. The reason you could not find this project, or me, in your computer search yesterday is because we did not want you to find us – yet."

If not physically, at least mentally he raised his eyebrows.

"We too have done our research, but with a little more success. It shouldn't surprise you that we have access to SIPRNet." she continued. "Your career, social skills, marital woes, financial situation, all_are in a file we have assembled. Naturally, it is not the only file the agencies have on you, but it is the secure one that we have. Based on this you have been invited to join an elite team.

"Almost all of our activities and dealings are legal. Notice I said almost. There are forces at work which we feel are at odds with our intentions and we are not above going around a few laws to straighten our path. On paper it looks like this shouldn't bother you?" This was a question.

"Not yet." was his response. Lacey had noticed she referred to the Secret Internet Protocol Network using the unusual acronym for the intelligence community's e-mail. She noticed he hadn't touched his coffee.

"Allow me to give you a quick introduction. As you know NASA has a branch referred to as DARPA: The Defense Advanced Research Projects Agency. Beyond doing the research that delivered the Internet and other wonders, the good folks at DARPA have a hidden budget. Within the incomprehensible budget of the Department of Defense is an equally incomprehensible (because their work is top-secret) or invisible chunk of money. Some of that is about to come our way.

"In the near future, the President of the United States will declare a State of Emergency. This will be a declaration based on the state of our finances and he will be addressing the issue of the runaway defense department spending while we have runaway education department obligations. Five of our states have declared their education departments unsound and in need of emergency relief. So, the President needs to find emergency funding and he is targeting the defense department.

"A committee will be appointed to audit the defense department. A committee whose findings we already know. The results of these findings will allow the re-organization of certain defense department procedures. One of these will involve the return of all heavy equipment we have left over-seas after some of our most recent conflicts. Are you with me so far?" He nodded.

"All branches of the armed forces will be charged with an accurate inventory on what armament they have and where. Also, we will need to know the weight of that equipment. Then the Navy and Air Force will do the heavy lifting and bring it all back to the United States. They will re-task carriers, C5-A's and jumbo jets. The order will be to get this done ASAP. But where will they put it?

"I should mention that in all the political confusion of this massive re-organization, presidential permission will be given to establish a power generation station in Wyoming. A parcel of land will be leased on a long-term basis by the Wind River Indian Reservation and a parcel donated to the reservation by the State. The Bureau of Land Management has some and a few acres will be bought or otherwise acquired from private owners. The finished plot will be enough to house the world's largest wind/solar power plants with some surrounding facilities. Like a town with an industrial base and an air-field."

At this Tom finally spoke: "How much territory are you talking about?"

"Well, maybe it will finish out at about 200 miles square" she replied. He whistled.

"Legally, all this territory will be part of a Native American nation. The United States through the BLM, will border the Nation along one 20-mile stretch. The State of Wyoming will be most of the remaining border. Infrastructure in this new territory will be a combined state, national and Native American effort. This is where you come in - if you want in. We are going to take some raw land in Indian hands and turn it into the largest electricity source on the planet. And do it fast, with little fuss."

He again spoke: "Little fuss as in . . ." his voice trailed off.

"When we get all our stars in alignment, very little has the potential to slow this construction down. We will control the land, the manpower, the materials and the funding. Naturally, we will have a lot of balls in the air and that is why we are bringing together the best jugglers we can find. If you wish, I shall continue and outline your team for you."

"Before we do that" Tom stopped her "Let's go through the why-in-the-hell would I even think about moving to Wyoming question."

"AH" she interpreted, "A variation of the what's in it for me question. Sure. But stop thinking so small. Who said anything about moving? As far as the public and your old friends at the BIA are concerned, you landed a plum deal with NASA at DARPA.

Beyond that, you will be off-the-grid unless you need to be found. What we have in mind is putting you in charge of a large aspect of this project. We have negotiated with the Native Americans, but we need a face. The wheels have been put in motion to get millions of tons of steel dropped at our feet, but we need steel mills and experienced workers. We might be building the largest concrete tank ever imagined and we need engineers, workers, materials, train tracks, you name it.

And then there's the town."

"What town?" Lacey inquired.

"We call it Urgent for lots of reasons. It doesn't exist yet, but it will, and it will be an important factor in the ongoing operation of what we are building. Urgent, Wyoming will need schools, infrastructure, air field, communications, health facilities and houses, churches and stores. It will all be yours! In a unique situation like this, you don't need to ask for money. We will be issuing you a blank check.

"You need to put together a supreme team of security minded research people. You sign their paychecks. Your travel from point to point will be in your private jet or whatever other mode of transportation you need. Your stack of credit cards will be so unique, and unlimited, that most transactions won't be questioned. The merchants will phone your office and your staff will cut them a check. You will almost be your own government.

"As for moving, you will live in as many places as you need. Keep the apartment in Washington or buy a mountain cabin in the other Washington. Steel mills are usually located on rivers, so I see you getting at least one boat. Beyond the jet you should have a few helicopters in hangers in strategic locations. We strongly suggest you outfit a couple train cars too because of the nature of some of our negotiations."

She paused - the coffee was cold.

"Do you really think I know enough people to pull this off?" he asked.

"No. But we do, and we can make some fairly accurate assumptions about who would fit nicely in this team. Our algorithms dig into psychology, personality, honesty, etc. We get pretty good results, if I do say so."

"And you believe you can keep this a secret." That was a statement.

"For as long as it takes."

SIX

● — — ● — ●● — ● — ● — ●●

"Dad, this phone just dropped another call. Tiffany was cut off just when we was deciding on what stores to see at the mall today. Can't you help with this?"

Senator Rodd Parmenter treated daughter Thea as his prize princess. After attempts too numerous to mention, he and his wife had been blessed with a baby girl 14 years ago. All that in vitro research and testing had paid off. His wife didn't need to know how his friends and colleagues in the senate had smoothed the way for that complicated and expensive procedure.

It had all come together. They had Thea and today it was time for back to school shopping. In prior years he had gone shopping with them. Watching her grow in her decision making and fashion sense was one of the many pleasures of being a father. He couldn't go along today, though. There was that damned pre-session meeting called in Sacramento by the committee chairman.

He had to agree with his party on this issue. California was basically on sound financial footing: what with last session's budget cuts to education and administrative overhead. His staff didn't like their stagnant salaries, but he had compensated them with some of the perks the lobbyists had sent his way. Of particular help was the staff retreat at Lake Tahoe.

Formally, the money was spent on the California side of the lake. Realistically they ate, played and gambled on the other side. Everyone in the office started with $1000 in casino money. Some lost it on day one. A result that funny money was designed to cause. Others were ahead when the outing ended on day three. They all ate well, as did their fortunate spouses.

Today they would earn their money. In response to this emergency, he and the staff had prepared a convincing, lengthy presentation on the California economy. As the next in line for chairmanship of the finance committee, he was assured a spot on the agenda and as much time as it took for Q & A.

The California governor had appointed a bi-partisan committee to advise on his State of Emergency. The Attorney General had recommended this approach as a safeguard in the event the issue ended up in court. The elected officials on the committee are representatives of state citizens and empowered to make decisions on the citizens' behalf. It follows that any court review would be influenced by the decision of the State Emergency Review Committee.

The senator had been appointed to that committee, and he knew he had the votes to stop this emergency issue. California was not going to be seen in an emergency light. Governor, or no governor, Rodd Parmenter was going to prevent the implementation of this State of Emergency. His creative calculations guaranteed this result.

His legal advice was to tread lightly since there was no precedent, no roadmap for him to follow in fighting this issue. However, there was no precedent to this fiscal State of Emergency either, so he figured he had it made. He was a good spokesman.

"Thea, honey, you are going to the mall this morning. Have them look at it and if there is a better phone, buy it. I've got this big meeting today, so I really can't help. But you and Mom can get your brains together and solve the phone problem. And Thea – it's *were*. We were deciding on what stores to visit. Please take a deep breath, calm down and practice talking like the daughter of someone in the public eye. I've got a car waiting outside. See you tonight."

The trip from Redding to Sacramento takes less than three hours: freeway all the way. The interstate is an easy road for back-seat studying and last-minute preparations. Rather than arranging for the expensive airplane he could have used he had chosen to travel by car.

Besides, it was an early afternoon meeting. At this hour there would be no traffic to slow them down. The limo could glide right into the secure underground parking. One hour into the trip his cell phone rang. When in the car, communications were secure, and he answered by picking up the handset located in the central armrest in the back seat.

"Yes."

"Senator, this is Sharon. Your family has been in an accident."

"What accident? What kind? I just left them at home. Phil – turn this damned thing around." He shouted to his driver. "Sharon – what have you heard? Tell me everything while I catch my breath."

"I just got a call from the RPD dispatcher telling me that they have responded to a car fire incident at the Central Valley Mall," she said. "Dispatch says your car was damaged by a car in the next space that caught fire. However, they can't find your wife or daughter."

"What do you mean can't find? They weren't in the car then?"

"No sir." she responded. "But there seems to be some confusion as to what's really happening in that corner of the parking garage. A few cars are involved. Some witness saw a white van pick up a passenger or two about the same time the fire was reported. And your transponder stopped sending."

"What witnesses? Pick up who? Where are the cops? And what do you mean stopped sending? That thing is bullet-proof."

"Exactly!" said Sharon. "That's why we are concerned and trying to locate your family. As for the police, Redding Police Department is on the scene and the CHP has been placed on a standby alert."

"I'm coming back. Alert the CHP that I expect an escort ASAP. Phil, get to speed plus 10 and when the CHP picks us up I want more than that. Sharon, call Senator Cohen and tell him I won't make the meeting today. We have the votes and my presence is not as important as my family."

"Yes sir. California Highway Patrol says they are eight minutes out from your location. They will pick you up at milepost 603, near Willows."

"And Sharon, get me the Redding police!"

At that moment, Thea Parmenter was leading her mother through a series of underground hallways below the mall. She was following family emergency protocol. A few minutes earlier, the senator's driver, Phil, had called and instructed her to go through an exit door. The one next to the Banana Republic store. The door with the round, yellow symbol with the red "X" in the middle.

She was following the route marked by a series of those symbols.

Down some stairs, around some corners, and past small doors with numbers and delivery hours printed on them. They were on a route that, according to Phil, would lead to a waiting car. But Phil had not called. She had responded to a text that signaled "emergency – follow protocol".

After four or five turns and self-closing doors, they entered a room with a window. To reach the exit door next to the far window they had to let go of the door through which they had entered that room. Click! At a fast walk Thea hit the bar mounted on the exit door. The door did not open. They both tried the bar and the door itself with their hands, shoulders, and feet. Nothing they tried opened the door.

"Thea, honey, stand still for a second. Don't panic. Please, let me see your phone."

Joanne Parmenter was thinking logically, but logic wouldn't work. There was no cell phone reception in this particular room. Now she had to convince herself not to panic.

"Let's see if we can retrace our steps," she thought out loud.

No – locked door there too. Next to that door were a few cardboard boxes that were just the right height. She instructed her daughter to sit down and began to survey the room. Along the left wall was a line of tall, wire storage racks full of more boxes. Next to their seats was a collection of white buckets that looked like they contained paint, or cooking supplies: she wasn't sure. Under the window, on the far wall, was a grate on the floor that looked like a long drain. Nothing was stacked on that steel device.

"What do you suppose is out there?" she asked while pointing at the window. They got up, grabbed the handle of one of the buckets and dragged it to the grate. After testing it for support, Thea climbed on the lid and looked out the window trying to peek though the waves in the wire reinforced glass.

"Mom, I see a dumpster right in front of this window. Beyond that there is a cement wall. Off to that side (pointing right) is the opening where the truck drops the dumpster off. There might be some trees way out there. I think I see green, or it's the high-up part of the movie theater. I think that's green too."

"All right honey, please get down. It appears no one would hear us if we screamed. Let's look at what else we have to work with." - still thinking out loud.

They examined the labels on the paint cans, the contents of the boxes they were sitting on, and started on the boxes on the wire shelves. After about half-an-hour of searching Thea noticed a partially hidden piece of pipe coming down from the ceiling. She called her mom to help move the heavy cartons, so she could see where that pipe went. It was a fire alarm. Thea pulled the handle.

Outside, Senator Parmenter was examining the blackened hulk of the family sedan. He had been on the scene only two minutes when the police chief approached him.

"Senator, we have an unusual alarm the mall security is responding to. There is a box in a storage area in the far basement level that has just squawked. It could be a faulty unit, but we will know soon enough. Their cars are on the way."

"Show me! Phil, let's go. Follow him!"

The limo followed the police car around the outer perimeter of the mall. The speed was too slow for the senator, but his driver knew the safety of mall shoppers was important too. It took five minutes to reach the location where the mall security car was parked. There was also a Redding fire truck idling; the red lights on both vehicles were flashing.

"Quick response." the senator thought.

As he jumped out of his car the security guard approached.

"Sir, please stand back. We have a situation with a large dumpster jammed into an exit door. Rather than wait for the usual truck, I'm going to ask the fire department to hook their engine to the dumpster and pull it out of the way. I need you and your vehicle to back up a couple rows."

"Phil, back the car up. I'm watching from here – no questions."

The police chief introduced himself to the security

guard and advised that the well-dressed gentleman was a California politician. They left him alone. As soon as the heavy metal doorstop had been dragged out of the way, the door in the building popped open. Thea's foot immediately followed. Obviously, she had been practicing her karate moves.

Her mom immediately exited the room. They both ran past the still moving garbage bin and joined the senator. Husband and wife hugged. Daughter Thea was studying the collection of flashing lights.

"Dad, what's the emergency?"

"You are." he replied.

"No, I mean why the emergency text? Was this a protocol test?" she asked.

"What text? Let me see your phone!"

After examining the message on Thea's device, he called the police chief over. The chief volunteered to contact his dispatcher, and the California Highway Patrol offices to see if any public official knew of any emergency. He was on his private phone while the Parmenter parents softly spoke of their concerns.

The family moved out of the California sun, into the calm air-conditioned comfort of his limousine. The senator wanted all the facts. Before too long the chief asked Parmenter to join him in the police car.

"Senator, I can find no one that can confirm any type of emergency or any reason for your daughter to receive that message. Where do we go from here?" he respectfully asked.

"Back to our offices." was the reply. "But I want a word with the fire guys first."

As the police official turned to leave, he hesitated. "FYI sir, this incident will be reported to the Feds. We have protocol that requires suspicious activity involving an elected government official. The Federal Bureau of Investigation in San Francisco has a web-site they use. We will visit that link immediately."

The senator nodded his agreement and entered his limousine. They drove back around the mall to the scene of the burnt automobile carnage. By now, the chief of the fire department had arrived and was examining the ruins. He was told the senator wanted to speak with him. They met under the shade of the parking structure.

"Senator, it looks like the car in the stall next to yours was leaking fuel and that liquid started burning. We don't yet know how, but both vehicles suffered severe damage, as you can see."

"Find out how." Parmenter said. "Would you like me to have the CHP forensics team sent in?"

"I can do that if I get in over my head on this, sir

"All right. We're going home."

Two hours away, in Sacramento, the committee was voting on the California emergency proposal. Without Parmenter to break a tie, the emergency was a go. As unusual as it was, one of the senator's associates, a San Diego county commissioner, had reversed his agreed upon decision.

The night before the vote, this county commissioner had received an anonymous text suggesting he check out a website. Once on that site, he followed some links that led to details about the funding of public schools. His interest was piqued since his two children were students in San Diego Unified. One website showed an in-depth history of the cuts in the funding of education in each of the 50 states. The California statistics astonished him.

The nickel here and dime there had not been a concern to the general public, but the accumulated overall shortfall from a number of years was a large number. In addition, the editor of the site had included data illustrating the real dollar amounts if the trends continued. That would be too much, said the father to himself. He had attended public school and his children would go to public school.

The commissioner knew there were options via charter schools. Usually a for-profit venture, very few of these schools delivered an education without asking for financial support from the parents. Furthermore, very few lasted long enough to actually deliver the education promised in their charters.

He flew into the state capital the morning of the meeting. Upon entering the office building, he ventured into two rooms that housed a couple of his closest allies on the State Emergency Review Committee. He wanted to get some support from like-minded members in swinging this decision.

The attempt was to no avail, but he was adamant. When the time came, he cast the deciding vote. California would declare a State Emergency.

SEVEN

•— • • — —• •— •— • — ••

The room was full of the most political power seen in the same place at one time in ages. With exception of the Vice-President and some upper cabinet members without security clearance, the players were all present. Sean Crockett had called this unusual gathering and made it a mandatory event. Generals, Admirals and out-of-towners had all flown in as requested.

"This room may not be as large as we are used to," the President began "but security and technology make this the logical place to start this project. I trust you all are comfortable. Now is the time for more coffee, or to use the facilities. When we start you will not want to leave your chairs."

When they finally settled in he continued: "Those of you that have been visiting the moon might be surprised to learn that the states of Pennsylvania and Illinois have declared a State of Emergency. Their financial situations are so tenuous that the governors feel it will take emergency action to balance the books. It might interest you to know that three more states will follow suit within the next two weeks."

There were murmurs throughout the room.

"After New York, California and North Carolina release their announcements, roughly one third of the nation's population will be under those emergency conditions."

"That's quite amazing." said one of the generals.

"It is also quite timely." Said the President. "It gives us the precedent to do the same thing."

The murmurs were louder now.

"I have run it by our best legal minds. Consider it similar to a declaration of war, only a war on our economic situation. We are on an unsustainable course, and in a runaway situation. Our economists fear global instability if we do not get our house in order, and we are such a big part of the globe that we must take responsibility and action."

He continued:

"On the screen at the end of the table is a brief description of where our money goes. There are no dollar amounts, only percentages of what we spend on various departments and agencies. Just to sum up our trends, we have also illustrated what those numbers were a decade ago. I won't read to you, just ask you to look at the data.

"Naturally, there are changes in needs and technology that result in changing responsibilities and increases or reductions in the appropriate budget amounts. But the trend is meaningful. Education is going one way and defense spending is going the other. At this meeting we are not going to get into any fixes or discussion about why one agency is doing fine while another is off the rails. I called this group together to let you know that we are going to announce our intention to resolve this issue. Right now, the management at the Internal Revenue is drafting a temporary set of tax laws.

"These laws will set the tax rates for the upcoming year at the same rates as last year, negating the tax changes passed by my predecessor during his final budget negotiation. That is the quickest way to guarantee our tax folks understand the tax law. We are doing this because a large portion of IRS personnel will be on temporary assignment. Our plan of action is to have these financial minds audit the books of all your departments."

The room erupted. He waited. As the usual suspects got louder, Sean just stared them down: one by one. Finally, silence.

"I am giving them one year to bring in an audit that is a close as they can get to generally accepted accounting principles. In fact, five senior CPA's from the largest accounting firms will be put on retainer for a year to help with the logistics and details. And folks, I want you to also know that this will be a fair and honest effort. No partisan politics can come into play."

Looking at the director of the FBI: "I expect a thorough security check on all players sent to us by the accounting firms. Criminal record, subversive connections, addictions, the works. These folks will be clean."

The Education Secretary started to raise her hand. "Later." the President said. "The audit of your department will reveal data needed to correctly allocate funds to you. We will get those school districts and institutions in your jurisdiction back on track."

Finally, he settled his gaze on the Secretary of Defense.

"Mister Secretary, this will be an almost impossible task, but we will audit your people.

To the Joint Chiefs, you had better start calling some meetings as soon as you leave this building. On the QT you may get started a bit ahead of the announcement – but only to advise your next in command to make some room and arrange transportation. Line up pilots and drivers to chauffeur a few civilians around. I demand upmost secrecy and trust you all to do your duty.

"You should know that a real audit looks at assets. Unlock your records and help these people analyze the Navy's mothball fleet and the ground forces' rolling stock both obsolete and left behind. We will place

URGENT STATE

a value on armament abandoned in the field of battle, used as mementoes in some villages and as honored as monuments in others. In one year we <u>will</u> know where our money goes and how much can continue in those directions.

"Tomorrow morning, I will be holding one more briefing on this matter with a few of you in this room. In a week I will make the emergency announcement. That gives each of you an opportunity to rearrange your family priorities if you see fit. In some departments a special audit represents no additional work. Your record keeping is meticulous, and the numbers will be easy to find.

"Other agencies, however, had better start cleaning house. This might mean the cancellation of some vacations and management overtime. So be it. Take one for the country and buckle down. We will do this."

The stunned group filed out of the room. Sean remained seated at the table He made eye contact with the Admiral and motioned for him to stay. Wordlessly, the rest of the Joint Chiefs complied and joined their boss in adjacent chairs.

To a person these esteemed members of the armed forces knew this day was coming. Patriotic service men/women, and millions of citizens, were surprised it took so long. The Defense Department, when in the news, was usually in that news for being over-budget. Bloated some would say.

The President had always watched defense spending, even while a state senator. When the magic number passed half a trillion dollars, he really took notice. Once he was appointed to sit on the appropriate committees, he began to quietly research the destination of all that money.

The public knew, or believed, that the newest of fighter jets was needed by the Air Force. Those same persons had been convinced that the Navy's fleet of old carriers needed to be replaced in order to handle the new aircraft. Those perceptions kept the politicians busy negotiating around a very large numbers of dollars and bargaining for some very large orders to be filled by our nation's defense contractors. Of major concern to Sean Crockett was the rest of the money.

There was money for the building of nuclear weapons in the budget of the Department of Energy - Why?

- Why did the Department of Veterans Affairs have a line item for war related expenses?
- Who put that same line in the budget of Homeland Security?
- But the big question was the black budget of the intelligence community!

The Joint Chiefs were all seated.

"You guys need to know that after the audit we are fully intent on reclaiming tons of weapons and material. I will be asking you to reroute some of your troops to the areas where we can conveniently retrieve this ordinance. If we can't fly it home, we will ship it. Tow the mothballed ships, or cut'em and haul'em by barge." He said.

"Assuming you want to give some of your commanders a heads-up, I suggest you fly them in for a briefing. Their supply people will be big players in this effort. Their in-house records will help in the audit of scrap yards and supply depots. Plus, they can assist in the retrieval efforts. Finally, you should concentrate on shipping to the west coast if possible and flying into a soon-to-be-built runway near Casper, Wyoming.

"You may need some additional manpower to help with this project. I will be giving you the authorization to encourage some of the team to re-up and entice a few to join. But be aware that this is just a loan. The audit will undoubtedly reveal a little fraud and theft. You will dismiss these personnel but go lightly on the sentence

The salaries saved will pay back the loan and we don't need a bunch of opportunists filling up the cells during this exercise.

"The United States of America has a defense budget that is so large that they say it can't be audited. Bullshit! This is the taxpayer's money and their defense department. We will be fiscally responsible to these people. Don't worry.

"Tomorrow morning my meeting is with the alphabet intelligence agencies. They have the same problem you do. Although their clandestine operations may suffer for a while, there will be no more cash payments to countries, or spies, or informants until we get this under control. In the morning, from your various bases, you will be able to hear these guys scream. I don't care.

"There are 17 major players in the intelligence community. To many in top management, they can act without fear of accountability to the public. Yet it all is funded by tax-payer dollars. Some of this money is going to dry up and you better believe that there will be some agency consolidation, or evaporation.

"The stories about having a shipping container full of cash dropped in Iraq might be true. But that will not be happening for a while. Our foreign relations people may need to get more creative, since this monetary emergency is serious.

"Now let's talk education. Your top brass was the first to complain that the average IQ of the all-volunteer recruits seemed to be slipping. I'd say the entire education system is slipping.

"Even at the academies, I hear reports of the quality of recruits being sub-par. If we waste a year doing what the public schools used to do, where are we? When we need to educate the new employees in the work-force and the first timers in the military our efficiencies are way out of whack. You don't want an under-educated pilot for a wingman any more than you want to share a foxhole with a guy that can't break down his weapon. This audit will release funds we can allocate to education.

It should be that simple."

His calendar called for a meeting with the intelligence communities on the following day. Those talks went as the President expected. The day after that, however, his plans took an unexpected turn.

While discussing the audit and manpower situation with Treasury, one of the senior tax advisors asked if he could speak freely. Receiving a positive response, the inexperienced speaker shakily started to describe a pie-in-the-sky idea he had been working on: a tax code suggestion box.

As he saw it, the existing tax code was:

A – Not fair

B – Complicated

C – The third-rail to politicians

To seriously revise that nonsensical system (at least non-sensical to the masses) would require getting outside the political sphere. All in the room agreed.

His ingenious concept was to ask the brand-new graduates of all accounting schools in the country to submit one idea of how to fairly simplify the tax code. Those ideas would be reviewed by a committee ("I'm not sure how you would form that group") and the top 20 concepts, or so, would be declared the best.

The tax expert added, "The accountant, or graduate if you will, that had a winning idea would get a job at the IRS and be assigned to study the implications of that idea further, with federal employee guidance. So, while most of our staff is out in the field auditing branches of the government, the tax staff has some fresh blood and fresh ideas. These efforts will certainly result in overtime pay for newbies and mentors, but well worth it in the long run.

"I feel that, during the course of getting their education, these former students heard stories of tax code interpretation from their professors. Those old-timers have been through a lot. Much of that experience having been in the arena of muddy regulations and downright fraud. The fundamentally honest individual will remember such incidents as something not right. Cheating leaves a long-lasting memory. If we can get those stories and put a positive twist on them our tax code might be equitable and less complex."

While various items in the tax code were under scrutiny, the audit of large departments of the federal government continued. The resulting fact vs. fantasy rumors that flowed through the White House began to disturb the President. As is the case with all large institutions, there is the public communications and then the grapevine. The actual effect of the suggestion box idea had been positive. However, the publicity delivered and paid for by the special interest groups was all too negative.

Rumor was that impeachment talk was getting under way. As anticipated some members of Congress from the other side of the aisle were on the news every night talking about how illegal this emergency order was and that the country was actually on a sound footing financially. They repeatedly claimed: It's just that the other party was cooking the books. General Accounting Office budget be damned, they were in the President's camp and falsified those statistics.

What was not anticipated was the movement from business as a result of the freezing of the tax system. High-paid, vociferous executives were spearheading a movement to circumvent Congress and go directly after the executive branch. There were large sums being spent on legal research and a few lobbying firms were on board as well.

The President and his advisors knew Wall Street would be complaining. The executive order to halt all computerized trading of securities held less than five trading days was scheduled to be implemented soon. In addition, one expected the lobbyists to push back. Their activities were being brought to a halt since no budgeted money could be re-directed to any new target. But experienced lobbyists knew that things were likely to return to normal someday. So, who was convincing them to join in the fray against the White House?

The President knew he had all his troops scrambling. Those that usually were able to help him in research were busy. He considered it bad form to ask any of the agents on the government payroll to investigate others within the system. It was time for another meeting with the philanthropist. He made the call on a secure phone.

EIGHT

•• — •   • — •• — ••••

Air Force One flew into King County Airport in Seattle in response to a political matter. The King and Queen of Sweden were accompanying their daughter to a cancer treatment center in the city. President Crockett wanted to greet the royal couple since they were on United States soil. These leaders had lunch together at a yacht club near the university's medical center, and then shook hands good-bye. Crockett's motorcade headed south, back to the airport.

As usual the press had surrounded the President as soon as he allowed. To justify an overnight stay, the reporters were told that Air Force One was having mechanical difficulty. Since the plane was built in Seattle, they would have it fixed there.

"The mechanics have assured me that we can fly out in the morning." he said. "Right now, I am going to do a little sightseeing. After that I will spend the night on-board."

Adjacent to the south end of the runway was a popular attraction, The Museum of Flight. Just out of interest, Sean Crockett decided to tour the museum and told his staff that he wanted minimum security with him. After all, they had closed the area to the public. How could he get in trouble inside the building? The secret service agent in charge agreed that his trusted aide, Mark Madison, would walk with him.

Earlier in the day, during the well-publicized lunch with the Swedes, few had noticed an executive jet touch down at King County Airport and taxi directly into its hanger. A few minutes after that the occupants of the sleek jet were driven around the end of the runway, to a back door to the Museum of Flight. The car returned to the hanger with one less passenger.

Steven, the philanthropist, worked his way to the basement of the building and entered his personal code into the keypad by the door. . He was working on his secure computer when the door opened again.

"Good afternoon Mister President." He said while rising, "In case you don't recognize me, I'm Steven. . ."

"I met you a couple years ago at a fundraiser in Washington. Why don't you call me Sean."

"As you wish – Sean. Have some wine, or whisky. We're clear until tomorrow morning."

There were over-stuffed recliners in the room and all the comforts of home - however no windows.

Steven had wanted to share his operation with this sincere leader. Sean had, politically, wanted deniability. But now the operation was underway, and it was obvious that it would be a fight to see the end of his term. The more knowledge the better. Deniability was a non-issue. They had all night to bring each other up to speed.

They decided to start by trying to trace the players behind the impeachment movement. Steven spent a few moments at the keyboard.

"OK. I have my best computer guru on the line. He's talking as he's looking and walking us through his routes. Most of this will be gibberish to you but suffice it to say that we are doing the same gleaning that your spy agencies do.

"We can follow the money, track credit cards, analyze

facial recognition and visit most closed-circuit cameras that are hooked to a live feed. While we have fewer personnel than the FBI, we are quicker and quieter. No one knows when we are in there or that we have even been there.

Let's have a sandwich. We've got some fruit here too."
The laptop chirped. Steven entered the password and switched on the monitor. Sean was watching as the startled researcher on the other end recognized him.

"It's OK son. We have some real work to do and I am not above getting involved, as long as we can keep it amongst ourselves."

"Uh, yes sir Mister President."

"You were saying?"

"Uh, I found our guy. He is a well-known left-over from that legislative wannabe outfit from a few years ago that was writing language in advance and trying to get it enacted anyplace. Name of Vern Osburn. He gets around Washington and used to make serious money. Now he hires out on a contract basis.

I'm tracing the funds right now. It looks like they change hands a bit, so your real funder doesn't want to be known. Not to worry – we'll get him."

"Then we'll sign off for now." said Steven. "Thanks."

"You can't say this is a surprise, can you Sean?"

"Honestly - no. It's just that they got organized so quickly. For some reason I figured they would take a while to bring it all to bear."

"If it means anything," the philanthropist continued, "I think this confirms that your action has the potential of being more effective than originally thought. You are hitting them where it hurts."

"I guess you're right."

Steven's movements directed them to return to the meal.

"Yeah, you have rattled a lot of cages. You may have heard the rumors, and I can tell you many of them are true. The public is deeply divided on some of the issues your emergency orders bring to the table. Not the least of which is executive compensation."

"Those greedy..." Steven interrupted, "Excess-u-thiefs."

"Cute." The President responded. "Or excessive-thiefs depending on who you talk to." said the philanthropist.

"The proposed restrictions on these CEO's that pull in super-money and the tax penalties if they continue, really has them crying foul. As always, the loudest voices are the worst offenders. Just as with the crash of 2008, they brought it upon themselves." Steven stated.

"There is not a bad guy involved, but the machinations of big business with bad, or no, self-control. The board gets itself stuck in this whirl-wind of more and more compensation for the wizard CEO that will do something to drive the stock price up. The wizards revolve within the cores of those large, complex businesses.

"Lately, the CEO to worker pay ratio has degraded to over 300 to 1 in our country's top 350 publicly held companies. What choice does the government have? These excesses are not sustainable." Said Steven.

"But don't worry − Now that you have stopped the downward spiral, there is an opportunity for some intervention by corporate finance people with long-range views.

"I have already heard of mutual funds that are carving out investments in firms headed by those greedy guys. The millions of citizens with money in those investments can speak quite loudly if they all speak together. It will be interesting to see how the market treats the corporations that have the balls to limit executive compensation and instead, divert these extra monies to a use that helps the business, not help the guys brought on-board to bleed the business."

When the computer came to life again, they learned that Osburn was on the payroll of a far-right lobbying firm. A partnership that had a great deal of interest in the tax code. In fact, they had been at the table when

IRS rules were written for the past six years in a row.

"Input into six years of tax code revisions is one serious entry on anyone's resume'." Steven surmised, "No wonder they were worried."

"He and his wife live in a suburban Maryland neighborhood. House is paid for and the kids are out, with their own kids. She used to teach. No major commitments. Sort of homebodies when he's not under contract. Then he's a bulldog."

Steven assured his dinner partner that nothing would come of the impeachment talk. Lobbying firms actually worked for clients, and the connections his foundation had with big business nationwide would work in their favor.

The President did not need to know what specific businesses used that lobbying firm. Sean acknowledged that he'd seen enough. He did not see the typing "TURN OSBURN" before the laptop was closed.

"Sorry about that, but I think our snack is approaching room temperature."

"Not to worry." Sean said, "I've been on worse picnics. Let's eat anyway. I am anxious to use this time constructively. This is the first quality, quiet time I have had in the two years since we started this project. Please bring me up-to-date."

"Well, Sean, there is a lot to share, and we only have a few hours. I think it would best be spent by providing you with the talking points you might need to quiet down those loud voices we know are lurking.

"I'm sure you're aware that the public will not argue with the redistribution of wealth. Your number-crunchers can give you an average income ratio of executive to laborer in various industries, by nation. Not that the rest of the world is always right – nor is the United States. If you compare democracies and leave the rest out of the equation, you will have a good starting point for this conversation.

"A mandate to spend more on education can also be

easily backed up. Test scores provide some of the data. Many countries share those scores, plus graduation rates. Although the tests may not be the same around the world. You have great minds that have access to great data on numerous aspects, and all levels, of education. But it might be interesting to get input from thousands of the nation's largest employers.

"I might remind you that you are one of the largest employers around. What is the feeling of your military leaders, your regional offices, your forest service? Get specifics from those that hire some of your two-million white and blue-collar workers. Are they satisfied with levels of education?

"While carefully examining education, you may be able to support the states that have decided to remove certain tax giveaways. You will recall that after declaring emergencies, three states generated new revenue for their education departments by removing, or changing, corporate tax breaks. They are now faced with threats from these large businesses. Moving out of state is the most popular bargaining chip.

"The government could join the conversation with a proposed tax break for the business that hires a recent graduate from an institution within that state. Entice the business to stay put and employ the better educated citizens produced by the local system.

"Before too long the public will begin hearing about the government's deal with the Native Americans on the Wind River reservation. That conversation will allow you to emphasize climate change in a big way. Read energy production into that response.

"Generations of our ancestors produced and harnessed energy. The impact of energy use occurred on a local level. However, after the conclusion of World War II and the arrival of nuclear energy, we were now impacting the entire globe.

"The rise and partial fall of nuclear was joined by massive increase in fossil-fuel based production to result in pollution. That is pollution on such a scale that the weather on the entire planet has changed. Beyond air pollution we have done a good job in damaging our waters also.

"Check with scientists on the factors contributing to those dead zones in the Gulf of Mexico. It isn't all about that immense oil spill of a few years ago. Our rivers are transporting nasty ingredients to the oceans.

"I don't need to give you the data on average temps, or wild-fire activity, or hurricane strength: your emergency folks have had to respond to it all. In addition, the sea level rise from melting continents is now an accepted fact by all who really care. Data from various government agencies can be used to confirm our need to shy away from conventional energy sources, and steer more towards renewables. Many will argue, but this needs to include nuclear – just build them safer.

"This country, and planet, is faced with catastrophic rate of CO_2 level increase. Scientists have data that models problems in areas such as food insecurity, mass migration, more wide-spread epidemics and deadly heat waves. We know of few industries that will not be impacted by upcoming climate driven problems. Short-term thinking executives may need to be reminded of some of these facts.

"One final thought: my brief synopsis had been a US based scenario. There are other parts of the planet that have it worse than we do. Remember, this is all interconnected at some level. If your audience tunes out because of lack of interest, just change the channel."

The President had sufficient input to guarantee he would not have a restful sleep.

NINE

— — — — ••• • — • — —

Vern Osburn had been a bit preoccupied lately and his wife was happy for the respite. His life had been one short gig after another since those corruption investigations into that group that sold legislation. When he went hunting or fishing with his buddies there was no telling when he would return home. He seemed to be drinking more than usual and acting gruff. The time and conversation she used to enjoy were spent somewhere else now, not with his wife. Therefore, she was not worried when he failed to get home for dinner.

By the next morning, though, she was a little concerned. Mysteriously he had been missing overnight years ago, and it had taken all her wifely wiles to extract the truth from him. His lobbying activity had lured him to a secure location owned by some bigshot. Absolute secrecy was demanded, and a few jet pilots were the only ones that were aware of the meeting. Without any prior warning, the rooms and roommates were assigned, roll-away beds were set up, and everyone in that compound spent two days out of touch. No choice!

Anne Osburn had been suspicious of that story. She found out the truth a few months later when the company held a summer B-B-Q at an executive's house. The wife of one of the lawyers introduced herself to Anne and they decided to sit under an umbrella at the far end of the pool. There they began chatting and drinking a colorful punch out of glasses laden with fruit and topped off with little umbrellas.

The two got tipsy, and talkative, and Anne asked about that lost week-end in the spring. Mrs. lawyer confirmed that her husband had also dropped out of sight. When later confronted he admitted that his legislative group had a client with ultra-deep pockets and security concerns bordering on pathological.

The executive of the lobbying firm had been whisked away to a secure setting and endure their client's detailing of a scheme to overthrow the government. They had no advance notice of the amount of time this adventure would take, and were sworn to secrecy forever after. Naturally, the scheme didn't work, and the big money guy found another group to try to do his bidding.

Now that the legislative group had been chased apart, Vern had become sort of a maverick. The couple of Vern/Anne had not socialized with any of the members of that organization for at least three years. Who could she call? She had to think long and hard to decide who she might call to ask if Vern had been seen or heard from. The phone number she finally called belonged to an older retired judge that shared an interest in the outdoors. He and Vern had done some hunting together and occasionally Vern had mentioned his name.

A short while into their conversation Anne advised that Vern was unaccounted for. She voiced her concern and the judge offered to make some calls for her. He could dig deeper into Vern's activities because he had previously been a lobbyist in the DC area: he knew those people. She thanked him, and they disconnected. Her knitting was waiting for her in the living room.

After retiring from teaching, she had returned to knitting. Watching some screen was white noise while her hands were occupied by the needles and yarn. Where was it all going? As a public-school teacher, she had taken homework home to grade and spent hours in that exact living-room spot planning the next lessons or talking with confused parents. That was meaningful work.

She had been a staunch advocate for children and fought many battles with mis-guided administrators. What were her meaningful activities now? Even her knitting was pathetic. Ever since Vern lost his job, he had asked her to donate her work to charity on an anonymous basis.

He was so embarrassed at his involvement in that failed organization that he wanted to drop out of sight for a while. She couldn't agree more. The publicity surrounding that corruption and those negative influences was intolerable for those with a conscience. They both sincerely wanted to do the right thing. Could it be that they were too easily influenced?

She would wait one more day for the judge to call her back. After that, even though she had no faith in them, she had to contact the law. She did not sleep well that night.

The morning brought a telephone ring. Their old-fashioned land-line still worked. They had refused to give it up. She answered.

A familiar voice responded: "Good morning Sweetie."

"Vern – honey, I was so worried."

"I know" he said "and I'm sorry – but listen carefully. At exactly 9:00 a white pick-up with a Sears sign on the door will pull up in front of the house. The driver will exit the vehicle and knock on our front door.

Please answer it and invite him in. Between now and then you need to pack a suitcase. Plan on three nights away from home. Don't worry about anything other than personal belongings. Before you leave with the driver, put the full suitcase in the hall, near the back door.

URGENT STATE

"I can't explain more over the phone. The driver will fill you in on the few specifics he knows. One thing I want to emphasize is that I love you and that there is nothing to worry about."

"Vern." she said.

"Yes Annie?"

"I love you too." she hung up.

TEN

•—• • ••• •—•—• • —•—• —

As soon as the plane touched down, the intercom announced, "Welcome to Wheeling". When the jet entered the hanger, Anne Osburn saw her husband through the window. He was with another man. Both were clean shaven and alert. Vern was wearing his usual, solid colored shirt while the other guy had on patterned flannel. The engines went quiet and the wood paneled door swung open. She walked down the stairs and hugged him.

"Oh, Annie. I have so much to say but this isn't the place to say it. This is Tom Lacey. You heard a bit about this flight and our safety from the driver this morning. Tom is our new boss and he has a room for us across town. Let's get going."

Their ride was a small, Ford pick-up. This truck was similar to the one Anne rode in when leaving her house in Maryland. They drove to a clean, six-story hotel on the edge of a mall near the West Virginia, Ohio border. Their suite had a small kitchenette with two chairs and a table. Including the chair that sat at the built-in desk, each of the three had a place to sit and talk, around the small table. Lacey got some soft drinks from the mini-'fridge. Tom proceeded to tell Anne the story he had already shared with her husband.

The dream about the future and the facts that the project had started. At that moment there were recruiting activities taking place and the results would be students for the proposed schools: volunteers from the surrounding hills. At new education centers, the pupils would be participants in the building, learning and sharing with other generations.

Through his networking and employment, Lacey had access to credit, security, employment and criminal histories. He had researched the Osburns and personally chosen them for this position, as a team, if they wanted it. Both or neither! He continued, and Anne listened even more intently.

"We have the traditional chicken/egg problem facing us." Lacey said. "Our team is actively recruiting students at this very moment. We would like to have some young people and a force of more mature pupils. The youth have the ability to learn quickly and are flexible: physically and mentally.

More seasoned individuals have experience, social graces and the capacity for deeper understanding. Both age group, however, will require extensive teaching. They are the laborers, cooks, drivers, nurses, and more, at our two education centers."

The description of the activities in the centers brought excitement to her that she had not felt in years. There was more meaning in what they were going to accomplish than she could imagine. Not only would her husband be by her side, but she would be his equal. And he knew and accepted that fact. His management skills would be needed to gather and train the manpower to physically build the center. Her years in education would be needed to teach and train both the workers and students.

She knew how to cook, but Vern would build the kitchen. The large financial decisions would be his, but he hated bookwork – she would do the arithmetic. As a couple they were about to enter their retirement years with a lifetime of work to do. The most difficult part of the decision was to agree that, for as long as they could, they needed to deceive their friends and family.

"We need a few years head start." Lacey had said.

"We will set you up with a cover, just like in the movies. You will get a motor home and we will register it in your name. The story is you will be traveling for a while as a 50th wedding present to yourselves. We can photoshop you into wonderful scenes all around the country. We can postmark letters for you. Our staff will pay the bills on the house in Maryland and you can fly home to visit once in a while.

I'm sorry but this ruse is in the interest of national security. It sounds funny due to the scope of this center I know, but we really do want to try to keep things quiet. With your help we can.

"None of us were alive then, but before World War II the United States was funding, building and testing the atomic bomb. Word of this project could not be made public. In fact, due to fear of espionage, we even kept the public in the dark as to the cities we had built around the research facilities.

Today, Oak Ridge, Tennessee (which grew to population 75,000) carries more of a mystique than it did prior to the war. The bomb built that town and hid it for years.

We need to do the same, for the same reasons. Although we are not building nuclear devices, we still do not want the public aware of our activities and dropping in for a visit. I will explain in detail later."

Anne was asked if she thought she could follow those instructions. Her immediate, affirmative answer told Lacey all he needed to know.

The Osburns were brought on board as the team to build and manage the Appalachia School. Lacey opened his secure phone and typed in a few letters.

Immediately the driver of the white pick-up put down his magazine. He had been reading in the lobby of the hotel and now he rose, approached the front desk and asked to see the manager. There was no question the unannounced visitor would be received. The area vice-president of the hotel chain had phoned earlier to instruct the manager to be on site today.

The driver sent a quick, short text of confirmation to Lacey, and then strode down the hall to the manager's office. Lacey excused himself to the Osburns and also departed for the manager's office.

They reached an agreement, before dinnertime, to have this facility used as an interim bedroom for the recruits in this region. When needed, extra cots and linen would be supplied. The entire location was on retainer and was to always have no vacancy. It was bought and paid for.

Tom Lacey was driven back to the airport in the little white truck and flew home. "Vern, honey, How . . ."

"I know Annie." he interrupted "It's an interesting story. Is it just lucky timing, or (more likely) has Lacey been watching me? Anyway, I was about to get in deeper with some shady guys in the lobbying world when he kidnapped me. Literally, picked me up against my will, and took me to some secure location.

Before I could try to escape, or steal my phone back to call you, or do anything; he had me sold. You heard the man. But beyond being in the big leagues, we're on the right side for once. Or at least I am. You have always had the reliable morals in the family. Now I get a chance to work alongside you on very worthwhile project."

Anne asked, "Vern, do you know what this entails? We have been asked not only to do some building here to set up a half-way house, if you will, for new students of this center as he called it, but also to write the curriculum for both this place and that center.

Who knows the ages of our students, or the education background? You and I, together, will be affecting the lives of every young person that strolls down these halls – forever.

"Thank you honey", she said as she threw her arms around him, "Thank you."

URGENT STATE

ELEVEN

• •—•• • ——• •— —• —

There it was again, that feeling of uneasiness. Jeff Foster was too familiar with the sensation – but it had always been associated with the scene of a fire or other incident. Why the unsettling sensation now?

He and his wife Ellie had met at work a generation ago and had since worked at different fire stations within Local 1004 in the Milwaukee vicinity. Both had exemplary careers, a couple of great kids and now this exciting new job. Yet Jeff still had the knack of picking up vibes from most locations and, at this moment he had the strange gut feeling that things were not quite right. Nothing you could identify, so no need to bother Ellie, yet.

It was similar to that feeling he had six years ago after a bunch of the guys at the station had decided to close their bank accounts in protest of what was happening with their new governor. They knew he was not acting in their best interest, or the interest of the average citizen.

Thousands of like-minded citizens visited the capitol to protest. When it was discovered that the local banker was a big supporter of the idiot-governor, a group from Local 311 in Madison visited the bank *en masse*

73

and closed their accounts: withdrew all the cash. Jeff's West Allis workers in Local 1004 joined them, then put out a call. Firefighters from 520 in Minnesota, 362 – Indiana, 413 – IL and more joined in. That day numerous first-responders closed their bank accounts while others cashed personal and/or travelers checks. The bank had to shut down that afternoon to prevent a more serious run.

They knew the governor could arrange for some unpleasant things to happen in Wisconsin if he wanted, but it looked as though nothing did. That, in itself, became unnerving. A message had been sent by the unions and they waited for a response from the union-busting politician. The gloom, as if something was about to happen, lasted for weeks - then something did.

One of the captains from Local 311 in Madison saw Jeff at a union gathering. Pulling him aside the captain related the story that he was being followed. In their travels in-and-out of the station, his men had been commenting on a familiar car parked around the corner. That suspect vehicle was never occupied, but the coffee shop across the street always was. One keen eyed, B-shift, paramedic noticed the same man, at the same table.

Further observation revealed that the watcher was only there when the captain was on-shift. Someone had their schedule. Someone had tracked the captain from the protest at the capitol steps, to the station. They concluded that their involvement in the political situation at the capitol had earned them surveillance.

Jeff was disturbed that he was now aware of that same feeling. Then it surfaced – a sudden recognition. That maroon F-150 was the same pick-up he noticed yesterday. Here it was in the mall parking lot, two rows from where he and Ellie decided to park. Nobody was in the driver's-seat, but Jeff didn't care. It was the truck he recognized, not any occupant.

Normally he was not a car guy – he was a firefighter. It was a search he did a couple years ago for an old-fashioned, stick, two-door pick-up that resulted in his glancing at all late model trucks. His earlier efforts had been almost fruitless. All the popular truck makers manufactured those four-door, automatic transmission high-dollar rigs. He had been looking for some low cost, newish two-door with a stick.

He felt he had better control of the vehicle with those features, but he sure did not have control of what was available. The big three all stopped making basic pickups a few years earlier. Even special-order rigs were not available. He got a used truck, and an overdue lesson in who made what in what years. So, today he knew it was the same truck in the mall parking lot.

Brian Knight had mentioned the possibility that Jeff's new job might generate an amount of curiosity in some ranks and result in him being watched for a while. It sure hadn't taken long, had it? To date their job had been to talk with cops and firefighters: to educate fellow public servants on the difference between credit unions and bank. What was threatening about this financial dialog, and who was feeling threatened?

They didn't know exactly who was concerned about them, but their being followed meant they would soon be able to answer that question. Should they turn the tables and do some of their own following, or just proceed with their shopping trip? Now that he recognized the threat, he became more comfortable in his surroundings.

Jeff Foster had a reputation, well deserved, for reading his surroundings. He described it as each scene having an aura. Most noteworthy was his ability to read a fire.

Once, as a young recruit, he cautioned a more seasoned veteran about walking any farther on the roof of a burning building. The caution was ignored and two other team members with the help of the ladder truck barely got the seasoned man out in time. Since that incident, no one ignored Jeff's sense of calm or foreboding, and no one at a response with him had ever been hurt. His current calm registered with Ellie. She picked-up on his change of mood. They were now receiving regular paychecks from Brian Knight and the two had been excitedly spending a wad of that money. The couple had set aside this morning to test drive some reclining easy-chairs. That's why they were driving Jeff's pick-up. She didn't question him when he whispered that he needed to make a secure call to Brian.

The truck, as modified by Brian's team, was communication secure as long as the phone call was through the blue-tooth via a specific frequency on the AM dial of the radio. On the off-chance that the truck had been bugged, he asked Ellie to help him put the salmon in the ice chest while he rearranged the other bags of groceries and camping gear they had just bought. There was no salmon or ice chest and Ellie understood. They met at the back bumper of the pick-up/camper for a quick chat.

Once back in the truck cab, as discussed, Jeff drove past the parked maroon F-150. Ellie leaned over to give him a loud kiss on the cheek and made a mental note of the license number she saw out the window. Then she dialed Brian. Automatically, an ultra-high (UHF) frequency wail was broadcast throughout the cab. This would sound similar to a police siren to everything listening except the secure phone equipment. Human's couldn't hear it.

In the length of time it took the satellite phone to connect, Jeff had effortlessly executed enough turns within the mall parking lot, and out onto the public street, that he knew he was not being followed. As a former member of Engine Co. #5 he knew which islands within the parking lot were wooded, and long enough to allow for some visibility cover – you always knew which turns the ladder truck could not negotiate. He headed away from their home, drove onto the freeway and began explaining the situation to Brian Knight.

"Where are you now?" Brian asked.

"We're headed east in I-94, a few miles from the lake."

"OK." Brian continued "Get to the museum and into their underground parking lot, the camper will just fit under there. The parking garage shouldn't be too busy right now. I'll have a team meet you within a half an hour and they can sweep your truck. Leave the vehicle and walk around above ground until you get my call."

"Not to worry. We've been expecting this." He disconnected the call.

The Milwaukee Art Museum is on the grassy shore of Lake Michigan. It was a romantic spot and a beautiful day, so they decided to walk along the edge of the lake. A little more private there, too. They were partners in this new experience, and no secrets were kept from each other. They both started to speak – he allowed her to proceed.

"You realize this means we might need to move on." she stated.

"Yea." he replied. "Brian did warn us that we could be asked to relocate. I'm not sure I fully agree with his interpretation of our presence being a dangerous distraction. But, it is his show and he does pay the bills."

"I have been thinking about this a lot." she continued, "and want you to know I am behind you 110% on whatever we are asked to do. Brian and his guys, whoever they are, have one serious endeavor and we need to help them. More than our lives are at stake. It's big."

"I know." he replied, "It's just that you and I have memories, family and friends here. To leave it all without saying a word comes hard to me. You know how much of a home-body I am. There is no question we will take off. Please give me a little time to think and sort a few things out."

They continued walking in silence. An inviting park bench offered a perfect seat to watch a little informal regatta of small sailboats on Lake Michigan. His cell phone vibrated.

"I have made arrangements for you to tour the Blue Ridge Mountains. One-one-five is waiting for you. I suggest you take the camper down I-74 to Cincy, then across 50. Fewer big rigs that way. I'll call again. Start driving the day after tomorrow. Swing by the gym on your way outta town. Have a safe trip."

It was as they had suspected. He told Ellie, "Here we go. Brian is sending us to southeast Ohio. The guys from Columbus will undoubtedly meet up with us as we get closer and provide more details. We have a day and a half to wrap it up here.

The story for the neighbors is that we are touring the Blue Ridge mountains. I know some guys at the station I can ask to maintain the house: do grass, mail, leaves, etc. for as long as it takes. Who knows, we might even come back. Are you ready?"

Over the years, as a result of various conventions and union involvements, Jeff had memorized the numbers of the firefighter's locals. Those that were not in the union still had numbers to him, just zip codes. Brian had told him that his old buddy from local #115 was his contact. Jeff was just to drive. He knew they would find each other.

He also knew that the guy in the pick-up in the mall was trouble. Such a quick response to a little surveillance could only mean that somebody out there was quite interested in their doings. Brian would know who. Jeff did not want to know. That would come soon enough. It was time to think about what to do, and what to pack and take on a vacation knowing that you may never come back.

Although it was only a few months ago, it seemed closer to a year since they had been approached in Las Vegas to work with Brian's team. A lot had happened; mainly a lot of education. They were quick to sign on to saving the planet, but the new office in Milwaukee and the security behind it all was hard to get used to. How does a guy that plays with sirens and bells become accustomed to working silently? He realized that secrecy would make the upcoming project much easier to complete.

At the request of Brian Knight, Jeff had kept his membership in the local gym active. They had some equipment not available in the exercise room at the station, so this fit into his retirement plans. He did plan on working out whenever he could. Brian's advice that Jeff swing by the gym could only mean there was material to pick up from the locker in the dressing room.

On their way east, they did in fact visit the locker and retrieve a gym bag. Once back on the road, Ellie unpacked a cell phone, license plates for Ohio, West Virginia, Virginia and Kentucky, a hotel key-card and $10,000 in cash. This would be some road trip.

TWELVE

••• • — — • — • • — • • — ••

The big camper pulled in behind the non-descript hotel. As instructed, Jeff used the key-card to enter through a back door and found his way to a room on the first floor. He knocked. The door was opened by a large yet gentle looking man who introduced himself as Vern – no last name was offered. Jeff replied in kind and was invited into the room.

"I've been expecting you." said Vern "Have any trouble finding the place?"

"Nope." He replied, scanning his surroundings. "It's nicer than I expected."

"That seems to happen in these circles." The host added "I'm getting used to this luxury. That is, when I'm not on the road. I'm glad you are here. I need the help."

"Can we get my wife outta the car first?" asked Jeff.

"Take her to room 266. It's at the end of the hall and closest to the stairs down there. That key will work on the door and the room. In fact, it will open every door in the building. Have a shower and help yourself to some of the goodies you will find waiting for you. Whenever you feel like socializing, wander back here - both of you."

Jeff returned to the camper and grabbed an armload of bags, trash and his gym satchel. Ellie picked up what she could carry, and they proceeded through the door, up the central stairs and down the long hall to room 266.

"Honey – I need to change plates on the truck before I do anything else. Come with me and keep watch then we'll clean up." They went back down the stairs. He moved the truck for security reasons, backing it into a space closest the back door at the far end of the hotel. The stairs at this end of the building were a straight-drop below room 266. He opened the tool chest built into the side of the camper and retrieved a screwdriver. Then he changed license plates to the Ohio version he had found in his gym bag.

Ellie had already determined where they were to hide the $10,000 cash they also found inside that bag. Earlier, she had activated the satellite cell phone she discovered nestled next to the cash and received instructions on the route to the hotel.

For now, they were to keep their real identity and keep the truck licensed accordingly. Ohio computers had been altered to align their vehicle with their ID and a street address in a town called Ironton. They would visit home soon enough.

After a shower and some food, they stepped out and downstairs to Vern's room. There they met Anne and were invited to join them at a conference table in an adjoining room. The interconnected suite had no bed but was outfitted with a large table and a map on the wall. Jeff noticed the electronics on a side table.

Vern began by welcoming the newcomers. He softened his speech so as to not appear too excited or bold. Anne had told him that his loud booming voice was as imposing as his size, although he noticed that Foster was just as large. He had been advised of the importance of first impressions. He wanted this couple to be impressed.

He then laid out the project, as he knew it, and the shared participation that was required of everyone in that room.

"I guess you could say we need to recruit recruiters. It's almost impossible to locate qualified workers in a community, from outside that community. There is not only the outsider aspect, but the lack of familiarity with the neighborhood and individual prospects. We need to have one-on-one conversations with real prospects, without wasting a lot of time."

It was hard to stop but he needed to make time for Q & A.

Jeff started "So we are to build a recruiting network and funnel these young people to you for education."

"Right."

"As I understand it, my connections with firefighter locals and not-so-organized associations will start this process and hopefully, these guys are savvy enough to keep it quiet."

"Right, again."

"Whoever set this up has been doing some deep thinking. I can almost guarantee that we can recruit the retired guys that I know in these organizations, and I'm sure they can keep a secret. Plus, they will love the involvement in something this beneficial to their community. I see keeping them going at a realistic pace to be the problem. Their tendency will be to speed things up as they get familiar with the organization and logistics."

"We can work on that together when need be" Vern said,

"How involved can you get around here, for example?"

"Can I use your computer?"

The others talked education and travels while Jeff worked in front of the screen. During their get-acquainted chat, Ellie and Anne discovered a common interest: teaching the testosterone fueled male: regardless of age. It was funny, and timely, that at that exact moment Jeff backed away from the side table and joined the party.

"Here are the quick numbers. Let's use this map of Ohio. I can guarantee a guy I know here," said Jeff as he stabbed the map with his index finger, " who retired ten years ago. He belonged to a station in this town, but to a union local that encompassed these three communities. He is one of 23 guys that are retired in this local. They all meet regularly at regional gatherings.

This Ohio River region covers this territory and contains 15 locals plus 83 volunteer organizations, all of which belong to another association that I know well. They never retire and are dedicated, trustworthy men and women.

Most of them are empty nesters and would welcome an opportunity to assign duty to some rookie substitutes and hit the road. So, the final numbers look like I can get you 800 to 1000 recruiters in this Ohio, Kentucky, West Virginia area, and this is around Appalachia. Did you want me to examine the deep south too?"

Vern whistled. Even Ellie raised an eyebrow. She knew her husband went to a lot of union meetings, but . . Jeff continued:

"Your recruiting message calls for some quality interview time. Each potential student must be given enough information to allow them to make an informed decision. Not every young person will be willing to leave home. Not every parent is able to send their child off to save the world. It can be done but we will need to be patient."

Early the next morning Vern was on the phone. This was exactly the data Tom Lacey was waiting for. After he hung up Lacey sent a message to Marina Whitehorse. The wheels started rolling to get beds, food, tools, and everything to south center. They were going to bring in recruits and put them to work.

The message came back down-stream to tell the Fosters to get started. Green light all the way. A message also came through that their episode with the F-150 in

Milwaukee was over. The pick-up had belonged to a hired gun that the governor's people had used to track the dissenting firefighters.

That communique suggested that they "Rest assured the governor, or owner, would never see that truck again, nor the four others they had just discovered that were following different firefighters."

THIRTEEN

• ••• — • — •

Sean Crockett had called together his closest advisors. Regardless of their official duty, he wanted to talk money. To help interpret his wishes he also had three tax lawyers in the room and some serious number crunchers.

"I'm not sure where to start this, or where we may be going, but I need to share some information with you and ask for your help."

After explaining some history behind the declaration of emergency, he continued.

"Let's not kid ourselves. Exercising this kind of Executive Order will guarantee I'm a one-term wonder. To some of you four years may sound like a long time: sufficient time to accomplish every item on our wish list. I don't think so. Assuming we tackle this agenda, there is no room to spend a year campaigning. I can't imagine being re-elected based on performance alone. Since we know I'm going down, I need to go down in flames. It is my intention to start the process of fixing some serious issues. I need your advice.

First, the emergency order will include language prohibiting Wall Street from the practice of instant electronic trades. We need all stocks to stay in the buyer's

85

hands for longer than five seconds – like a week. I have read enough to know that it is just not fair that the big boys and the market makers have the computer power to execute these trades while everyone else is on the slow boat. We need to slow down and level the playing field for a while."

Taking a break from furiously making notes, a Wall Street executive raised his hand.

"Please hold that question until we get deeper into this." The President advised, "I guarantee there will be more. While on the subject of the stock market, we need to change the rules of the trades and earnings made by the folks that add nothing to the economy.

"As I understand it, some derivatives and hedge fund managers are making money for guys who only trade and make money from making money. There is no value added to the economy, just dollars added to their coffers. Look into tax penalties for investors in those types of trading. If they know how to make money without working, or providing a service to mankind, then we need to tax more for that easy scheme. That again, is the big boys gaming the system."

Crockett shifted his gaze to one of the Treasury Department division Assistant Directors.

"Speaking of big boys, we need a serious investigation into the spending of the defense department. How many of you knew it is the largest single employer in the nation? Until recently, me neither. In addition to the massive payroll, they dole out close to $110 billion each year to a select few defense contractors. Too many of these businesses expect, and regularly receive, this money. Too many of our senators and governors are awarded these dollars without negotiating, or even bidding, for them. But beyond building weapons, do you know where a large part of this money goes?

"We have military bases at 787 sites throughout 88 foreign countries. At home we have over 600 bases, depots, etc. scattered around our 50 states. You talk about a landholder. No wonder we have such a huge budget. We have better infrastructure at foreign bases than we do in some cities in the south. I think it is time to concentrate on better jobs and roads in the United States.

"I have had one meeting with the Joint Chiefs, and I intend to have another one. It is not my job to tell them how to run their armed forces, but it is my job to try to balance the budget. I want more money spent at home and on projects that help civilians, as well as the military. It would seem logical that the construction crew on the base or fort could use manpower from the local community to build roads and bridges within that community. However, I'm not suggesting that we go back to the CCC days.

"I am suggesting that we can use civilian contractors on a small scale to work on joint infrastructure projects in local communities. The need to fly a US contractor and crew to the Persian Gulf to build an oil refinery will soon not exist. But the need to help local folks get a job and learn a skill will always exist."

The President needed to stretch his legs, and stood.

"I know we can't encourage base commanders with tax breaks but figure out what carrot we can use to encourage them to shift the paradigm. More specialties in both military and civilian labor are turning towards electronics and computer science. However, we will always need some laborers. Can't we help them move from manual labor to skilled and, in the process, appreciate that they have a future?

As for the military future, more of that will be on this continent. No one will admit it, but our need for global superiority has changed. We will never again be required to police the oceans so we can safely import our oil because, lately our production is greater than our imported supply.

In addition, we will never again need to station submarines beneath those same oceans, so our missiles can reach their targets. The sophistication of drones and satellites make long-range weapons obsolete. Therefore, we don't need the expense of those 787 foreign sites I mentioned earlier.

I'm going to task the military leaders to tell me what foreign bases they will leave open if they have a 25% budget cut. Based on their answers, I'm going to ask you to run the logic and numbers by each other. This is going to be an interesting exercise because not all our military brass knows how to think smarter: they only know bigger and harder.

We have mini-drones now that we can program for specific targets: either through facial recognition, or many other algorithms. These wristwatch-sized weapons can carry a shape charge capable of blasting a hole through a brick wall. Ten of them in a row and you're through a concrete wall.

If we can get a photo of everyone in a village in Afghanistan, the drone can neutralize an enemy threat without one American being hurt. Does that mean we can remove an entire base? Probably, if we spend some money on buying a photographer in the village. Weigh the difference in cost and the difference in risk. I want to see us return the village to the villagers."

"Mister President," interrupted one of the accounting office staff. "We can't just walk away from billions in equipment and leave these untrained civilians without protection."

"I will address theater exit strategies later." replied Crockett, "Our asset column should list personnel first - material second.

As uncomfortable as it is, we need to recognize that military jobs are a huge portion of our labor force. Not just our all-volunteer service persons, but the contractor's employees as well. When we bring the personnel home from a foreign base, we need to have jobs waiting for them.

Put your heads together on that problem. One thing we need to do to help soften the nation's financial woes is eliminate the early retirement system the military has.

"All federal employees need to work towards a retirement at an age that is fiscally responsible. Sure, we grandfather the existing service-persons out of new requirements, but enlistees from here on out can consider it a long-term proposition if they want to retire from our United States military. Age 65 as an absolute minimum to earn 100% of salary. With respect to those retired from the military, give some thought to how to refine the tax-rates for double dippers.

"We know there is a large number of public servants that have retired more than once from tax-payer supported jobs. Is that what the tax-payers deserve – to pay two complete pensions?

"One area you also need to examine is the process of awarding work to the defense contractors and the administration of those contracts. We spend just shy of a trillion dollars a year on this complex industry. That is too much money for any of this spending to be automatic. The money received from United States taxpayers will not be taken for granted.

"It is of primary importance that government contracts be awarded only to reputable firms. We need to define that not only in terms of corporate guidance and reputation, but also the reputation of the owners if it is a wholly-owned com-pany, and board members assuming it is a corporation.

"We need limits on executive compensation and limitations on cash on hand. If our contractors are not spending their cash on benefits or research, we need to tax excessive reserves. They can do business with us, but they had better not just accumulate surplus without planning for the future or keeping up with technological changes. I'd like to see a federal financial report card for defense contractors.

"Let us prepare and publish these analyses as a way to let the public know when a company is in danger of losing its government credibility. The way I see it, Wall Street has established precedent by publishing whether or not a stock meets expected performance. Those experts that predict performance are not from the company that issues the stock, but from Wall Street.

"It follows that the government should have the right to tell investors when the government thinks its vendors are not meeting expectations. We can only hope for the day when investment firms give financial advice to help a company earn a specific government certification: a better grade.

"Allow me to finalize, then we'll get to questions. Most of you are aware that many of these changes have been made public. In fact, some have been instituted. However, none have really been fine-tuned and a majority of the rules have not been written. I wanted to get your input before we got to that step. FYI, it's rapidly approaching."

The President took a breath, sat down and thought about the amount of work to be done in such a short period of time.

"As I mentioned earlier, I don't know what I'm doing. We have an opportunity to take this country back to the levels and values it had before it recently began always favoring the rich. We don't have all the answers and you can bet that all these proposed fixes may not get going. However, I am damned sure we need to correct our course.

Any of you that feel otherwise may bow out at any time. If the heat gets to you, just jump ship. No hard feelings. By using this opportunity, we may be sealing our fate. My biggest fear is the outcome if we do NOT take drastic action."

He was certain these major changes made him unelectable. He was wrong.

FOURTEEN

• — —•— ••— •• — —•——

This most recent chapter in Joseph's life had started innocently enough. His son had come home from college with an idea. More of a project actually, since Junior (when was the last time he was called Edward?) was an active participant when the two first discussed it. Amazing what those classmates come up with when given time to study and time to – don't they call it network?

There is no question that his athletic abilities had paid off. The full-ride scholarship allowed him to pursue his studies and run track as he (and the coach) saw fit. It was at a track meet when he was a senior that this younger kid had started those almost forgotten conversations. That was years ago but Joseph recalled when he first was told about the interest the younger student expressed in his son. Not in their mutual passion of long-distance running, but in mining and technology. How those subjects came up between those two young men was never addressed.

Edward's approach with his dad was simple. At university he had met this younger student that had revealed a deep curiosity about the tribe. Not so much in the history and working of the Nation, but details and specifics about the land.

"Dad, Harold is so enthusiastic about our geography and the site of the reservation that he has asked to come home with me on spring break."

Between their last two quarters, most seniors in college chase the opposite sex at some sunny locale. What was wrong with this white guy? What harm in entertaining one of Junior's friends rather than paying for some junket to Cozumel, or other exotic Mexican destination? That was the introduction to Hal, as he called himself. He visited for a few days and nights.

The boys had slept in one of the tipis, rather than in Edward's room in the house, and put hundreds of miles on the jeep. Spring was a good time for visiting the Great Plains: not too hot yet and the days are longer than the nights. The two college kids went everywhere, then went back to school. That was that, but it was the beginning.

Joseph had forgotten the interval between when his son had last brought Hal to the reservation and when it was decided that the father (Joseph) should meet Harold's influential older brother. Not forgotten was the honesty and depth of that first meeting; and its length. They spent all night talking. The young bucks went to bed while the real men had one long powwow.

Every member of the Nation believed in man-made climate change. Every member felt hopeless when discussing it. Brian Knight had come forth with a plan of action that involved the tribe as deeply as they wanted to be. Plus, there was a design to introduce meaningful jobs, expand their boundary and create new wealth.

Although vague in long-term details, the ideas brought up in their first conversation appealed to the old chief. It was obvious that these issues would not be resolved in a single generation. Fortunately, Joseph and his son had a relationship that included the sharing of dreams and expectations.

Whether hunting together in the high-country or building a house for a tribal member, this team was constantly sharing feelings and thoughts. Edward (or Junior as everybody called him) was dedicated to returning to Wind River after college. The chief knew a tribal leader was being groomed – not just a son to follow in his father's footsteps. Joseph had faith in his son to continue the efforts started during that long night.

For some unknown reason, he also had strong faith in this new acquaintance. Brian Knight spoke with authority but was not an employee of the government. He referred to a very healthy non-profit foundation yet did not try to educate Joseph in the ways of such a business. They spoke as equals, yet this young white kid was the age of the chief's son. He admired that confidence in youth.

Joseph did remember that they had scheduled their next meeting to be held in a most unusual spot: the small reservation runway. The decision was made to meet there after discussing the second-class accommodations and the availability of the single hanger. The appeal was its remote location.

Brian had emphasized the need for security and the chief began thinking of various steps needed to have this gathering be private. Private, as in the chief and two elders visit the runway, but only Joseph would go aboard the jet. He had never been on an executive aircraft. "I wonder if they have a bathroom?" he asked himself.

FIFTEEN

—• •— — ••— •—• •— •—••

The swamps of Alabama are not friendly. If you don't know what you're doing, you can get in serious trouble. Yet that is how many of the first Urgent workers got their early education. They were raised to survive in those conditions.

The recruiters for the new town had been encouraged to bring their new recruits to the reservation in a timely manner, but better educated in the ways of their new lives. Not only were warnings about families and drugs and alcohol to be passed along, but teachings in social, financial and gender tolerance as well. For this reason, the trip from home to Urgent had to be long, yet memorable.

Hurricanes in the Gulf States leave wreckage everywhere. Things that float seem to get particularly battered. In the aftermath, salvaged boats are cheap, and the Urgent team bought a few. When shopping for this transportation the requirements were simple: it had to float, and the engines needed to run. Those parameters made boat buying easy. Then the teaching started.

Always traveling in two-boat sets, young southerners were driven north from the Gulf along the Tenn-Tom waterway: an inland link that runs parallel to the Mississippi River, but is less commercially traveled. The better of the two vessels was chosen as the galley and master quarters: the other as the workshop. From day one the recruits started working. The driver of the work boat (to be called skipper) was accompanied by one trained mechanic. Classes were held on that vessel. The subject was the needs that arose to keep the 40-foot boat safe and moving. Recruits were transferred from one boat to the other regularly, except for sleeping. Couples had a berth on the better vessel, whichever one that might be on that particular night.

Days were spent charting the way through the South, navigating the Tennessee Valley Authority maze of lakes and locks, and into Kentucky. The Ohio River would then carry them on to South Center: their destination. Along the way everybody learned the basics of low-voltage wiring, plumbing, woodworking, and fiberglass repair. All hands also shared the boating needs of navigation, communication, and safety. Every afternoon they swam instead of showering. Those that did not know how to swim when the trip started, knew how at the end.

When in port a few youngsters would accompany the skipper on a shopping trip. They learned social skills in buying, taxi riding, clothes shopping and public conversation. Back on-board they learned, and were evaluated, on personal grooming, hygiene, even writing letters writing back home.

It took about a month to follow those calm waterways. In that month the non-stop education was molding a more complete person, soon to be delivered to the training center. At that point the adjustment to community living would be less stressful than it might have been. Stress was still a part of their new surroundings, though, because of the larger number of fellow trainees

Once disembarking on the edge of the Ohio River, and entering the South Center, the new water-borne joined those that had made the same trip before them, plus the young people that arrived overland from Appalachia.

Recruits that came through the hotel in Appalachia did not experience the water teachings. Their specialization became roads and highways of America. Towns along the way, exits, campgrounds, state parks and monuments, freeway loops and beltways: all became familiar terms and encounters.

The Osburns had succeeded in expanding the cooking capabilities of the hotel but dining room seating was at a premium. In fact, the recruits ate in two shifts. Six floors of lodging, at 50 rooms per floor, was just too much for the downstairs meeting/eating space.

A few of the hotel rooms had been altered to allow for seating of smaller more intimate classes. To some, having one's own bathroom was considered a luxury. Each room had a television, but the cable had been disconnected and local programming was not too exciting.

Due to evening classes and exercise hours, there was not a lot of time to watch TV anyway. In addition to social education, the recruits' powers of observation were under constant evaluation. How quickly did a student learn the surroundings and how accurate was the reaction to that environment? The guides/teachers had been instructed to get to know their travelers well enough to determine who had street smarts. Who could read the circumstances, or land, and what was their reaction.

When they started their trip – their education – most recruits had biases. Even prejudices and racism were evident. One month later those negative analyses of other individuals had been replaced with a healthy attitude and positive thinking. Yet many individuals still needed a realistic analysis of daily events. The trainees that best exhibited mental flexibility were to be identified. At first, the most astute were those that were allowed to move from the hotel to the center.

Life at the centers was much more work related.

URGENT STATE

Construction was top priority for many years. It did not take long before all labor was performed by the residents. Concrete work, carpentry, roofing, grading, road building, glazing; almost all work. Cooking was in-house, but the food was brought in. Utilities were needed initially. Soon solar power added to the independence of the centers.

After work and after dinner, groups gathered to discuss various topics and solve problems. The varying subjects kept conversation from getting stale. The schedule called for games two nights a week, but these were educational in nature. Although the group was laughing at antics, or incorrect responses, the byproduct of all entertainment was learning. Movie night meant documentaries or films loaded with moral stories and hidden meanings.

Not evident to the new students was the fact that a large part of their curriculum was science. The future work of these young people would involve the need to understand the basics of the origin of man, and the planet he lives on. It was not unusual to introduce a young, believer to the theory of evolution. Heated discussions would involve arguments from both sides of a question.

When the origins of the planet were brought into the mix, young minds began to understand the real meaning of time as astronomers viewed it. The time required for man's evolution became easier to accept. For those that exhibited a thirst for knowledge, the teachings were guided towards the present environmental condition of our earth.

The history of mass extinctions was used to reinforce how close we are to repeating such an event. Warming oceans, atmospheric CO_2 concentrations, carbon levels in the sea, ozone layers: all real science was readily brought into the picture and talked about. The students were never prohibited from supporting their beliefs.

They were, however, expected to listen to the other side of the argument.

The center had a non-denominational chapel, and anyone could worship at any time. Religion, though, was not in the daily teachings of everybody. Sharing ideas about religion was, but in a universal sense. A young Catholic might read a fable from the Bible and could enjoy a response from a Jew that knew a similar story. The centers' teachings were that no religious teachings were wrong. albeit, some were out of date. The group was taught why that might be and why religion might be so slow to respond.

Native American beliefs were emphasized. For obvious reasons, all citizens of Urgent were to be knowledgeable in local traditions and lore. The culture of family life, dating, dancing, singing; all was to be taught to everyone.

The saving grace of Urgent, and possibly our planet, was that it was located on land that was part of another nation: not the United States of America. All citizens would respect that fact.

SIXTEEN

•• —• ••• •——• •• •—• •

Tom Lacey had researched out-of-the-way places to build the centers he envisioned: midway points on the route to Urgent. In addition, he felt there was a social midway point needed. A large part of the population (therefore the future leaders) would be from deep poverty and deep in their traditions. Exposure to money and other cultures was necessary if the future meant living, working and learning with strangers.

The rolling hills of southern Ohio are covered with dense, hardwood forest. A few farmers have cleared fields over the years, but the terrain is not conducive to large farms. It is home to logging, mining and lots of outdoors activities. With the canyons and hollers separating these hills, it's hard to learn one's way around. In fact, years ago the nation's famous Underground Railroad operated throughout this region.

The project called for a location that could house future participants while the town was being planned and/or expanded. The geographical confusion is the exact reason some of this land was under construction. The scope of this endeavor dictated there be two such centers. Call them schools for lack of a better term: one in the south and the other near a Great Plains Nation.

The southern location was being established on the Ohio/Kentucky border: deep in the woods but near the river. It would be built first.

The availability of transportation via water offered maximum security. It would take hundreds of shipments of construction materials to build this center, yet Lacey wanted to keep it quiet. The local citizens might spread rumors about a religious cult or compound, but very few would visit and realize how large the center was. Building materials could be brought in by barge and by truck. Even the pupils could arrive by either water or land.

Sure, people would talk. The locals within the river communities always had great grapevines. However, the rumors would grow silent once the project generated enough revenue to bolster the county and township balance sheets. The amount of activity would certainly be a topic at various local meetings.

In an effort to speak to these concerns, Bo Elliott traveled the local meeting circuit to be a face for the project and to confirm the benefits to the community. A recent transplant to this area, his new job was to distribute the facts.

Rural roads would need to be widened. Local coffee shop and diners would need more help. By activating previously abandoned rail lines, nearby dormant businesses might also be reactivated. It would be announced, or leaked, that the fees for building permits and leases had already been paid. This unexpected growth was all above-board, and all transactions were public.

Bo's usual location was sitting in his office, on the side of a hill, watching the construction below him. He knew it was organized - he organized it. Yet there was a certain disorganized appearance to the pace and crossed paths of the workers. A hard-hat on a forklift would be in sight, heading east, and suddenly disappear behind some trees. Popping out from a tree line on the other side of that meadow would be a bobcat carrying a load of dirt, or some material. No obvious choreography. At times he wondered why all those people were following his plans.

What special qualifications did he have? When Jeff Foster first approached him about doing something rather than work until retirement, he was curious. "See where curiosity gets you" he thought. Not that he minded. This was actually enjoyable. And these efforts took his mind off the fact that he was single again. "Damn breast cancer!"

When she had died, he promised himself he would get involved in some worthy project and dedicate his efforts to her. This was certainly worthy. Foster had sold him on the concept and Bo figured he would never leave Alabama anyhow, except for this opportunity.

He and Jeff had met years ago at a regional gathering of volunteer firefighters in Pensacola, Florida. Although Bo lived in rural Alabama (Monroe County) they usually went to Pensacola for meetings. The two were on a panel together and ended up talking afterwards for most of the evening. Neither had ever visited the other's country and comparing notes was the entertainment that night.

Jeff had made the first telephone call a year ago. Bo had remembered him and received him at his home a few days later. The subsequent recruiting effort by Foster had been endured by Bo as a form of community service, uncomfortable but necessary. He was too young to retire, but he dreamt that anything he could do to better the future for these unfortunate kids, he would do. At least he had the firefighting experience in the Navy to give him the needed education. Without something, these young people would be stuck in rural Monroe County and add another generation to the rolls of welfare, under-education and lethargy.

Right now, folks around here die young. He thought he could change that. But to do so he would get them away from here. His own recruiting efforts had been very rewarding. He interviewed kids and asked the smart ones who else was smart. Then he asked the independent ones who else was independent. He overlooked a little trouble making. Teamwork and problem solving were admired. To have a chance, these smart free-thinking youngsters needed to leave the area.

Politicians in these parts did not value their citizens. Even the governor was on the side of money and big business. Alabama had some universities with great football and basketball teams. There was money for that, but nothing for rural and other folks. No one even noticed when the recruits started leaving town.

In these small up-river villages, the population cooperated and made do by itself. In the big picture however, they were invisible. One even doubted if these lost citizens were counted in the unemployment statistics. Bo was happy to help the cause, and he was good at it.

He remembered every kid and remembered which boat they traveled on as well as who the skipper was. The neighborhood, school, dates, references, all were in the old memory bank. Every parent was aware of the adventure, every guardian advised. While not being an absolute in each recruiting effort, secrecy was strongly suggested. To a person, the adults agreed. They saw no need to share with authorities or peers the whereabouts of the missing young workers.

After over a year of recruiting, Bo asked a question in a phone conversation with Jeff. The tentative "let me think about it" answer had later resulted in a "get ready to move" order. They decided to put recruiting in this part of the South on hold and install a new project supervisor at the South Center: Bo Elliott. Well, OK, but all he had asked for was a stationary position on land. Bo folded his Alabama map and went out to buy one of southern Ohio.

Some dorms had been built first. Actually, they were big military surplus tents. They kept the bugs out and were portable. The canvas tents were plunked down anywhere there was not a building and moved when they got in the way. Under Bo's supervision, the first real structures were the classrooms, then some warehouses for materials. He appreciated that education was first, even in the early stages of the center.

The young people from the deep south had been thrown together with those from Appalachia. The different races now ate, worked together and attended class together. They laughed at the way some words were pronounced and grimaced as they learned how some foreign foods were prepared. But mostly they worked.

After a one-month probationary period, the new recruits underwent an in-depth interview. Their compatibility with the ideals of the project was the main subject. Work ethic and social skills were discussed as well. For those that decided, or were allowed, to continue, enticing new information was shared.

The near future would involve more building, more classes, and hard work. As a sort of graduation present, they could look forward to being moved to Urgent. Based on Bo's recommendation, a regular trickle of promising citizens had started moving to Wind River.

Describing the new village as a work in progress was an under-statement. Relating that there were challenges, opportunities and a bright future also understated the facts. Among the issues to be addressed:
- There was initially no need or room for personal vehicles, transportation was at the site.
- There was no place for babies in this wild-west town: oral, birth control was mandatory.
- Until further notice, the place was dry: no alcohol.
- Communication with home was to be kept at a minimum.
- All paychecks were be automatically deposited in a bank account set up for each worker. There wasn't any place to spend money anyway in the early stages of growth.

Not everybody agreed to the rules. They were given a ride home.

Not everybody obeyed the rules either. They too were given a ride. The team that remained at South Center was adapting well and getting along. Bo was proud of them and what they had accomplished. But there was a lot more to do. Building materials were arriving faster via the river, now, and he needed to train some tugboat skippers. Then there was the logging.

The plans indicated the clearing of a few more acres and those trees could be milled, the lumber used after it dried. He needed to find another old-school guy that could cut trees. The last one was lost to alcohol. "Damn booze!"

Plus, he wanted an experienced boat captain to help move the logs around. Bo knew the handful of skippers that ferried his recruits up from the south. He put a call out to find which recruits had shown an affinity for boat handling. After a few days he had a list of six names and brought these prospects in for interviews and auditions. He chose Courtney Jones to be the new tug boat skipper.

Her grandfather began taking her out fishing at an early age. She fished the rivers and streams in southern Alabama, and out into the gulf. She had time at the helm of a variety of boats, but none of the big stuff. Her sense of speed was uncanny and her grasp of terrain and location, virtually perfect. Show her the chart at first and let her travel that route. After that no chart was needed. Her memory was amazing. The twinkle in her eye was mesmerizing.

To Bo Elliot's astonishment, she was only 17. He would have sworn she was older than that. Bo had been about to ask her to skipper one of the recruit boats, but he would not send a teen-ager back into rural Alabama to guide new teenagers north. He kept her on the Ohio River. He had no children, but he told himself that she

was exactly what he would want his daughter to be like.
When Courtney wasn't at the helm pushing logs around the river, she was in his office studying. She was particularly interested in her surroundings and what grew there. He brought her some reading on local history and regional flora and fauna.

One memorable day he decided to take her to the library with him to trade her old books for new ones. She had exhausted the material at the small local branch. He opted to visit the next largest library: in Chillicothe, just north on the highway. Courtney had never seen such a large, light building. The glaze of this shiny structure had her looking at everything.

At one point, inside the building and between the stacks, she said, "She must have a nice car."

"Who are you talking about?" Bo asked.

"That woman in the white shirt."

"Why should she have a car?" he continued.

"Well, I saw her on the sidewalk downtown. How else could she get here as fast as we did?"

"Are you sure?"

"Oh yea, I saw her face in the café door."

"You saw her face?"

"Yea, I'm not real good at colors, but I always remember faces."

"How can you not be good at colors?"

"A teacher at school called me blind one day."

"You mean color blind?"

"Yea, that's what he said."

"OK" he continued, "but what about the face thing?"

"I just remember them."

They checked out some books and left the library.

The first thing Bo did when Courtney went to dinner was call Jeff Foster. He had thought Jeff might be interested in Courtney's ability. He was right.

When that conversation ended, Jeff phoned Brian Knight. "Yea, what about that face thing?" he mimicked.

SEVENTEEN

••• • •—• • —• •

Tom Lacey originally met with Chief Joseph on the reservation. The chief told him of their lone hanger, and short runway on the west plateau. Lacey had the jet cleared to land at Jackson Hole, which was the closest real airport to his destination. The jet-set that frequented that area would not look twice at another unmarked plane. Then he borrowed a helicopter to get into the Wind River reservation.

A table with coffee and sweets was set up, just out of sight of the wide rolling hanger doors. The aircraft and its passenger were inside. The pilot sat in a seldom-used detached office structure. His guide, and guard, was a tribal elder. There was an intercom wired between the two buildings, turned off at the hanger location.

To build a city is no small undertaking. To do so with a minimum of publicity requires some careful planning. They were at the first of many stages. Both realized that a handpicked team would do the real work. Their job was to do some initial legwork after defining a mutual vision: to look forward, past their lifetimes, at the community and, more importantly, its leaders.

There was a philosophical agreement that, if at all possible, the multitude of laborers needed to do this job should be those in need of a job. There were only so many tribal members of that generation still available. Of those, how many were capable was yet to be discovered. Importing such a work force would require careful selection. It would also require visits to various communities and hundreds of interviews.

Large blocks of unemployed and undereducated are found in big cities. There was no way to recruit there and be sly. They discussed visiting rural, impoverished areas and using that labor pool. Local politicians might not realize the reduction in population until it was too late. The Deep South and Appalachia regions of the country had such a populace. Plus, they had too many politicians that didn't care about, and would not miss, some citizens.

The two men felt it necessary to talk about the traits, attributes and rules they would need:

-- No drug or alcohol addictions.
-- No children.
-- No record of violent crimes.
-- Focus on able-bodied people.
-- Amenable to intense education.
-- Mandatory participation in community activities.

Education would be part of continued employment and a reward for effort. They weren't sure exactly how, but married couples would have no choice in remaining childless. There would be jobs for everyone. Counseling, classes and community activities would be mandatory. The daily routine would be varied but completely fill waking hours.

Joseph began voicing his concern about unemployment among tribal members and the need to fix it. Just to the east of them was South Dakota. Four of the poorest nine counties in the US are in South Dakota: each of them home to a Native American nation.

"We need to work with the Cheyenne, the Sioux: all of them in offering employment as soon as their people can handle a job. Even the Crow could use our help. Right now, they make millions from a coal mine or two on their land yet still have nearly 50% jobless rate. They sit on over two million acres and quite a bit of fossil fuel, but what will happen when that market dries up?" Lacey knew the chief was not expecting an answer. It was late in the day. They had some dinner brought in from an elder's house and continued talking. The next day they scheduled a ride around the reservation in the chief's old military style 4-wheel drive Jeep.

Their mutual vision told them it would be a difficult task. Wrapping up a few hours of driving, they both still thought it formidable. To site a city near the river would require new roads. To build manufacturing facilities would call for laying new railroad tracks. If hundreds of wind turbines sat on that ridge, then those peaks needed to be moved or removed. And then there was the boundary question.

The reservation ended at a most beautiful place; this happened more than once. Joseph felt that the need for property acquisition made this seem like a mission destined for failure. At one particularly troublesome location, where the river made a sharp bend, Tom Lacey spoke:

"Chief, I have been given this project by some very quiet, yet powerful people. None are paid by the government but are well known by those in political circles. Let me make some phone calls."

Joseph had a question in his voice when he responded, pointing:

"That land is owned by the State of Wyoming, and the section over there by a mining concern. We have tried to buy even just the river bank from those miners, to no avail."

"We have a couple options." Lacey replied, "The area on the east side of the canyon could provide access by rail from those existing lines coming south. We might trade some acreage in the hot springs region for a chunk bordering the lake. Also, the reservoir is so far removed from any population center, it makes sense to trade it for the building of some recreation area farther east, like near Cheyenne."

"Do you really think so?" asked Joseph.

"Only one way to find out." He took out his phone, leaned back in the passenger seat, and pushed some buttons. Joseph drove in silence back towards the runway. He knew the helicopter was refueled and waiting. He also knew there would be no answers to these hard questions today. The phone calls would start the process, but decisions would take some time. Or so he thought.

He was taken aback when Lacey spoke after taking an incoming call.

"About the swap with the mining guys: that can be taken care of before the quarter is over. The answer on getting title to the Wyoming land will have to wait a couple days. It seems the governor is out of town. I have been told we are always able to swap land if the receiving party thinks the deal is too good. So, the recreation area near the reservoir is ours whenever we want it.

Naturally, we won't lock it down. We just want to make it part of the Nation, with the legal title. The public can still fish, and water ski, swim and whatever. It will comfort you to know that we will go beyond the US government when registering this agreement. There are world courts that receive notifications such as this and have some powers that nations have agreed to. Once we grow our borders, we will keep them. Period."

"I am really impressed," the Chief volunteered. "When you say you work with some powerful people you speak the truth. My experience with your government has been nothing like what I just witnessed. I guess that shows how little power the chief has in the white man's eyes."

"Our government," Lacey analyzed, "has gotten off track. The people you have been forced to deal with are the same people I would deal with if I did not know their superiors."

Knowing he could trust this man, he needed to share: "I should mention, though, that when we face an immovable obstacle, and can't go around it, we will bury it. We do not have the luxury of spending the time needed to educate some people. As we discussed last night, this is about our survival. The greedy businessmen (and they mostly are men) that want to control the world are too busy to notice us. That's fine.

"Along the way we could encounter an observant management type that suspects something. We will try to put that person to work or prevent them from working. It may be their choice, or not. You will never know. In fact, I doubt if I will be told.

"When I first was asked to join this project I, like you, was impressed. When you realize that this undertaking could happen, you, like me, will feel overwhelmed. I was told to share the job with someone of my choosing and to ask him or her to do the same. The simplification of duties to that one mission makes the actual, mammoth goal seem attainable. I suggest you try thinking like that. As the leader of your people, you have experience in delegating and evaluating fellow tribal members.

"You will need to evaluate them through a different lens than before, but I know you are up to it. There will always be someone on the end of a phone line to cover your back. It's up to you to face the front. If you need help, we will be there. It may take us a while to dig through our files to get you exactly what you need, but we do have some impressive files. We are forced to do a lot of listening, and watching, to determine what we are up against, and that is not an easy task. Primarily because there is more than one force opposing what we stand for.

"The years have created many different social and/ or political groups with different ideologies. Any one of them could raise hell with our plans. So, we need to keep track of them all. There is not one opponent, but many.

"You can see how more than one investigator might be trying to find us. Unless we break some serious or highly visible law these investigations will be only semi-official. These are explorations ordered by committee members and their hired help, not the big letter intelligence agencies. That means we constantly monitor all committee members as well as the usual suspects."

Joseph asked about these listening capabilities. He was told that they had started monitoring conversations around Washington. Certain officials used secure communication lines and those were open to Lacey's computers. As were all satellite signals. It was harder to get information from old-fashioned landlines, but access to the computers of those individuals that used landlines usually was rewarding.

"It's amazing what you can discover if you have a copy of the daily calendar and the secretary's cell phone circuit. We also use the oft-derided, human intel. A few of our senior players are not that far removed from jobs in Washington. They still have friends and have great relations with former colleagues.

You have met Brian Knight, the one that arranged this meeting. He is a former Washington type. We only work with individuals that are smart enough not to burn bridges. They maintain access."

Lacey climbed out of the old Jeep and boarded the helicopter. As the engine wound up, he reached in his pocket and retrieved a business card. Handing it to Joseph he said: "I never turn the phone off."

EIGHTEEN

•••• — — — — • — — — • — •

It had taken longer than expected, but Joseph received a phone call two weeks later advising that the governor had agreed to the land swap at the reservation. "The state is willing to work with us towards the goal of getting title of the entire lake into native American hands." Tom Lacey had been a man true to his word. He also advised that he was gathering a group of people to get the party started.

In the early morning light, the unmarked private jet was touching down on the runway at Jackson Hole. Although not a particularly long place to land, this aircraft had been built for such performance: short take-offs and landings. Just off the taxiway was an empty hanger with large doors that rolled closed as soon as the plane was inside. The fewer that saw the tail numbers the better.

Marina Whitehorse had not visited this particular reservation. During the flight out, she had been studying the dossier provided her. Now, as she boarded the helicopter, she packed the computer inside her soft-sided briefcase and allowed it out of her sight. She knew there would be no screen time on this leg of her journey.

Waiting for her to arrive were Joseph, his son Edward

and long-time friend Harold Knight. The two younger ones were quite curious. They had been told months ago to get their affairs in order and prepare to work in the Nation for an unknown length of time. Each had a short-time love interest they needed to apologize to, and short-term rental housing agreements they needed to void. Chief Joseph has said he would handle the latter.

It had been a couple of years since they had seen each other, so last night had been a late one. They were bunked together in a bedroom at Joseph's house in the village (Edwards old room) and talked until well into dawn. Hal fondly remembered his time spent on the reservation during those college days visits. He had been reminded why Edward was called Junior, he looked exactly like his father. The two former roommates were again a team by morning.

Half-way between the landing strip and the village, was the tribal facilities building. This well-used basic wooden structure had modern conveniences (power and water), and an insulated, small meeting room for the mechanics and drivers to gather. Nestled against a slight rise on a small plateau, tribal facilities was out of sight of any eyes in the village. This was their first destination of the day. This building had been scheduled for the chief's use and there would be no visitors.

Wanting to avoid curious onlookers, the chief advised he would bring them lunch at about noon. He excused himself and drove home in the well-worn Jeep. His circuitous route through the village guaranteed that most tribal gossips knew he was back home.

At the shop, Whitehorse retrieved three laptops from her luggage, gave one to each person at the table, and looked around for something like a screen to project on. A map of the reservation on the far wall would work. It was hanging and had a white reflective backing. She turned it over and turned her computer on.

"Chief Joseph knows all I am about to share with you.

He doesn't need to be here for the particulars. Allow me the cliché, 'He is the chief and we are his Indians.' I am going to confirm first, and certainly will remind you many more times, this is highly confidential. As of right now the three of us are the leaders of a massive project that only a select few are aware of. Fill up your coffee cups and listen."

When Joseph returned with lunch, she was almost finished. He sat down and allowed her to continue, uninterrupted. She looked like a young version of his late wife, although he knew she was from a northern Nation.

"And now it is up to us. There are forces at work out there starting to gather and move personnel. We need to get ready to receive them and give them something to do. I'm giving you guys a week and we will meet back here.

"The only real guidance I can give you is to say that your workers will be qualified and will be approaching from the south and the east. Site your roads to allow for easy access off the existing interstate and state highway systems, with exits avoiding the populated locations. The heavy materials will be on rail cars coming from the west.

"The best rail lines will be those leading to the Powder River Basin and used right now by hundreds of coal trains. We can use those lines but getting from there to here needs to be carefully laid out. Don't forget we will need infrastructure leading from the town to the generation site and to the tank.

"Oh, and the steel mill will need to be near the water yet down-wind from the town. It's going to be one, challenging puzzle, but that's why you get the big bucks. Let's have lunch."

While eating the sandwiches, they discussed the next phase of their research. The boys would take the chief's Jeep as they had many times before and be gone for as long as it took.

Village elders would remember when Junior and Hal had roamed the reservation in that vehicle, leaving Joseph to walk and/or call for some help. Those kids – just like in the old days.

Those kids were anxious to get started. They decided to head north and west, then loop back to the Powder River Basin and plot rail lines from there. What they saw on the computer were views from above that showed a two-dimensional view of the land. From space it was hard to determine angles of grades and curves. They needed to look at the terrain for themselves.

They loaded the old Jeep with the necessary camping gear, and enough food for a couple of days. They knew that their wanderings would not take them away from civilization (including a food source) far enough to miss too many meals. After working their way south, the study narrowed in focus.

The future city and all transportation routes met near the canyon, and south end of Boysen Reservoir: the lake. Saving this area for last, they drove east and south to familiarize themselves with Interstate 80 and I-25, along with State Routes, three or four of which approach the reservation from the south, off I-80.

"It sure would be nice if we could bring rail into the plateau on the other side of the canyon." Junior said, "We might even join that area with new roads coming in from the south and cross above the canyon below the existing reservoir."

"I can see it." Hal responded. "What's to say we can't put the mill and the wind farm on the open side yet site the town on this side of the canyon? That's not that far a commute. As you said, we could even bridge the river somewhere nearby. There would be room to expand the generation station over there, and a cleaner layout with the town on this side."

With rail coming in from the east it makes sense to terminate trains at the mill on that side: bringing them near, or through, the wind farm. Trains aren't so wide that those rails would really interfere with the efficiency of either solar or wind power generation."

"If we did that," Junior responded, "We would have room for that tank beyond the mill. What was it Marina said - two football fields long? We can only hope there is not solid rock in that location. Let's get a geologist, or someone to come in and test the soil."

"We will need to get the entire area tested anyway." Hal stated. "Rock or no rock, that is the region we will need to dig deepest. We need to know the composition of that land. I'm guessing we probably won't need two football fields anyway."

He was so wrong.

NINETEEN

● — — ●● ● — ● — — ● —

In the middle of the game she heard the phone quietly signal. The device was not voice activated because she had turned that feature off. The game was too noisy. Ruth answered the call forcing her opponent to disappointedly halt play. He had been winning too. Her intent listening, and her body language told Stretch that Ruthless, as he called her, was finished playing. These lengthy conversations often resulted in travel and work for them. That thought agreed with him.

"We gotta get to south Texas," she said as she hung up. "White truck and the van. Wake him up." He headed towards the back of the small warehouse where the housing area had been built. He had almost reached the door that was the entry to their living quarters when she ordered: "And Stretch, load some food and get out at least ten-K."

Ruth headed the covert team of diversion experts. The all-but-invisible young athletes were adept in the magical operations of slowing people down. Ideally, this resulted in their targets missing meetings or flights, with little or no harm done. Their allegiance was in accomplishing the mission.

In the early rounds of negotiation, she and Brian

Knight had quickly agreed that they should locate this group in Phoenix, near the university campus. As individuals, in a smaller, public setting her team was far from unobvious. Ruthie was above average height with jet-black hair and too much ink. At 26, she was seriously street wise, clean, straight and well built. She fit in better in a college-like surrounding.

Undoubtedly one of the best gamers on the planet, her hand-eye co-ordination and offensive attitude had won her many a gaming championship. The famous rub your tummy, pat your head challenge was child's play to a woman who could advance her troops on the electronic battlefield with such efficiency. In the arena of gaming, there are a few players that actually make a living at it. She had been one of them.

These sharp-eyed youths are so coordinated, so fast, that when a big-pot contest comes along they travel to the country that is hosting the contest. Any place else and the speed of their responses is slowed down due to the distance the electricity has to travel.

Brian Knight first heard of Ruth through a contact in Canada. He found her, offered her the position of a lifetime, and she was on board immediately, providing her second in command could be Stretch. He was equally as obvious due to his height, slender build and race: he was Chinese. After the necessary security clearance was received, they began assembling the team and locating their supplies.

The financing and logistics of running the team were turned over to Brittany, Brian's next in command. She set them up with a place to work, some vehicles to start with, ID and licensing; and some cash. The team was to be difficult to trace, and the use of only cash for everything helped achieve that goal. That is why Ruth asked Stretch to retrieve ten-K, as in thousand dollars. He was entrusted with the combination to the safe.

It is about 1200 miles from Phoenix to Houston. Their destination was near Houston: a city called Beaumont.

They would study the map *en route*. In long distance travel, they would loosely follow each other, but use different places to fuel up and different freeways to loop city centers. The two vehicles they drove for this trip were non-descript. White American products old enough and dirty enough so as to not attract attention; with the exception of the dark windows, which could be electronically lightened with the push of a button.

To discourage curious eyes, the windows were always darkened when the engines were shut off. Obviously not a factory-installed window treatment, but the team needed the security due to the contents of the cargo van and the truck's camper.

In crossing New Mexico on the way to Texas, they would be out-of-state for only a short time. It was decided not to waste time putting New Mexico license plates on the rigs. They put in a call for Texas plates with the thought of later switching when they got to Texas. These supplies were to be given to them at a rest area in West Texas: as were the specifics of the target and the timing.

Both vehicles contained communication systems that were secure, and invisible. The stock looking AM/FM/CB radio contained two-way encryption that made long distance contact secure. Unlocking the Citizen's Band conversation feature was impossible unless you were schooled in its workings.

Stretch was driving the van and Ruth was in the seat next to him. They pulled into the well-manicured rest area about an hour and a half beyond El Paso. The contact, a local friendly, was in a similar, white van. Stretch parked facing the opposite direction, at the far end of the double row of parked cars.

Behind his seat was a blue, gym bag. He picked up the bag, put on an orange and blue Houston Astros baseball cap and tee shirt and got out of the van, "I'll meet you on the other side of that building." Ruth said as she pointed to the rest room structure.

Stretch went into the men's room. When he walked out, he proceeded directly to the passenger side of the "friendly" van, opened the door and got in. After a short conversation he exited that vehicle, still carrying a small, gym bag. He went back to the men's room.

Ruth was now waiting on the other side of the restroom building. She saw Stretch emerge wearing a blue and white Dallas Cowboys baseball cap and tee shirt. He walked to the van. Stretch jumped in the passenger's seat and they drove out of the parking lot. Changing clothes and parking places was standard security protocol used by this team.

In the back of the van, while motoring along I-10, Stretch described to Ruth, and simultaneously by encrypted radio to the pick-up, the contents of the gym bag that was given them in the switch back at the rest area.

"First things first. Let's stop and change these plates. Looser, are you in place?"

"Affirmative Ruthless."

Thirty minutes had passed when the Van pulled into the next rest area on the freeway, parking only a few slots away from the stall containing the pick-up. They quickly put Texas license plates on both vehicles and left the secluded rest stop.

Once they all were back on I-10 Ruth announced," We've got a Houston representative that is visiting his daughter in the Beaumont area the day after tomorrow. We're set up on the north side of Houston with a home for a few days. Looser, you take I-10 to 610 and loop around south. I'm taking the north side and up State 59. Our destination is out 59 a ways, south of the airport. We have a largely unpopulated industrial area damaged by the last hurricane. Not too many prying eyes."

"Affirmative Ruthless."

The traffic was light, and they reached the destination without complications. Once inside the musty warehouse, it was apparent that Brittany and some work-er-bees had been hard at it. The otherwise empty space contained a parallel row of workbenches with an array of tools and compressed air. There were folding cots for each of the team and his and her portable toilets had been delivered.

What would serve as a kitchen and worktable was next to a full-sized refrigerator and shelving unit with dishes, cups and utensils. The only things missing were TV and alcohol. There was room for both vehicles inside the dark building. Although this was their first operation that took them out-of-state, Ruth was again amazed at the thought that went into outfitting her team.

Brittany's crew had even set up some short walls to block the view of the inside from anyone peeking in through the dirty windows. Yet light was allowed over the walls and helped brighten the working interior of the warehouse. They started to unload the van.

"We are going to do a RailOp followed closely by an AmpedOut. This is an industrial location so I'm guessing the cell towers will be easy to spot. Stretch, haul the drones over here and let's double check the status. Looser, I need another battery check on the bots and an ID check."

As with most covert operations, a minimum amount of material is left behind. That which must remain on location, must be clean: untraceable. With magnifying readers on, they all looked over every part of the bots to verify they had removed any identifying symbols or marks. They also oiled any fingerprints off each piece. The drones were used in the delivery of the micro-bots but would return home and be used again. They were also oiled and tested.

The next day the team visited the region. Their earlier computer study revealed location of tracks and crossings, but they still needed to see it for themselves. Their most visible weapon, the RailOp, resulted in stopping a train. Their quieter operation, the AmpedOut, blocked all wireless communication. Precise preparation dictated they see the rail crossings in advance, and be within the sight line of communications channels on the day of activity. They finally found one ideal spotting location: a parking lot behind an abandoned building. They would have a partial view of the railroad crossing that needed to be blocked.

The timing of the train was easy to control. They had access to the electronic system that signaled when the cars were filled with oil and when the train was complete. The first few sections of this track were only for outbound units from Beaumont and would roll as soon as cleared. This was the largest oil port in the country and the refineries were always anxious to send loaded cars on their way.

From their vantage point, their departure would be protected for a while since the stalled train was between them and their target. However, there was no guarantee that help would not approach from the other direction: behind them. As an advance warning device, they would position the pick-up a couple miles up the road in the parking lot of the bowling alley. The pick-up would be silent and not move, unless something went wrong.

They returned to the warehouse and called the other flyers to join them. In the morning they plotted:

- Flyer 1 would monitor the limo. As soon as the car started moving the two closest cell towers are to be draped.
- Stretch stands by the refinery fence. Install the cut-bot. Get the pick-up across the tracks and to the bowling alley.
- Flyers 2 and 3 are to each drape two towers upon command. Consolidate transportation and get to the Shreveport airport.
- Ruth and Looser are to drape the three towers on the north side of the tracks and get the van to location and jam radios.

The thoughts about the next morning's activities meant everyone in the warehouse had a sleepless night. Their RailOp would disable an entire train of filled tank-cars and block an intersection for a period of time. To prevent a phone call by anyone inconvenienced by that broken train, an AmpedOut procedure would disable any amplification devices (like cell towers) that enable such phone calls.

They would know soon enough if they needed to disable communication at nearby businesses. The senator was not to make a public phone call, either at the bowling alley or other location. Fortunately, he never tried.

It was at times like this that Ruth wondered if Brittany, or anybody, knew how much she liked her job and her fellow workers. She had negotiated to include Stretch on her team, and he was as useful as he was careful. He and Looser were an item: they lived and traveled and worked as one.

Also a world-class gamer, Looser was a loyal friend to those that deserved it. In addition to electronic games, he was a bit of a gambler and known for making many, quick large bets with unwitting foes. His Mid-west parents had quietly paid their gay son to stay out of sight.

Therefore, spending their money on unlikely wagers did not bother him at all. He was undisturbed if he lost - but opponents knew not to refer to him as a looser. His response to such a derogatory taunt was to increase the rate and size of betting until the foe was driven into shame and total defeat. His close friends called him Looser - their ultimate term of endearment.

By their nature, young people that get seriously involved in gaming are introverted. Kind of nerdish, and social misfits, they have spent thousands of hours by themselves, in front of a screen, studying not only the response of the screen to their input, but also the responses of their opponent.

When they get successful and compete at the highest

levels, they know not only the game, but some psychology. It's just never called that.

Ruth had been in contests against quite a few superb opponents and had their numbers in her phone. The flyers she had at her disposal were still active in gaming, or recently retired. She knew them by pseudonyms and trusted them because the true gaming clique was trustworthy. If they were in town they would respond to a request for help: they had.

Ruth had a cadre of elite flyers, as she called them, that she had tested and trained. They all had extraordinary coordination, but to drape a cell tower required more than that. There was special hardware, connected to unique software, and a need to understand the different targets. It took her a month of practice to feel comfortable with that joystick and its response to her movements. Once self-taught she offered them three months of paid practice and her team was trained.

They were, indeed, a unique fighting force.

TWENTY

● — ●● ● — ●● — — — ● ●●●●

The brakeman had been working for the railroad just long enough to know something was wrong. The slight change in the sound of the big electric motor warned him before his gauges did. The train came to an abrupt and complete stop.

"What the . . ." said the engineer at the same time Cable exclaimed:

"Shit!"

Both knew that the catastrophic failure of the train's braking system would put them way behind schedule.

"Big Mac" McDonald had worked his way up to engineer, and he was good at it. He was observant, alert and determined to be on schedule. In the engine with him was Raleigh Hutchins. The white guys on the shift called him cable because of his dreadlocks. To seasoned railroad folks that hair looked like steel cable. He had been honored when they started using that nickname for him: a sign of acceptance.

"OK, Cable. Start down the line looking at every hookup. I'm going to get on the radio and find out how far away help is."

The braking system on a railroad train is powered by the engine: the locomotive. In the event that system is compromised, the brakes lock up. There is no chance of a runaway when all the cars apply their brakes. There is also no chance of pushing that much weight along the tracks to clear a crossing.

This particular train was over one-half mile of tank-cars, carrying crude oil. They had been filled at the refinery/terminal near Beaumont, Texas and were on their way to Oklahoma. The train was at a dead stop, blocking the road that leads to Beaumont from Port Neches, on the bay.

As Cable examined the brake line connection between each tanker, he noticed a uniformed officer walking up the road his chain of tank-cars was blocking. It was none of his business, so Cable continued his inspection. The Texas Ranger headed towards the engine. Big Mac saw him approach and jumped down from the engine.

"Good morning." Mac said.

"Hi – I'm Don Wilson. Down that road, about 25 vehicles or so, is one of our State Representatives we're escorting back to Houston. Any idea how long you'll be blocking the road?"

"I've got my best man on it right now. We need to figure out where the brake system broke and fix it. Trains don't move if the brakes don't work. Usually a loose connection between cars is quick to fix. Half-an hour or so. I was just on the radio trying to find out where we might get help if we need it, but there seems to be some static. You wanna come up and I'll try again?"

"No thanks." said Ranger Wilson "I'll get back to the Congressman. He's kinda antsy about moving along so he can vote at some meeting." He walked back to his waiting car.

A quarter-mile into the inspection Cable noticed a break in the brake line. There was a clean, perfect cut and the pipe had separated a couple inches. Not a hard fix, he thought. When he tried to radio BigMac he only got static. He crawled out from under the train and started walking towards the front of the train.

After a brief conversation, both railroad workers returned to the location of the trouble. They suspected that one part of the brake pipe must have slid back due to weakening mounting brackets. They crawled under the car to examine the fastening system. Cable noticed a two-inch section of pipe lying on the ground, between the tracks, under the adjacent car.

"Mac, look at this." he exclaimed as he retrieved the piece, "It's been cut."

"What?" McDonald crawled back to Cable's location. "How's that possible? Did you see anybody running away from or near the train?"

"Nope."

"Neither did I. Let's work our way farther back and see what the next few cars look like."

Examining a train car from underneath is as difficult as juggling razor blades. The rock used to make the railroad bed and support the ties and all that weight is not polished; it's sharp. In addition, the inspection is extremely uncomfortable because the person beneath the train can't stand up. In fact, the position is a cross between a duck-walk and shoulder-blade crawl. When one does lie down to crawl beneath the axles, the sharp rocks cut into the clothing and the back. It took 25 minutes to carefully examined the connection between, and line beneath, another 20 tank-cars before they found an unusual object on the ground: a metal object.

"Look at that Mac. There's some little motor with a cutting wheel and a little gear like thing with small teeth. Do you suppose this could make those clean cuts?"

"Only if there was another cutting wheel or something like it to hold it on the pipe and balance the forces." Mac said. "Let's keep looking."

Meanwhile, Congressman Renton was in his limo still trying to phone his office. After making ten attempts, with no call having been completed, he walked to Ranger Wilson's patrol car and asked him to make radio contact and get some help. The officer had to admit that his communications were down, too. Renton was getting flustered.

He was expected to be the tie-breaking vote on a land swap issue up in Wyoming. He had not really read the brief but knew his would be a no vote because his job was to obstruct anything the Crockett administration tried to accomplish. His fellow politicians in the Dakotas were counting on him.

Throughout the years the coal and moneyed interests in the Powder River Basin up north had helped the oil and wealthy interests down south. It was his turn to help maintain the status quo. Without his vote the thing might pass and too many deep pockets would wonder where Renton's voice was. Yes, he was flustered.

The two railroad workers, on hands and knees, started crawling under the cars towards the back of the train. In a few minutes they found another little wheel with teeth. Then they discovered a small battery.

Mac spoke: "This looks like sabotage. Don't pick that battery up. We had better tell that Ranger to radio for some help and investigators. And tell him we'll be here for a while."

By now the backlog at the crossing was about a mile. When Ranger Wilson still could not make radio contact he decided to drive for help. The Congressman asked to go along for the ride. Renton thought he could get picked up by helicopter and still make the vote in Houston. He had an hour, and Houston was not that far from where they were stranded.

The patrol car, with lights flashing, turned around and made it just to the first bend in the road when they encountered a tractor/trailer rig doing the same thing, but those big-rigs can't turn on a dime. It was in the middle of what must be a ten-point turn and blocking the road, the shoulder, everything. They waited again.

When they saw more trucks farther down the road executing the same maneuver, the ranger told the congressman that it was going to be a long trip back to civilization. Renton knew there was not enough time for him to make the vote! He also knew that, even though he could not hear it, his phone would soon be ringing - and not with callers sharing good news.

"It's been an hour, Ruthless." said Looser.

"OK, cut the line." she replied.

On his control panel at the back of the van, Looser pulled up a series of images on the monitor and clicked on a local map. When the curtain icons appeared, he pulled a scissors tool from the margin and released it on one curtain. He repeated this move seven times.

Outside the van, the electronic signal that these clicks created caused small bots, similar to the one on the train's brake line, to sever small plastic cables. These cables were high up on cell towers and attached to a curtain of Mylar that the team had hung on the towers earlier. This is how cell phone communications were affected.

A day earlier, the team had pulled up a map of cell towers in this part of Southeast Texas and determined that seven strategic towers would disable the cell system. That resulted in their asking for three more skilled flyers to be brought to the scene. Ruthie coordinated all activity and hung three herself.

It took a particularly adroit person to hang these curtains. Attached beneath a drone, the Mylar shield was carefully framed, and draped so when applied, centrifugal force would cause it to flare out. It could then be dropped over the cell phone tower and cover the antenna array. This took serious skill.

The challenge was that to generate centrifugal force, the drone had to start spinning. By itself, this is not an easy maneuver to initiate. Let alone spinning while decreasing in altitude to cause the Mylar to drop on target. For this reason, hand-eye coordination of at least one member of each team was of paramount importance. On this team it was Ruthie.

The small, cutting micro-bot that Looser activated was installed at a point on the plastic cable that was a gathering of many smaller plastic lines. Each line led to a corner of a Mylar panel. Many of these panels made up the curtain. When this line was cut, however, each panel floated free from the others and the tower. They all fluttered to wherever the wind took them.

Also on Looser's monitor were the controls for their jamming device. The team had been disrupting radio signals within two miles of their location. This was a directional system, meaning they had to have their antenna pointing in the direction of their target. Naturally, when they stopped the jamming signal, radio communication was restored.

That was when they started driving. The three visiting flyers had done their job and left earlier. Ruthie's team headed directly back to the warehouse and drove inside. Within minutes they were making their escape.

TWENTY - ONE

..—. .—. .. . —. —.. .—.. —.——

The van and pick-up traveled at the legal speed limit *en route* to Shreveport. Arrangements had been made to meet on the outskirts of the city, near the university campus. The smaller, northern most airport was nearby, and the college-types would ignore unusual looking figures, and the Texas plates on the truck and van. Flyers 2 and 3 arrived earlier and were waiting in the largely vacant parking lot near the baseball practice field.

The vehicles destined to join them had taken the usual two-rest area precautionary measures. Ruth had received new instructions and a new gym bag. Back in the van she opened the bag and verbally disclosed the contents to all parties: cash to get home, new Texas plates to change immediately, and new ID for a new member of the team.

They drove to the small hotel on the other side of the freeway, as per instructions, and proceeded around back. Looser, being the cleanest white guy, registered under the name he had just been told to use. He went up to the room, then he down the back stairs to let the rest of the group into the building. The rented suite had two bedrooms. The boys immediately claimed the largest one.

The flyers were invited out for a meal at a local restaurant. They discussed the just completed operation in great detail, emphasizing timing and stealth. When the debriefing was completed, all said good-bye to the flyers and Ruth's crew returned to the hotel for a good night's sleep.

The following morning, they ordered from room service because they did not want to join the other guests at continental breakfast. Showers and some clean clothes and the team was almost human. Before they had a chance to finish watching the morning news there was a knock on the door.

Looser opened it and saw one striking, deeply tanned, or maybe black, woman with piercing eyes and jet-black hair. She whispered "Looser?" while holding her index finger up to her lips. He nodded, and she stepped into the room and closed the door behind her.

Quickly taking in her surroundings and the others in the room, she said, "Sorry but the security guard was on the elevator with me and I'm not sure he wasn't listening, just around the corner. I'm . . ."

"Courtney." Ruthie said, finishing her sentence. "Welcome to Shreveport, and the team."

They exchanged pleasantries, had more coffee and listened to each other's instructions. In short, this was Courtney's first field assignment and her expertise would help the team get safely back to Phoenix. Looser went down to the front desk and paid cash for the room.

During the first part of the trip home, after they changed the plates, Ruth drove the pick-up and Courtney rode shotgun. The boys were in the van. It was explained that during the operation just completed, Stretch had been seen on closed circuit TV, planting the bot on the train. The fact is, the refinery had cameras along the fence line. This development dictated that they take precautions on this leg of their trip.

Stretch had worn his disguise: super fat rimmed, dark glasses, a thick Fu Manchu mustache, a goatee and plastic ears. But when video gets the license number and description of the truck, the vehicle needs a disguise too. They had been prepared.

The first step was to change license plates again. The second was to put women in the same vehicle. They removed the custom-designed camper from the pickup and put it inside the van. The ace-in-the-hole was Courtney.

Their route took them around Dallas proper, and across the rest of Texas. While they did not encounter a roadblock *per se*, there was often evidence of law enforcement. It was the invisible enforcers that had them worried. They knew there was no electronic trace of their activities. It would take physical contact to disrupt their journey. They remained vigilant.

An hour west of Dallas Courtney spoke: "That's the second time for that black car that just passed us."

"That's a dark blue car if you mean that one." said Ruthie, pointing.

"Sorry, I'm not very good at colors. But I know I've seen that car twice."

"Forgiven. Let's keep our eyes open and stay off the radio."

She clicked the send button on her CB set three times signifying turn the car radio off for 45 minutes. They rode in silence. Ten minutes later a similar dark car went slowly by. Both the driver and passenger were seriously studying Ruthie's ride. She didn't like the looks of this.

She broke her own radio silence. After three attempts at a series of two quick and two normal clicks she received an identical reply. She spoke into the microphone now, "I need some light in Dallas."

The speaker in the truck chattered. "Bright light?"

"Nope – sun bursts should do."

Click click.

They rode in silence for another 15 minutes. Courtney then noticed a parade of three cars, all about the same design, like the ones she had earlier seen, proceeding in the other direction quite quickly. Ruth smiled.

"FYI," Ruthie said, "that last radio transmission was a call for help. Even though the radio in our vehicle is secure, we don't take any chances. In case someone translates our electronic transmission, we still use code in these conversations. That knot of police cars you just saw going the other way means they are responding to some activity our people got into near Dallas a couple minutes ago. Probably a TrakTore on the freeway."

"TrakTore?" Courtney asked

"Most of our rigs are carrying some homemade spikes. Like the jacks you played with when you were a kid, only larger and sharper. At some choke point in the road, a toll booth is primo, the jacks are carefully dropped onto the road just behind the vehicle. A few more are slowly spread out into other lanes to be eventually picked up by other cars. Before too long you have two, or three, or six cars with flats that really screw up traffic for hours. The police immediately drop what they're doing to help clear the traffic jam."

Courtney smiled – sunbursts she visualized. She liked this group and their organization.

The two pairs leap-frogged across the rest of Texas. When they entered New Mexico, they felt safe enough to switch drivers and passengers. By the time they were in Arizona the whole team felt comfortable with Courtney as part of their world. She was a little less comfortable.

Ever since she left the safety of her home in the south she had been with a variety of people. During that long boat ride, she bounced back and forth between the two vessels, the two skippers and six young people about her own age. It was the first time away from home for all of them and their conversations had always had a common thread of wonder about this adventure, the side trips and the characters they encountered.

The first months at South Center had been more of a get acquainted session with the surroundings. Yet the group that had come north on the boats managed to stay in touch. Even if only brief eye contact during some class, they acknowledged each other, therefore recognizing their common ground: being from the south.

When she was tapped to drive boats for the center her time was spent with various skippers, new recruits and Bo Elliott. There were common roots with the kids, and a mentor/student relationship with Bo. Bo with his missing canine tooth. Bo with his out-doorsey tan.

But with this team there was business and risk. She was definitely out of her comfort zone. Bo had told her this work was important. He had taken her aside one afternoon and advised her of the need, as uncomfortable as it was, for her to have an adventure.

"Courtney, please don't share this with anyone yet, but I have been asked to leave the center and help build the facilities in Wyoming. In case you need confirmation of the rumors, the pace with which Urgent is growing is faster than anticipated. It seems my talents might be better used on that project."

"Don't you need a driver, or skipper, or go-fer?" she asked.

"Please let me talk. This is hard. I have been trying to figure out why this is so difficult and have admitted to myself it is because I think of you as more than a student, or fellow worker. You may have similar feelings too. I see something in your eyes that must be a reflection of what you see in mine." She shyly nodded.

"Our age difference doesn't mean a thing to me. I am learning that what's inside is more important than years on the job, or in school. But I feel strongly that there is a big world out there and every young person needs to see some of it. I also know that the project that brought us together needs our talent.

"When it comes to companions, people are basically

selfish, I think, and I'm no exception. That is why it is really hard for me to ask this, but I believe it of major importance that you and I apply our talents to the tasks at hand for a little while. Those duties will take us apart.

"I told you that I have been asked to move to Urgent. As part of my job, I have also been asked to tell you that you have an opportunity to join a group of young people that are helping in a different way. I have not been told any specifics, and I don't need to know. There is an interview scheduled at a place near Cincinnati if you want to learn a bit more. I think you should."

Now, here she was. A thousand miles away from Bo, or any mentor for that matter, for the first time in her life. Ruth was her superior? She was told to give it a chance, and she would. She had also been told she could bail any time she wanted.

"Can you fill me in a little about Looser and Stretch?" Courtney asked. In response Ruth shared her interpretation on the personality, motivation and expertise each of her male team member possessed. She then asked her co-pilot to do the same.

Courtney related the history of her escape from her childhood, in the form of a boat trip to South Center. "Low income, underemployed father with too many children and not much honor." Before her brothers, or brother's friends started feeling their testosterone, she got out. She had too many friends, including her wild, younger sister, that got pregnant before they finished high-school. In fact, most did not finish.

Lately her dates had been trying really hard to get beyond first base with her and she was not having any of that yet. She guessed that her hormones would kick in later. So, she got on the boat and had not been back since. She did write her mom every once-in a while and kept up with the family gossip.

"What about you?"

"My story is a little like yours," replied Ruth, "in that

I got away from home. Not because of guys my own age, but because of incompatibility with my parents. When I was quite young, I got hooked on video games. Then I got better and took on other challenges. This involved thousands of hours in front of any screen I could find. At first, I played on my parents slow, old fashioned computer.

"The one at school was better so I switched to it. Then the library got a couple faster PC's and I wore them out. A friend in the gaming world told me about the machines the colleges have, and I started visiting the computer lab at the local community college. It was there that I met Stretch.

"The two of us were an item for a few dates, but neither really wanted to devote much time to anything other than gaming. We were getting really good and started entering competitions. I tried my best to explain this life style to my parents, but it just would not sink in.

"Whenever I needed to spend a night traveling to reach a certain destination or computer, I was continuously reprimanded, accused by my parents of all things nasty and then punished. I did manage to finish high school, with a better than average GPA, and pretended to go to college.

"Actually, I moved in with two other gamers in some crash pad. We didn't need much room because we were on the road, gaming, all the time.

"I got so good that I needed to fly to the country that was hosting the game. Why? Because the response I got from the keyboard and controls of the game were faster if I was in the same town as the origin of the electrical signals controlling the game. Can you imagine that? I'm so fast that the speed of electricity is too slow for me at times. When in the zone I'm like a machine. I can click hundreds of moves a minute. My folks still don't understand. I'm still not welcome at home for more than a meal or two."

"What about boys?' Courtney asked. "I'm asking because I think I have some special feelings for this guy I met on the boat."

"That's so cool. I've never had that experience. Sure, there have been some one-night stands during an outing or two, but nothing serious. No kids – no STD's. Just routine stuff for someone my age. Tell me about him."

"Well, that's kinda hard. We split up just as we got started. In a way, I was working for him on the boat and at South Center, then it became a different type of work. He knew it, and we briefly talked about it. Then he said it had to wait. This work was more important in his mind. I like his mind, so I went along. But I do think of him a lot."

"South Center?" questioned Ruth. "Tell me about South . . ."

"Hey Ruthless." the radio interrupted "Yeah?" "It's S & S time."

"Liquids?" "Both OK." "Working."

"We need to find a place for the boys to stop and swap driving duties – the S & S Stretch was telling us about. I asked about liquids. He would have told me if he needed in or out, as in to take on fuel or pee. Since we still won't have both vehicles within miles of each other we need to coordinate these stops.

"You've been watching us navigate long enough. Try your hand and see what the GPS reveals within the next half-hour or so. We can use any exit that allows them to pull off, take at least two turns off the freeway and then get back on. We need a similar arrangement with the next few exits, but not consecutive ones. Oh, and we need a gas stop."

TWENTY – TWO

.— — ——— —. .

The partnership of Edward and Harold Knight had been the catalyst for the formation of Urgent. The growth of the centers led to the growth of the village. The small community became a town. In the four years since President Crockett was elected to his first term the distance from one side of Urgent to the other had grown so one needed a half-hour to walk from the west side to the canyon edge.

Tom Lacey had once dreamed out loud with the chief about getting control of sufficient territory to build his project. Some dream. Lacey got the trades he wanted, one way or another. He had traded with local governments, and with the federal folks too. The reservation boundaries now included the town, the industry, miles of roads and rail, the beginnings of a dam at that narrow canyon, and miles of open space on the other side of the canyon. It extended across the Wind River and the new limits were miles east, towards Casper.

Years ago, there had been some concern among members of the tribe that this large manufacturing facility would ruin the environment. More specifically, their concern was that the operational mill would heat up the water in the lake and reservoir to the extent that

139

there was no more fish, or fishing. Chief Joseph's people love to fish. His people love the water. There had been nothing to fear. The fishing was fine. Joseph was proud that his trust in the outsiders had paid off.

He was prouder still of his people and the changes they had made. The dramatic expansion to the reservation had given them a life changing confidence. They could do big things. At one of the elders' meetings, the discussion got heated when someone brought up the policing of the new territory.

"Why should we? It's a non-tribal event?"

"Wrong" Joseph had exclaimed. "This is our land now. We have signed a treaty. More importantly, we have title to it and have filed that title in a world court. We wanted to make sure that the untrustworthy US Congress has no choice but to recognize us as a sovereign nation – in our newer larger configuration. It's ours and we will govern it as needed."

He had continued:

"Your children and your children's children will benefit from our actions here. We will figure out how to, and get the vehicles needed to police this land. Our children will have new schools built which they will attend with all children of all races that live here. Other nations may be stuck in the old ways, but this land is being used to save those tribes and their lands. We have the honor of being asked to work with a visionary group of men who think as we do: that mother earth is worth saving.

"If we survive, not as a tribe, but as a species, the world will know we played a small part in that effort. If any of you or any of your relatives find this not to your liking, you are free to move. We have an agreement with our brothers in the Arapahoe nation to smooth the way for all such members. They will help find housing and have some knowledge of the local job market.

"Come back to visit any time. I should mention that we are going to use your house, but your friends and relatives will have beds for you. Trade with our businesses, fish in our lakes. But if you choose not to work here and help in this growth, you will not share in the rewards, whatever they might be. Oh, and be prepared for your children to leave home at an early age. We all know how the young follow the new and exciting."

Joseph was being prescient, again. Urgent was new and exciting. He envisioned the opportunities to participate in the growth as an enticement to keep younger members of the Nation at home. The community would someday urge any young person interested in college, to follow that dream. College would be paid for provided they brought their skills back home. A vibrant and growing home, worthy of them.

Slowly, during the past three years, the opportunities at Urgent had benefited the industrious members of other tribes. The rate of influx of workers from other Nations was gradually increasing. The demand for clean, educated tribal members, prepared to work, was affecting all Great Plains tribes. The unemployment rate was falling and graduation rates were increasing. It was obvious: they now had a future within their culture.

To those that follow the financial news, there were two headlines that would have caught their eye: although not appearing on the same day. The first was an application with the appropriate authorities to form an Indian Bank.

It would be called a state bank within Wyoming. The charter called for all Native American investors and board members. While the Nation is an independent entity, the founders wanted the support and involvement of the surrounding communities. The citizens of Casper, Thermopolis, Rawlings and other local towns would be able to become members of the bank. It would be founded in Wyoming.

The second financial announcement would have been seen only by those in the insurance industry. Negotiations had been started between the Nation and a specialty insurance company to ramp up their coverage. A New Mexico insurance company that specializes in providing benefits for Native Americans, and is wholly-operated by tribal members, was shopping for a company to insure its insurance: reinsurance.

To the trained eye, this was a sure sign that there was about to be more growth in the value of all things insured on the Wind River Indian Reservation. However, those eyes were only trained on large changes in balance sheets and profits of companies that sell these policies.

The increase in covered risk in Wyoming was insignificant to the large-scale world-wide insurance business. The financial growth of this project was proceeding unnoticed. The total local control was also unnoticed.

TWENTY - THREE

●●● — ● — ● — ●● — ●—● ●

This was not unusual; Bo Elliott was waiting for Courtney. Her plane was scheduled to touch down at any minute and he was excited. This separation had been a few months, and he was pleased that it was her last one. She was coming to join him in Urgent.

For about a week now, hearing that she was done with her field work, he had been planning their future. He had the house and she knew that. He had the ring in his pocket which she did not know. He was arguing with himself about children at his advanced age but was siding with her on this issue. Being 65 when his child graduated college wouldn't be too bad.

Of utmost importance was the fact that he loved her and wanted to see her every day. To be with her every night. He saw the dot on the horizon and began smiling.

Courtney was sipping her drink and looking out the window of the jet. She was facing the front while Ruth was facing her. "What are you thinking?" Ruthie asked.

"I'm really sort of in neutral." she replied. "This last operation got me excited again and I need to unwind before I can get completely calm. There is a man I love waiting for this plane to land but I need some time to decompress, or whatever you call it. Bo will want all of my time initially, but I want some of my time too."

"I know what you mean." said Ruth. "I remember when I needed time alone after a particularly competitive gaming session. Usually I had some airplane time, but my folks wouldn't stop questioning and chatting when I got home. That's why I moved out and never went back."

"Never?" Courtney questioned.

"Oh, I have done a holiday or two, but never for more than three days at a time. I just have this need. Maybe I'm an adrenalin junkie or something. I gotta admit though – I don't know what waits for me either."

The door at the front of the airplane opened and Brittany exited the cockpit. "We touch down in about fifteen minutes. How are you folks doing?"

Ruth looked up at her, hesitated, and whispered, "Can we talk?"

Brittany sat down next to Courtney and waited for Ruth to continue.

"We have been chatting and realize that both of us are a bit unsure of what we are about to do and become. We need some time to think long and hard but are afraid that forces down there will not give us that time."

The cabin went quiet for a few minutes. The young ones were surprised when asked "Do you know how to ride a horse?" It was a rhetorical question – it didn't matter. They continued talking until the pilot announced that the jet was on final approach. Brittany returned to the cockpit.

Edward was driving the reservation Jeep and approached Bo as he was standing on the taxi-way, looking skyward. Junior jumped out of the open cabin (there was no door) and slowly walked over to Bo's side. They looked at each other and the driver nodded in the direction of his ride. The pair began walking towards the Jeep, with Bo wondering why they just didn't begin the conversation.

144

Once seated in the vehicle Edward started;

"Bo, I know you will understand because you are a patient man, and a loyal individual." The understanding man did not like the way this sounded. Edward continued, "The team on that aircraft has been involved in some serious and sensitive errands. You will learn about them in time. She will tell you when that time arrives.

If not – I will. Today, however, is not the time. In fact, today is not the time to meet that plane. As the elder in this situation, it is on me to meet alone with the leaders of our troop up there", pointing towards the sky, "and my conversation needs to come before anything else."

Holding up his keys he said "Take the Jeep and go home. Your needs are important but can be fulfilled tomorrow. Today they're mine. I will call you when she's back."

He looked straight into Bo's eyes and the mutual respect was affirmed by that graceful motion. Bo didn't need the Jeep. He had his own car, which he used to drive back home. Junior waited for the jet to taxi into the new, large hanger.

As the members of the Southwest team walked down the stairs of the jet, they noticed the sole member of the reception committee and were both relieved yet wondering. Once on solid ground Edward told Brittany to take the Jeep and drive into town.

Turning to the girls he said: "We're going for our own ride."

He picked up two suitcases. They grabbed their backpacks and followed him towards the business section of the hanger. Once in the back room and away from the hanger expanse he approached a clean workbench and set the suitcases on it. On the end of the bench was a pile of brightly colored, hand-made blankets.

He handed each a blanket and asked that they take clean clothes for one day and roll them up in the blankets. Leave all electronic toys in the suitcase. There's the bathroom if you need it. With a brief "I'll be out-side." he walked out the back of the storage room.

They did not need to clean up, the plane had con-tained all the conveniences. Each did grab a drink of cold, clean water and, with their bed-rolls, followed Junior out the back door. He was waiting there with three sets of reins in his hand. At the end of each set was a large, alert horse.

Letting go of one horse, he signaled that was his ride. The horse did not move. Approaching the other two, he took the hand of each woman and placed it beneath the nose of the horse he had assigned to her. Then he gave each an apple piece to feed to the animal and told them to introduce themselves to their companion.

"Place your open hands on the cheeks of the horse, stand back at full arms-length and whisper a five-min-ute story. Always keeping eye contact." During that five minutes, he was standing between the two ani-mals, gently rubbing their necks, feeling behind their ears, bouncing the saddles: just adding to the sensa-tions of the moment.

He helped each woman up into the saddle, mounted his horse, and started walking. The others followed. When planning Urgent, Edward had always insisted there be horse trails and/or walking paths. Following the path, they started towards high country saying nothing to each other. With the houses now behind them the trail widened. Edward slowed a bit and allowed Courtney and Ruth to ride along-side. He started talking.

The women were surprised that he spoke not of their escapades, heroics or close calls, but of the story of this land. They heard the history of the great plains from the native perspective. Story that had been handed down for generations.

-- Which were the warring tribes.
-- How they hunted the respected buffalo and why it was so important.

-- Where to camp when spring arrived or when fa
turned cold.

A few hours out he reached into his saddlebag and
pulled out a sack of sandwiches. They dismounted, sat
on the ground, and ate while the lesson continued:

-- How to secure a horse on the open range.
-- Where there are signs of water.
-- The places likely to have snakes.
-- Identity of birds while in flight.

They fed the horses another snack and rode on, ever
climbing.

Now they were riding into the setting sun and could
not readily see the landscape ahead. The horses are to
be trusted with each footstep, but their actual destination was a mystery. Not to their host.

Reaching the summit of a small mound in the middle of the plain, they noticed a cabin on the edge of a
stream. They rode towards their destination. The horses sped up a little, they seemed to know this place. He
suggested they slacken the reins and give the animals
their head. They would only want to head directly to
the watering hole.

Outside, the building was surrounded by shade-trees.
Inside, the cabin was thoughtfully outfitted. There was
indoor plumbing, a cook-stove and sink on one corner of
the great-room and one walled off bedroom. The women
would be safe after sundown. Although unspoken, each
already knew that. This man was showing them another world: a serene place.

After he lit a fire, and cooked dinner, he brought out
some wine (his one true liking of the white man's ways)
and began to tell more tales: this time of the present.

Far below them, in the big cities and big buildings
were big men with big dreams. He related fact and fiction about these people and how they got that way. Not
in the political sense, but in practical sustainability (or
lack thereof) he talked of what they had accomplished,
and of the consequences of those great deeds.

URGENT STATE

As a student of history with a better than average memory, Edward was able to outline the lesson learned by our society generations ago, and the way our leaders fixed the mistakes taught by those lessons.

-- The easiest mining in the early days was open-pit: then we learned to value the earth.

-- For eons we have been suspicious of and went to war with, those not like us: then we began to value these differences.

-- Generations ago big business placed no value on workers: then we learned that was bad for business.

Edward then told of the repeating of the same mistakes by today's greedy leaders. He proceeded to explain the unintended consequences of these actions as he saw them: step by step into the abyss.

The story of how we became mired in our present situation could not be told in chronological order of problems. They didn't happen in order anyway. Topic by topic he shared the dilemmas we were facing on this planet. There was scientific proof that we (man) is warming the place.

The world is big, but so is the population and so is the number of machines and fires we have built. Anyone with a basic understanding of mathematics can appreciate what will happen if we melt all the ice on earth. Most thoughtful humans that have ever noticed the difference between low tide and high tide, can imagine if those levels were dramatically increased.

What he often wondered about was the water in the sky. He recalled reading one day that if all the water contained in clouds was brought to earth at the same time, the sea level would rise by six feet. Was this correct and why had he not heard any more news about this?

There was more scientific evidence confirming the importance of trees. The oxygen we need to live is not an infinite element. As we use it the oxygen molecule become something else. It is up to nature alone to make more. We are burning forests in places to make land for farmers. We are logging trees to produce more furniture and houses. Sure, man can plant some trees, but they take a generation to mature. Do we have that much time?

"As the planet warms," he asked, "does oxygen stay near the ground or does it tend to rise with the heat? I guess I'm asking if the oxygen content of our air is the same, regardless of how warm it gets. Beyond that question is the confusing fact that an ever-increasing amount of gasses are mixing with the oxygen in our air, thus reducing the amount of oxygen. These invaders are being released by the thawing of frozen ground. How much area is thawing and at what rate? Can our plant life replace oxygen at a rate equal to the rate at which oxygen is being lost to this chemical process?

"We have an economic disaster on our continent, and it is infecting others across the oceans. There are published facts illustrating that the super-rich are getting richer, at the expense of everyone else. But how can there be a society if there is no everyone else?

"Forces at work would eliminate government unless part of that government provides something free to them, and only them. These foolish people believe that since they can buy health and health care, others can do the same. Yet the workers employed by the rich are underpaid and devastated whenever a health need arises: not an emergency, just basic needs.

"The same mindless people (I won't call them citizens) that can afford to hop on the family jet and visit a foreign land for lunch, would eliminate public places because there might be valuable minerals beneath the land. Imagine the buffalo in Yellowstone grazing around an open pit mine as big as the lake itself. Imagine the polar bear in Alaska trying to catch a fish near a noisy, pumping oil derrick. Then imagine the extinction of these species.

"Our entire world is an ecological wonder of parallel food chains. Insects, fish, mammals, they all have spent millions of years evolving into an eat or be eaten society. We have plants that help some animals cross boundaries, but the major food chains are pretty evident. The microscopic sea critters get eaten by the bigger ones, which real fish eat, and then bigger fish eat them until the whales (mammals) eat the biggest fish.

"Along comes man as another mammal and we eat some whales. That's not too upsetting, but our sport and rituals waste a lot of food and then our ever-increasing numbers throw the whole thing out of whack.

"We have millions of people dying of starvation in the middle of a big dry continent, and millions of tons of fish being wasted because we think only their fins are valuable as aphrodisiacs. I'd sacrifice an erection to feed a family in Africa, thank you."

The evening wore on and the wine had a relaxing affect. As everyone got settled and tired, Junior traveled towards his summation. That was the subject of man's priorities. The ever-advancing technology and need to understand it all was reorganizing our priorities, and not for the better.

"There are those in science that will state that his opposable thumbs are what makes man better than other animals. Some respond that our ability to speak is the key. I must tell you that I am firmly in another camp – our ability to teach. Man has the unique ability to learn from his mistakes.

"We are not the strongest animal around. The buffalo has much more strength. The antelope is a lot faster than we are. The rabbit is harder to see when he stands still. The snake is much more flexible. The bird can fly. How is it that we dominate these creatures that are in one way or another better than we are? We can teach our young how to survive and save lots of lives in the process.

"Each generation of rabbits must learn how to run away from the fox and survive to make more rabbits. Then the young rabbits learn the same thing from their parents or die. We compound our learning and advance at a rate unheard of among other species.

"Teaching has been a priority item for humans. Learning has helped us advance. The family unit is our security – call it a tribe or a congregation. As a progressing and growing society, we advance. The single tree gets taken down in a windstorm. The group of trees stand tall for generations. We have our priorities all wrong. "

It was getting quite late and Courtney excused herself to get some sleep. "I can't sleep well on a plane." she explained. "See you in the morning."

"I'm not there yet. You go ahead." said Ruthie as she smiled: totally content. This man was the most charismatic person she had ever met. He was more than spell-binding. His honest approach to everything and his thought processes held her captive. While she could not talk like him, she thought like him. She wanted more.

He glanced at the moon as it shone through the window. "The people that occupied this land for hundreds of years were very much in sync with it. The land the animals, the plants. I can't remember the exact pronunciations, but my father knows them all.

"There are Indian names for each moon. For eons time was told via nature. Spring is here during the Moon of Snow Blindness: it's cold but you are almost blinded by the sun reflecting off the bright snow. Then the Moon of Fattening is the time when the female animals are their largest, prior to giving birth. This is followed by the Moon of Planting, then the Moon of Good Berries. See the connections? Other cultures honor mythology. Our culture is this land."

On into the late night and wee hours of the next day the two of them sipped wine and shared stories. He spoke of the loss of his mother at an early age. She

151

shared the friction between her personality and that of her parents. He went to college. She attended the school of "hard knocks". He had a long-time friend that was his co-founder of Urgent. She had one friend that had just preceded her in getting some sleep.

A few stories towards dawn they had moved to the small, padded seating provided by the sofa. They closed their eyes at around the same time and did manage to achieve sleep, side by side, knee touching knee. When they woke up, and saw each other through sleepy, yet fresh eyes, there was a recognition. He slowly bent towards Ruthie and kissed her. She kissed him back.

The smell of cooking bacon woke Courtney from her dreamless sleep. She had been tired. The cabin was tight and cozy, allowing her to sleep in her favorite long flannel shirt she had stolen from Bo.

Opening the door into the main room she saw Ruth reading at the table and Edward at the stove. Both fully dressed in the same clothes they wore yesterday. When they noticed her enter the room both extended morning greetings. Junior asked how she liked her eggs. Something was different.

Courtney had always learned by observation rather than constant questioning. She just watched until she noticed that every time he moved around, or near the table, he touched Ruthie on the shoulder. Yep – something was different. She smiled.

After breakfast, Ruthie cleaned up and Courtney offered to do the dishes. "Fine by me." said Edward. "I have some horses to tend to." He left the cabin. Just as Courtney finished combing her hair, Junior returned. "All set?"

Again, riding three abreast, with Junior in the middle, the party started back towards the village. When the narrator picked up, the story had changed to the present time and the present place: the workings and mission of Urgent.

He stressed that he trusted them to not share these stories with others. Not that he was asking them to keep secrets. Those he knew they would not pass on. Rather, he was concerned about misunderstandings if some of his passages were taken out of context.

"The early generation, the founding workers (now the senior citizens) come from backgrounds far different from ours. The indigenous methods and pace used to bother the non-natives. It took years for there to be a common trust and unity. Not everyone is always going in the same direction, but the inertia carries us all through the rough times. Community is powerful.

"Urgent was founded on a few unique principles. To the founders, there is no question of right vs. wrong. There is just a valid reason for our citizens, at this time, to adhere to these fundamentals. In the future, a few rules may change, but slowly and with due diligence being performed. A good example is our insistence that all businesses be employee owned.

"Retailers, car dealers, power companies, large banks: they all would like to set up a branch here. Some in our community are not too sure if we are right and "they", pointing beyond the horizon, "are wrong: or visa-versa. Two things are worrisome with opening our business borders at this time.

"Of particular concern is the fact that the money involved in those transactions would leave the community. Not just the profit, but the cash flow in the many mom-and-pop shops that sell other stuff. If it was only about dividends we might think twice. It's about more than that.

"Second is the jobs. Contrary to popular opinion, and their advertising, big companies that make more money do not create more jobs. A bigwig from the big city would open a branch in Urgent and bring some assistants with him. They would train a few local folks and offer those locals advancement opportunities away from Urgent.

The talented locals, that is. We need that talent. There will come a time when we will allow outside interests into our village; but on our terms.

"What does it mean to have a zero-unemployment rate? That's us. This society we are caring for supports all its members so carefully that everyone has a job. Most even have a job they enjoy doing. The folks behind the counter at the store, own the store. The workers pouring hot steel by the day, are getting free education, baby sitting and entertainment at night. While the pay is not that great, neither are the expenses.

"There is no need for a car with our public transportation system. So, no car insurance costs, maintenance and/or repair emergencies. When someone wants to get away, they can borrow a village vehicle or go to the airport. Everyone is checked out on driving. Prior to any road trip, there is another safety lesson and driver's class.

"What would the big city save if their police force had no crime to investigate? While we are not exactly there yet, we are close enough so as to be the envy of most towns our size. The amount of socializing we do and the amount of public praise we bestow on all our citizens, results in everyone knowing everyone. That type of visibility and public awareness is just not conducive to criminal activity. Sure, we do have the occasional impulse action, but no one's shooting up a classroom.

"I would imagine there are a few out there that are shooting up a drug. The addiction assistance programs we have built call for anonymity, so I can't tell you any more than I already have. We're working on it.

"You should know that what I consider to be of primary importance is that we soon will be totally independent of outside energy. Within the next few years we will reach that goal. Following that, we will start selling clean green energy to the grid.

Our solar fields coupled with the wind farm and smaller hydro-power stations will make us unique and valuable. Almost monthly we get approached by a large, outside company wanting to share in our work and technology. No is still the answer.

"Our scientists are working on advancements in all these areas. We want to save weight in the building of the towers. We want to improve efficiency of the solar cells. We dream of electricity moving faster through special wires.

"We even want to study ways to limit our water needs. We are on the verge of sending our first students to the colleges of their choice. Books and tuition are on us if they study specific fields that relate to our goals."

He slowed down long enough for the trio to eat lunch and water the horses.

"One more topic and I'll engage in some Q and A with you. First, though, I want you two to know how this all came about. I know that question is in there (pointing to his head) and want to get it out before you need to ask.

"Urgent is the brain-child of a couple of really smart and talented people. Behind them is a group of philanthropists that started the funding and will continue to do so. Not totally altruistic, their reasoning is simple. If we continue down the path we have wandered onto, the species is doomed. What good is the money then? We have been organized based on that simple premise.

"More are doing more organizing. You folks have been trained and called into action. All to allow us to fulfill our mission. Along the way we have done what we needed to do and will continue to do so. Your team has been an integral part of this journey. If we had medals to give out I would personally announce your efforts to the world.

"We have recalled our distraction team. It is no longer needed. Individuals and forces that would prevent us from becoming have failed. We are here and here to stay. All the players know it, too. As to who those players are, we won't go into that. The handful of leaders that have that information may share it with you in the future. I have not asked and don't care to know.

Now, what else may I tell you?"

They silently rode on, towards Urgent. The sun was setting when Bo got the call.

TWENTY - FOUR

—— •——• • —• —• • ••• •••

The small helicopter slightly bounced as it set down on the helipad. The burley, well dressed passenger opened the door and jumped down to the ground. It was a short stroll to the group waiting beneath what looked like a tower of fire. After Agent Emmet Fitzpatrick introduced himself, he learned that refineries consistently burn off excess fumes on towers like that one. "Is that good for the environment?", he silently asked himself.

The walk to the ground floor offices allowed Emmet to stretch and get the basic questions out of the way. When the FBI had first been notified of the incident on the train there was little interest. It was the further explanation revealing how precise and untraceable the little gadget was, that aroused the curiosity of the local office. Once they discovered the involvement of a politician, they notified the special Los Angeles unit headed by Fitzpatrick: the West coast unit dealing with unusual incidents. Any report of an unlawful activity that could not be neatly filed under normal crime categories (conspiracy, murder, racketeering, etc.) would first be reviewed by Emmet's special team: the Odd Case Unit.

To disable a mile-long tanker train so perfectly reminded Fitzpatrick of other activities he had reviewed.

157

There was also the traffic jam a few hours later near Dallas. That was exactly the same event that occurred in Milwaukee a year earlier. There, the spikes had been used on a bridge causing miles of back-up and hours of delay. Who traveled a thousand miles to throw spikes in a Texas toll booth he wondered? The similarity in these interstate events is why a senior special agent was outside his normal jurisdiction.

The closed-circuit footage they reviewed in the refinery office revealed little more than he already knew. The tall, obviously disguised, figure got out of the Ford pick-up and walked over to the refinery fence line just as soon as the engine passed that point. The train was moving slowly then, so diving beneath the tank car was not a dangerous move.

Had the culprit been counting the cars? Fitz asked that they play the first part again. He really couldn't tell if the placement of the device was random, or on a particular target car. He did know that the over-sized ears, elaborate glasses and dense facial hair would play hell with the facial recognition program. The disguise told Fitzpatrick that he was watching no amateur. "Keep the tape rolling."

In real time, the Ford pick-up was empty for only four minutes. Once back behind the wheel, the occupant carefully drove off. The license plate grew into full view. Beyond that the white vehicle had no special accessories or marks. Fitz had the distinct feeling that something was not right about the tailgate, but he didn't know his trucks that well. There were experts in the "bureau" that could confirm his suspicions about the modification to the truck, and about the disguise of the dark figure. His guess on the outcome of info on the truck was a toss-up. What was it about a 10-year old, white F-150? Why was that familiar?

On the way in he had been studying a map of the area. He asked that the yard super take him around the neighborhood. Driving along the refinery perimeter fence he inquired if the security team had checked for any breach in that fence. The supervisor advised they had walked the entire length on this edge of the facility and found nothing.

"Well, let's go the other way then." Emmet ordered. The car turned around. In a few miles they came to an intersection. At the stop sign the driver advised "Downtown Beaumont is a short drive that way," (pointing left)" and north Houston suburbs are that way."

"Let's go towards the crossing. I would like to see where they found the device." They turned right.

Fifteen minutes later the car pulled onto the shoulder just before crossing a set of railroad tracks. They exited the car and walked up the country road.

"How far from here to the refinery?" Fitzpatrick asked.

"I'll get you the exact distance." the driver responded as he retrieved the GPS from his pocket. Fitz smiled. The young and their toys.

"And how fast is the train going when it gets to this point? I'll need to know that too."

They walked along the now vacant tracks, towards the refinery. Small ID tags had been planted on the ground at the spot where the local police had discovered foreign objects. The objects themselves had been retrieved and were at the police station. He would see them soon.

The tracks were laid in a shallow cut in the earth at that point. Fitz climbed out of the gully to the top of the nearby mound of and surveyed the landscape. Back towards the refinery were buildings, tall stacks and activity. He turned to look in the opposite direction. Less humanity, less re-construction of hurricane damage, more open space. "I'd like to take a look beyond those trees." he said.

As they walked back to the car Emmet asked: "Didn't I hear that some bigshot got caught up in the traffic jam?"

"Yea," was the reply. "A Congressman from Oklahoma that was down here on business. He had a Ranger escort and both cars got involved. Eventually, they turned around and made it out of here. No harm done I guess."

"I'll need to interview that officer."

"Will do, sir."

They drove across the tracks. Turning into the parking area of the vacant building he felt a sense of accomplishment. This often happened to seasoned officers. They never knew how or why, but that feeling was significant.

Fitz got out of the car and proceeded to walk around the warehouse type building. He peered into the structure through broken windows. Nothing unusual. At the back of the empty structure he noticed the crossing was partially in view. A careful inspection of the ground in this area revealed nothing. It was clean – too clean. Where was the litter, candy wrappers, rubbers, fast food evidence, anything? Nothing.

Returning to the refinery, Emmet phoned the local office to ask them to pick him up at their convenience. He was told that a team was already on the way and was at his disposal. At his suggestion, when the local agents arrived, they drove him to the field office. Once in the car, he stated that he wanted to view as much video as he could find from the area near the crossing.

The local office had a list of businesses in that area that had closed circuit video systems, certainly not a complete list, but a place to start. They sent a team into the field to retrieve this film and conduct interviews. Emmet needed to check-in to some hotel and clean up. He knew he was here for a few days.

The next day, one of the team was interviewing an employee at a local bowling alley. A waitress remembered a white truck sitting outside in the parking lot for quite a while. The footage from the closed-circuit cameras confirmed it was the same truck. The time stamp indicated the truck left later and drove off north. Fitz wasn't concerned with where it went. He was confident that was a wild goose chase. He wanted to know where it came from. The investigators decided to concentrate their efforts in this side of town: more legwork and interviews. Emmet had an afternoon appointment to talk with the Texas Ranger that got stuck at the crossing. Don Wilson was on duty and in uniform when he arrived at the bureau field office. He shook hands with Emmet. After each poured a cup of coffee, they walked to the conference room. One of the local agents would be in on this too. Jim Flagg introduced himself.

Ranger Wilson had a good memory. He told of his conversations with the train engineer and made a pretty accurate guess as to the timing of events. When he related the part about loss of radio contact, Fitzpatrick's warning systems connected. He asked, "Who lost radio contact?"

"As I remember it, Emmet, when I first spoke with the engineer, he said his radio had a bunch of static that he couldn't get past. When I got back to my car, I experienced the same static. It finally cleared up after we had turned around and spent about 20 minutes getting away from the crossing."

"Come to think of it, the Congressman's cell phone wasn't working either. He tried numerous times to get through to his Houston associates, to no avail."

"So, you're telling me," Fitz confirmed, "That from the time you got stuck, for almost 45 minutes you could not make contact by wireless with anyone."

"Right."

"OK, Ranger Wilson, thanks a lot. I've got to check on a few things."

"Roger that." They shook hands. Don Wilson left the building.

After three days of knocking on doors and looking at movies, Fitzpatrick decided to go back to Los Angeles. He was too far away from his paper files, his notes. Unlike the younger guys, Fitzpatrick's comfort zone was with paper records. New recruits seemed able to do everything on their smart phones and other small electronic devices. Fitz had not mastered those gadgets.

The local Houston guys would keep him posted. He flew home. Along the way his mind searched for threads of evidence that might connect his various ideas. His major concern was the disruption of communication. Why jam radios and cell phones? He remembered one witness in that Bay Bridge traffic jam last year complaining that he couldn't get through to his office on the car phone.

Fitzpatrick had written that off to the normal communications glitch when thousands try to use the system at the same time, like after a major rock concert when all cell service fails. Maybe that wasn't the case. How do you disrupt cell service?

He picked up the phone in the jet – it worked even at 35,000 feet.

"Agent Flagg." was the response on the second ring.

"Jim, it's Fitzpatrick. I'm not sure what we're looking for, but check the cell phone towers within two miles of the crossing, will ya?"

"Sure thing, sir."

"I'm landing in an hour and going straight home, so but won't be in the office 'til morning. Call me then please."

"Roger that sir." the line went silent.

The following morning, he arrived in the office early. He sent a quick text to Houston in case they needed more time, but Flagg responded immediately via telephone.

"Your hunch about cell towers had some weird results. We visited the group of towers within, give-or-take, a couple miles from the crossing. At three of them we found some rectangular pieces of Mylar on the ground or in the fence at the base of the tower. In fact, at one tower, there was a chunk of the stuff hung up on an antenna at the half-way level.

"I'm sending you some photos. Like you said, we don't know what we're looking at. I am also sending you a copy of the report we sent to the lab and asking for their input. You will get a copy of whatever response I get."

"Thanks Jim. I'm going to ask our guys in Washington to give it some thought."

The scientists in Washington, DC responded first. One technician had remembered a similar finding in their investigation of a Milwaukee traffic jam. There had been no crime, *per se*, but the FBI had been called in because the disruption caused the cancellation of a meeting between the Wisconsin Governor and a Chinese delegation trying to sell solar panels and ancillary parts.

"Agent Fitzpatrick, this is Washington lab responding to your inquiry about Mylar panels. We just want to confirm that our records indicate there has been another similar incident in the United States this year. Actually, it was last year but that's current enough.

"We ran a battery of tests and could find no identifying marks or chemicals on the subject material that could help identify where, or by whom, it was fabricated. The light weight line, which we presume is on the top, is generic fishing line. The heavier section of weight at the bottom is normal, stainless wire. The Mylar is not unusual. Even the adhesive securing these sections to the panel is everyday. We can't tell you anything definitive.

"You might be interested in knowing we checked the other properties of the panels. Our conclusion is that, if two panels were placed on top of each other, most cell phone signals would not penetrate the material. That is, a majority of the signal would be lost or disrupted by the time it surfaced on the opposite side. I hope that's somewhat helpful agent."

"It sure is." said Fitz.

"One more topic, agent Fitzpatrick. Your suspicion is, and some photos back this up, that this was hung on the cell towers. Our analysis partially confirms this theory. I say partially because we can't determine how to accomplish that. Assuming that the antennas get in the way if one climbs the tower, and that the perpetrator would be too visible for too long, what other means can be used. We see no way to get such a shielding up on top of a cell tower."

Fitzpatrick thanked him and hung up.

He immediately called Jim Flagg and repeated the findings. He then added," Jim, I think we need to widen our search and recover as much of this stuff as we can. Let's piece together whatever this is. I know that the wind can carry a piece of Mylar quite a distance, and that you have some weird winds in Houston. Still, we need to go out there and find it. Call me in about a week and let me know what you've accomplished."

"Roger that." the line went dead. What is gained by interrupting communications, he asked himself?

Law enforcement can consult with the National Crime Information Center (NCIC) and search for all types of criminal activity and criminals. The dropping of spikes on a road, however, may not constitute a crime. If it is, it could be handled by local officials as a prank or simple misdemeanor. Neither of which would get to the NCIC e-files. Where would he go to look for more?

The incapacitation of the train must be a crime. Who keeps track of these things? Can the National Transportation Safety Board get involved? He asked his secretary to get the NTSB on the line sometime today regarding this train case. She silently walked into his office a few minutes later as he spoke on the phone. She gave him a note that read: "The NTSB is ready to talk."

After finishing the one call, he gave her the nod and she returned to her desk. The phone on his desk rang.

"This is Emmet Fitzpatrick of the Federal Bureau of Investigation, who am I talking to?"

"Mr. Fitzpatrick, this is Charley Dodd. How can I help you?"

When Fitz had detailed the story, Charley Dodd spoke, "Agent Fitzpatrick, the NTSB investigates accidents in an attempt to promote safety in our public transportation. I'm not too sure you have told me of an accident. Let me look into our files on criminal activity. I might also suggest that you check with your legal eagles to see what they think."

"Good idea." Fitz said, and hung up.

The popular answer he received from multiple sources, was that if there was property damage or injury there could be criminal charges brought. That did not seem to be the case here. Devoting time to this might result in the inability to track other such incidents. All similar actions, if they were not crimes, would not be in any national database. Neither this Texas incident nor the Milwaukee traffic jam seem to be reportable crimes. He was back to square one.

As he normally did each morning in the office, he picked up the daily paper and read the headlines. He was on his way to the comics when a below-the-fold headline caught his eye:

Committee OK's land swap. Renton misses vote.

Renton, wasn't that the name of the guy in Texas? The Oklahoma Congressman?

He looked at his files. "I wonder," this time aloud, "is this about politicians?"

He pulled up the e-files on the Milwaukee case and started reading. The list of witnesses was long and the occupations hard to make out at times. When he finally had read the last name on the list, he sighed. No politician. Still on square one.

"Where was it?" Now thinking to himself, "There must be a connection."

TWENTY – FIVE

•• — •• • • — • — ••

Harold Knight had always been sort of a nerd. While not a true geek, he was known as being extremely curious: perpetually more interested in learning than most of his peers. His older brother, Brian, was old enough that they had only been in school together one year of elementary school. Then Hal was on his own and shy and near-sighted.

Coming from a family of educators, it was no surprise when Hal was awarded a full ride to Stanford. Although on the other coast, and away from home, Stanford's engineering schools were excellent and that was his interest. They also had a rowing team. That too was of interest. He was a lean, strong kid and his brother had always told him to work out and bulk up. He had read about rowing as a way to do just that.

While dabbling in various majors and fulfilling basic requirements at Stanford he was introduced to Materials Science. He became fascinated by this area of study and by his second year he was leaning towards that degree. While looking into the most reputable institutions in Materials Science he learned that Massachusetts Institute of Technology (MIT) offered a few courses that Stanford did not. He also read they had a fair rowing team. That cinched the deal. He transferred to the school on the other coast that was closer to home. He was a New Yorker, but Mass. was close enough.

In one of his classes he met an adjunct faculty member that he immediately resonated with. After a few classes, and some office hours discussions, Edward White asked Hal if he would run with him. Long distance runners liked company and Hal, through rowing, had serious stamina. They started running together and talking. As Edward described his home and the reservation, Harold listened closely.

The geology, the minerals, the metals and the canyon exposing it all would be something to see. Hal's receptive attitude sparked a friendship that would last forever. Other relationships begun at MIT were of a more professional nature, this was a true friendship.

The engineering studies offered opportunities to network and attend conferences and seminars in various locales. Many such gatherings drew an international audience, with students and/or faculty from other universities in attendance. Hal got to know experts in the field that taught at Oxford, Cambridge, Harvard and his former place of study: Stanford.

One Thanksgiving weekend, while still at MIT, Harold's brother Brian had sent a message to confirm that they both would be home for that holiday. Brian expressed a need to have a quiet chat. After Friday turkey sandwiches, Brian invited Hal out to the local pub for a beer.

They bundled up and walked a few well-known blocks to a popular tourist hang out. The tourists were gone for the season and there was room in the back corner to relax and talk. Only the periodic clack of balls on the pool table was loud enough to interrupt.

In confidence, Brian told the story of the plans to put together a new community. The younger brother listened intently, and he envisioned the scale and complexity of such a project. Realizing that secrecy and security were initially paramount only intrigued him more. It was after the second break shot on the pool table created a break in Brian's tale that Hal spoke.

"Brian, are you really looking for the talent needed to put this all together?"

"It started a few months ago. It has taken that long to wrap my head around this challenge and begin to realize what help I need. A big part of it could be yours."

"If you're talking about the engineering side of it," Hal quickly said, "I'm all in. I may not be the supreme commander of materials science, but I'm learning, and it sounds like we've got sufficient time for me to learn more."

"On the surface, what do you see?" Brian asked his brother.

"The solar panels, the wind turbine towers, the extreme temperature tank: all would benefit from the use of sophisticated materials. Particularly the tank, which you describe as being underground. You'd better know what you're doing if you make something that large and expect it to perform after you bury it for years. And the pipes - don't forget the miles of pipes carrying warm, or extremely hot fluids. Then there's the question of location. I may know of the perfect place."

"That's a done deal." Brien said. "Ever hear of the Wind River Reservation?" His brother was aghast at the coincidence. Both realized the communication breakdown caused by their increasingly tight schedules. They knew each owed the other more quality time. The two siblings walked back home and into a new future. Brian had his engineering expert with security clearance, Harold had a lifetime of challenging work. Mom and Dad would only learn of this partnership years later.

An early structure at the new canyon rim location on the reservation was the research lab. Money had been allocated to bring in not only the materials to construct this facility, but the manpower to do the research. The search for talent had been Hal's pleasure. His years of attending and speaking at engineering conferences had given him social and professional capital in those circles. When he phoned for an interview, the scientists listened.

Those willing to give up their comforts to move to a new, less than exotic, and somewhat, secret location, tended to be younger at first. His charter team in the research lab averaged less than child-rearing age. These pioneers studied the physical metallurgy: the mechanical testing of metals and some alloy analysis. The materials needed to construct the windmills required different properties than those exposed to extreme heat from solar reflectors.

The early lab acquired the equipment to help in these experiments. More often than not, for security purposes, this equipment was installed below ground. Only a select few knew that one phone call to Brian was all it took to get the equipment.

Occasionally, Hal needed to visit university testing facilities and work with foreign teams in their areas of expertise. Over time, his working knowledge in numerous specialties grew. His reputation as a scientist grew also. Within the scientific community, it became an honor to receive a phone call from Harold Knight asking for an audience. It also became known that, subsequent to such a visit, some researchers left the university and went to work with Hal. However, the exact nature of that work was often a mystery; as was their location.

The majority of those graduates/researchers dropped out of sight, even to the alumni list: into a black hole of scientists.

TWENTY – SIX

— •• • ••• — — — — — • — ••

At the regional office of the Federal Bureau of Investigation in Los Angeles, Emmet Fitzpatrick was in the middle of pushing papers. Senior agents spent more time chasing the coffee pot than chasing criminals. He was overjoyed when one of his associates brought him an internal brief of interest.

Call it karma, but nearly two years to the day, he was offered another chance for further investigation into his missed-meeting theory. The agent read a morning briefing item about a meeting of the Federal Energy Regulatory Commission (FERC) that ended with a surprising decision.

The massive renewable energy program being built in Wyoming needed clearance on an energy buy-back matter. The generation station anticipated producing such a vast amount of electricity that they wanted to sell any excess back to the grid in the Great Plains. FERC got into the act because the energy was being generated in another country: an independent Native American nation.

Hearings were held at various locations to discuss the impact such a power output might have on the supply of hydroelectric power from the mountain states and the west, and coal-produced power from the east. It was anticipated that the support the big U.S. players had would overpower the allegiance drummed up by the smaller foreign producer. The final outcome was not what had been expected, primarily because Senator Seasons from West Virginia did not vote - he missed his plane.

Emmet Fitzpatrick stopped what he was doing and looked up the specifics. The senator had been speaking in Columbus, Ohio and needed to get back to his home in West Virginia before catching a flight out of Huntington and getting to the meeting in Washington. His motorcade returned by the same route it had taken to the Ohio capitol. On the return, however, there had been a massive traffic jam on a high bridge that crosses the Ohio River near Ravenswood.

Not only were they blocked by a collection of cars, but it seems no cell phones worked. They had been unable to call for an airlift or other help. Fitzpatrick looked the site up on his computer. Too familiar.

He called the State Patrol in West Virginia and was referred to the locals. He was told that the Ravenswood police had been first on the scene, followed by the country sheriff, and they sorted the entire event out before anyone else interrupted.

"Kids threw some spikes on the road" was what the incident report said.

When Fitz asked about the lack of cell service the sheriff told him that some remote parts of Appalachia often lost cell service. This problem was not unusual. As a follow up Emmet asked the officer if he could take a look near some of the closer cell towers to see if there was any thin, smooth fabric laying around. He didn't want to bother with an actual identity of the material.

The reply indicated it might take a couple days because there was some heavy barge traffic coming up the Ohio and on busy weekends the back up at the locks usually required police presence. Fitzpatrick let out a long sigh. He did not want this case to get cold, but West Virginia was too far East, and in another jurisdiction.

When the Federal Bureau of Investigation organized their Odd Case Unit (OCU) they split the country into three sections and connected communications between the three via a unique system. All agents in the bureau could access that site, but it required effort. The result was a two-tiered network with the majority of FBI agents having immediate computer access to their type of case, but needing to dig if they wanted information on files in the Odd Case Unit.

To Fitzpatrick the computer worked another way: his files were those he first saw on the desktop when he opened his computer. After talking with the first responders in Ravenswood he sent a heads-up message to the Atlanta OCU office, which included his analysis and recommendations. The agents from that office would handle this incident.

The white van and white pick-up were driving at legal speed along the freeway near Charleston. They had West Virginia plates and were not overly concerned about being stopped. They were always vigilant, though.

They had been reluctant to assemble the team again after retirement, but all knew they were still young enough to enjoy a cross-country drive. Courtney was driving the van when Ruthie picked up her secure cell phone and read the text. "Get us southbound on I-81 and head for Bristol. Our condo is ready."

The guys in the truck were told of the message and turned to smile at each other. They had been this way once before. A great meal awaits. As traffic increased, Courtney was cautioned to not get caught up in the increased pace of the flow.

"Don't impede too many faster drivers but do go slow enough to cause the faster guys behind you creep up and ride your bumper. This temporarily blocks the view of your rear license plate." advised Ruthie. "It's a precaution I learned from the best." she added.

Ruth knew that cameras were becoming scarce in this part of the state, but they could easily be spotted from the air: fewer overpasses and larger spacing between vehicles. Never take chances, she thought, for good reason.

David Fowler, a Charleston agent with the FBI was in a bureau helicopter, working his way south. His associate in LA had given him a heads-up on this Ravenswood traffic jam and alert agents thought they spotted the two white vehicles driving south on I-77. On this heading, the preponderance of drivers would soon vector south to Atlanta, head east towards Raleigh, or proceed west towards Nashville. The bureau had agents in the air coming from all three directions.

Fowler was the chosen one today. He spotted the suspect vehicles driving southwest, on I-81 just north of the Tennessee border. When he asked the pilot to set down in Bristol and radio for a car, the response was: "Sir, you're going to need to go to Ashville to get a car."

"That's over an hour away. What about Johnson City?"

"I'm sorry Agent Fowler, but it's race week-end. Not only will you play hell getting a quick rental car but driving in this part of the country is impossible for three more days." Fowler did not follow NASCAR but did know about the popularity of these events. Stock car racing had its origins, and was therefore huge, in the south.

"It's OK – well find them. Let's call for a car, private if need be, and have them drive to Johnson City to meet us at the airfield. From there to Bristol is only 15 minutes. Lotsa time." He was convincing himself, "We'll find them."

The traffic started getting thick about 60 miles out of Bristol. At point the two white vehicles were within sight of each other, as spotted from the air by

Agent Fowler. Within 30 miles the average speed had dropped and the distance between the two was four miles. When they entered the hotbed of activity near the race track, they were half an hour apart.

As is the case near all large sports venues, entrepreneurs have struck with numerous businesses of various types. At Bristol these include apartment and condo complexes. There are miles of them on both sides of the road, on both sides of the exit to the track.

Gently working her way through the masses, Ruthie was now driving and heading for a familiar turn in Johnson City, south of Bristol. There was a sympathetic motel, just off the strip, with good food nearby and a superior view of two main arterials. As she entered the motel driveway, she knew the truck was already parked on the other side of the highway in a used car lot. She unloaded, then parked the van on the street three blocks away. She walked back to their second-floor room and flopped on the bed.

The helicopter had been on the ground for half an hour when the rental car and his chase car, finally showed up. "Sorry sir, it took all my knowledge of our country roads to get here even this quickly."

"That's OK, son. Thanks for the quick service. We'll get this car back to you as soon as we can." Fowler commandeered the pilot and they drove off towards Bristol. At any time, other than during the race itself, the average speed near a NASCAR track is average. However, on race week-end there are thousands of pedestrians, ignoring all traffic signs, and thousands of hot rods doing the same thing, creating an average speed closer to zero.

On the southern edge of condo row, Dave Fowler spotted a white van parked in front of a four-story residential building consisting of 80 living units. His heart rate increased when he saw a white pick-up parked around the corner, toward the back of the building. He got off the road. The well-dressed agent felt too conspicuous, even though he had taken off his tie and sport coat. He asked his passenger, the more casually dressed pilot, to jump out of the car, walk back and get the license plate numbers.

They then decided to keep an eye on these suspects. The condo complex across the street and up the road a few hundred yards had a slight hill behind it. The higher elevation of that parking area would offer them better visibility yet some separation from the target.

Moving to their new surveillance location, Fowler called in the license numbers of the suspect vehicles. They waited. In a few minutes the pilot acted startled. He squirmed in his seat, and sharply inhaled. When asked, he merely pointed towards the far end of the parking lot of the motel they were using for cover. There sat a white van and pick-up, parked next to each other.

"What?" exclaimed Fowler. A few seconds later: "I just wonder..." He got out of the car, clean-cut looks and all. The pilot followed. For the next two hours they visited all the condominiums along both sides of the highway, within one mile of the race-track. Not including the odd, real vehicle, they counted seven pairs of white, plain-Jane vans and pick-ups. When they got back to their car, they called for back-up and spent the night sleeping in the rental car. The reinforcements would arrive the next morning: race day.

Courtney was on look out early the next morning when she spotted five similar cars following each other along the arterial. She told the crew it was time to go. She had received a text earlier advised that the Nashville office of the FBI was leading the search.

Courtney wanted her team to get north to Lexington before heading west to Kansas City, thereby giving wide berth to Nashville. In KC they would leave the vehicles and fly back to Urgent. Others would hide the pick-up and van for a month, then ferry the white vehicle set back to the secure garage in Wyoming. They put on Kentucky plates while in Johnson City, then left 15 minutes apart.

All other vehicles in the area were stationary, their drivers watching the race, or some suspects. The FBI team knew that any group involved with the bait vehicles would also be stationary while the race was being run. Soon, it would be time to move!

Agent Dave Fowler met with the younger resident agents just after sunrise. They had gathered at his location behind the condo, and he briefed the crew on his plan. He was certain that, under cover of the race, the drivers of the pairs of vehicles would try to escape.

The bureau had run the plates and advised that they were all rented vehicles. Fowler deduced that one pair of drivers would be the team that was running from the Ravenswood incident. The FBI would apprehend and question them all. Each Nashville agent took up position near a white van-truck set. Soon the internal radio chatter started.

The agents observed how pedestrians would have difficulty crossing the busy stretch of asphalt, how others needed to drive around the building to meet up with each other, how there were consecutive license plate numbers, how Agent Fowler's rental car had a plate number within that sequence -WHAT? The chatter stopped"

By now they knew their search was to no avail. They were stuck in Bristol, in condo row until the post-race traffic died down. That would be four hours.

During that time, not one set of white suspects had been approached, yet alone driven away. To top it off, there was so much post-race cell phone activity that the system went down.

TWENTY - SEVEN

• •• — • •• — • — — — • — • —

The truth was that he was tired of travel. As the pilot announced a five-minute delay in their arrival into Milwaukee, Tom Lacey realized he was exhausted and just wanted to go home and go to bed. This had been a long trip. He thought back on other long trips he had endured. Do it again in a heartbeat as they say. Not so with this last visit to Washington.

Marina Whitehorse told him, years ago, to set up shop anyplace he thought necessary. Since he was recruited while living in Washington, he considered that home, for a while. It soon became obvious that the commute from there to Wyoming was too long a flight. Yet he needed anonymity and wanted to stay out of the way. The centrally located Milwaukee vicinity seemed logical, and it was.

Things got a little too close for comfort when he heard that people known to Marina had recruited local firefighters. However, she soon advised that the subjects in question were on the road and not likely to return. The Milwaukee office was remote enough to be secure. More importantly, his communications center and power source would remain where they were for a while. Good – less confusion for now, and the perfect spot.

Long ago, in the interest of security, Tom had decided to move these electronic tools from eastern Pennsylvania to Milwaukee. The equipment needed to gather all that data from satellites and other digital sources became a concern. Intelligence agencies were too close, and he did not want them accidentally scooping up any of his signals. Plus, his research team was growing, and his increasing power needs were likely to raise a red flag at the power company before too long. It was not that the physical move was such a hardship. It was the need to take it slow enough so as to not raise suspicion at either end of the move.

At the receiving location, the traffic around the airport was light and his people had quite a bit of freedom. Years ago, a large airline company pulled out of Milwaukee International Airport, after millions had been invested in a beautiful expansion. The terminal was extremely spacious for the foot traffic. The runways and surrounding infrastructure were under-utilized. Tom Lacey negotiated a sweet deal with the landlord and began quietly building the ideal data/research center.

The airports communications antennae array had room for his complex system. The warehouse neighborhood was scattered with empty buildings, all having plenty of parking and multiple entrances. He knew how to obtain, and divert, the crucial electrical power, enough for today but with room to grow. When he was involved with military intelligence, Tom had mistakenly designed the relocation of an OP center without sufficient room to bring in more power. He learned how difficult it is to secretly add electric capacity to an existing facility: a mistake he never repeated.

He spent a year weaning the area of his presence. He had not wanted some sudden hole in any patterns to be noticed as he abandoned the east coast When the move was finally over, he was fairly certain that no agency noticed the lack of digital traffic, just as no neighbors noticed the lack of vehicular traffic.

The state records remained the same: his fleet of vehicles remained licensed for one more year in Pennsylvania, even though they now all had Wisconsin plates and garages. He had kept the building lease and skeleton research staff.

Periodically he did visit this DC location for quality one-to-one briefings with all personnel. His understanding of the data they shared was more complete when he could ask direct questions and fine-tune their efforts. Plus, any human intel was centered around this location.

The visit he had just concluded was not particularly informative. The findings of his long-distance research from Milwaukee was merging with those of this Washington location. New technology knew no time zones. No, he really did not want to move again. If the timing was right, he would relocate one more time and that would be to the reservation.

At the same time, he would shut down this office. Urgent would be his last address. Through the years he had set up and dismantled regional offices in many locations. That was simple. Well, mostly. Now it was time to think about the last move and working fewer hours. He was slowing down and enjoying a longer night's sleep. That must mean something.

He had elected to participate in a Naval Reserve Officer Training program as a senior in high school. Once trained, he put in his time in military intelligence. After a full 30 and retirement, he continued with public service at the Bureau of Indian Affairs, deeply involved in data, research and intelligence. Now he could tack on nearly 12 years of this mission. Yes - he had earned a change of pace.

To Lacey, any move was a matter of timing. This last move needed to occur while things in Urgent were quiet. Those brief, sporadic incidents that drew the attention of law enforcement in various forms always meant postponing the move. The FBI or other jurisdictions had not connected these accidents to his operation, But why take the chance? He could not relocate if any agency was investigating one of their missions.

He fondly remembered the Texas RailOp, the first serious diversion for that new team. The NASCAR hide was a few years later and still unsolved. That long-ago car fire in Redding, his first out-of-state OP, would never be forgotten. He smiled at how his researchers had stumbled through the Milwaukee experiment almost, what was it, 12 years ago now

It was his intelligence gathering that enabled the team to even start these missions. The routine, day-to-day mundane job of an analyst was seldom appreciated. However, those valuable workers knew they were admired by their Tom Lacey. In fact, he almost treated them as family. He joined them in the lunchroom. They had office pools for every game during the Packers football season. He even took the winner of the to the next home game.

But the job was getting to him and he wanted to move. There was no big-league team in Wyoming.

TWENTY - EIGHT

— •• •• • — •• •• — —• • • —• —

The New Mexico incident had not gone according to plan. Due to the complexity of the scheme, they should have known. One of Ruthie's flyers, Rosita, was an experienced waitress. It was not difficult planting her in the Congressman's favorite restaurant in Taos. Nor was it particularly hard finding out what he ordered, and doctoring it with a drug.

Two days prior to his visit, Lacey and Ruth had arranged to erect a temporary construction site on a road they knew he would use. That faux-site was on the only road out of Taos and had been adorned with a portable toilet which, the drug guaranteed, he would also need to use.

The congressman had needed to stop at that porta-potty, and his limo did get bogged down in the soft earth in front of the toilet stall; exactly according to plan. What was unexpected was the speed with which he had managed to call for an airlift. Perhaps cell phone signal traveled farther up here, or his car had a satellite phone.

The team didn't know how, but he had summoned a helicopter and was quickly airborne. What they did know was that contingency plans needed to be activated. Rosita, who was monitoring the operation, called Brittany Odom.

Gordon Niles was a young US representative from North Dakota who proudly served his base. He bowed to the energy powers in his home state: the fossil fuel powers. Everyone knew he would vote against anything green As is often the case, his home turf included numerous Native American reservations, but he didn't consider them Americans or constituents. The oil and coal guys were the true Americans.

He had read that members from various tribes were slowly moving to the Wind River project in Wyoming. The population of young people from the Cheyenne, Crow Creek, Yankton, even Standing Rock reservations was dwindling. That was not his problem.

The concern here was the intrusion of a big environmentally friendly power source. In quiet, personal moments, Niles did admit that fossil fuel had to ultimately give way to other types of power. There was a finite number of dead dinosaurs.

Each year he stayed in office, though, was another year he could pad his retirement. Those fossil fuel guys had big pads. Congressman Niles had heard that this project on Indian land was getting built rather quickly. Somehow the permits were getting issued and some land swaps had been made between the Nation and the BLM, and/or the state. Anything he could do to confuse the issue, and or delay any part of their plans was his plan.

Also, he was concerned about their electricity know-how: network if you will. Neighboring Nebraska is a power maverick and Niles knew the rates in Nebraska were the most competitive in the country. How was it that they had built their own power association? A bit like a food co-operative, Nebraska cobbled together the publicly owned utilities, the smaller co-ops and some power districts, into a public power association. The not-for-profit group, elects board members, sets the state-wide rates, and establishes service standards. A few years back they even approved, financed and built what at that time was the nation's second largest wind farm.

It looked like this new Wind River generating station would be at least that large. What if Wyoming too organized an association? Could such an entity take all the power industry profits away from his supporters? Not if Niles could help it! In his role as a congressional representative of the committee, all variances of the rules of the BLM needed to be voted on. Normally, the other representatives on that committee wasted no time in approving all agenda items that appeared before them.

The Bureau of Land Management did not have many management issues. On this particular occasion the Wind River folks had asked for approval to run some new rail lines through quite a stretch of BLM land. Niles knew his negative vote would set this project back.

Regardless of what the load might be, hauling by truck and highways was slower and more expensive than moving the goods by rail. It was critical that he make this vote, stomach pain notwithstanding. There would be another bathroom at the airport. While in the helicopter he needed to hold tight.

The Congressman's flight was coming to an end. The pilot had radioed into the Albuquerque tower advising of landing location and getting clearance for the near-by limousine to briefly cross the taxiway to meet the politician. After receiving the OK, the limo driver was watching the helo to make sure he could quickly and safely cross the taxiway. He did not see the approaching drone. A bright flash near the tail rotor was his first indication that something was wrong.

When the aircraft started rotating, the chauffer knew there was a problem. As he turned to speak to the congressman's aide in the back seat, the sound of the changing pitch of the helicopter engine made him look back. The engine speed was attempting to counter the increased rotation, this meant that altitude would be lost. They only had 100 feet to lose before hitting the ground.

There was no fire, no explosion, like vividly shown in action movies, only the sounds of metal being ground and twisted, broken and sheared. There were no human sounds. Airport response teams were moved in seconds.

All flights were cancelled; even the jet that was on final approach and one mile out. Everything was diverted away from ABQ. The immediate response notifications went out to various federal agencies and each had teams that sprang into action. At the same time the message reached FBI HQ in Washington, it also reached all field offices. It reached the Odd Case Unit and Emmet Fitzpatrick.

He was above real investigating now. The latest promotion had taken him out of the immediate action arena and tied him to a desk. Eight years had passed since the last politician missed-meeting problem, as he called them, but he was still intrigued. Not just because the incidents were dastardly crimes: some appeared to not be crimes at all. He was curious as to who was doing this and why. This had to be a conspiracy, but to what end and who was doing the conspiring?

When he told his secretary to get the jet ready, she knew who to notify that the Assistant Deputy Director was flying, and how to get clearance and file the flight plan. The bureau had some latitude in notifications of the ultimate destination, but to get out of LAX required prudent planning. Even before he was airborne Emmet was in contact with the local office and brought them up to speed. He was told that the airport area was heavy with video cameras and all personnel would, thanks to his input, soon be looking for a pair of white vehicles: a van and a pick-up. One victim was a politician and Fitzpatrick knew he had to investigate.

The reactivated southwest team had been advised that this was a one-off gig. The growth of Urgent was proceeding ahead of schedule and soon all efforts to hinder the new project would be too obvious to be politically advantageous. They had also been advised that this guy from North Dakota was devious, tenacious and just plain nasty; he was not going to get to vote. Period. That was the story Lacey had told Ruth in requesting her expertise in this exercise.

Now the team was leaving the scene for one last time. The target had been immobilized, albeit in a much more visible manner than they liked. They would discover later that the drone missed its target. The intent was to disable the helicopter by crashing into the front windshield and temporarily blinding the pilot. At the last second, the pilot had rotated into the wind. The approaching drone could not change course in time and took out the tail rotor. After that, the pilot had no control of the aircraft.

Everyone knew this act required the law to pay attention. The incident would trigger an immediate inquiry by the NTSB and involve hours of questioning. Therefore, precautions started as soon as the van did. The guys would take the pick-up north, to Urgent. It would be of future use and could be well hidden there.

"Avoid Denver and Cheyenne by taking US and State highways." had said their instructions. They had plates for Colorado and Wyoming. The few miles spent on Utah roads were not of any concern. Northeast Utah had very few residents, and fewer state police. The more serious planning involved getting the van away from the scene. Ruth remembered they had a great contingency plan centered around Phoenix. She instructed Rosita to meet up with the drone pilot, Sara, and get moving.

Sara was an Albuquerque kid, familiar with the roads on the shady, south side of town. Her alert response to this situation got them quickly off the main roads and headed away from traffic and trouble. "Someday I'll tell you about growing up around here." she told Rosita. Half-an-hour after the incident they were going south on the freeway, exiting west onto US highway 60.

There was not a lot of traffic along this route which runs across the continental divide, through Fort Apache and into Phoenix and the valley to the east. All were aware that they could easily be seen but they would also be more able to see those looking for them.

Once off the interstate, the van bounced from village to convenience store, to rest area; hiding for a couple hours and looking for a tail. Their instructions were to start the descent into the valley shortly after sunrise. The van was not a fast vehicle. It also was far from unique. Without any special features it looked just like the millions of white vans produced the same year, years before and years after. From the air it blended in but alone on a desert highway it was simple to follow.

Sara was the better of the two drivers. She was behind the wheel during the descent into the valley from the high-country near Fort Apache. This gave her a view of the sky in her mirrors. Both she and Rosita were watching when she finally spotted the helicopter. She cleared her throat in preparation to speak, "I see him," Rosita said. "I'll send a message to mom." and she activated the secure radio.

The trip towards Phoenix was at legal speed and without incident. Rosita was looking out the one-way windows in the van keeping tabs on the police tail they had picked up. She counted three within sight and noticed one unmarked car at every other on-ramp, sitting still, but ready at an idle. The scrambled radio contact was constant, by now. Brittany was encouraging Sara to calm down and walking her through the series of events that were taking place about an hour in front of her.

Emmet Fitzpatrick was in the helicopter. He knew he could stop the suspects any time he wanted. His prize, though, was going to be the location and identity of whoever was in charge. That white van was going to lead him directly to his target.

He instructed the helicopter pilot maintain this altitude, high enough that Emmet needed binoculars to watch the van. He saw no indication that they spotted him, nor did he note any evasive maneuvers. All his agents and the police force were to casually follow and carefully watch.

The van approached Phoenix proper from the east and turned north on one of the many wide freeways that loop around that expansive metropolis. This freeway allowed quick access to the population north of downtown. In the northeast corner of this loop was a growing suburb. Years ago, this was all empty desert, then they built the Musical Instrument Museum.

Having grown into a popular attraction, the museum anchored industrial and residential growth there. Most of the houses were on the outside of the loop. The business expansion was on the inside, adjacent to the museum itself. Local city planners had left an open zone surrounding the museum, intended for future expansion.

The land next to that zone was under construction. Steel framing, parking lots, and foundation trenches were all there. The traffic pattern around the museum was interrupted by this construction. Heavy equipment was parked on the shoulder near miles of steel fencing and strong gates surrounding mounds of dirt. The area was dotted with small cranes, and well-worn dirt paths crisscrossed the land.

Emmet noticed the van driver activate the right turn signal. "She's exiting here," was his radioed warning.

On Sunday morning the Musical Instrument Museum was at its busiest. It was bustling with the usual out-of-town tourists, bus-loads of locals from retirement communities, fraternal organizations and other groups. The large parking lot was almost full causing traffic at the exit coming from town to back up onto the freeway.

This mass of humanity bothered the FBI personnel, and for good reason.

No sooner did the white van slow down to exit than a large explosion rocked the museum. One large mound of earth in the construction site disappeared. Soil, rocks and cactus pieces began peppering all the cars within direct sight of the blast. So much material flew skyward that the chase helicopter heard small bits of debris hitting the windshield and fuselage. The pilot immediately gained altitude and rotated away for fear of another blast.

Things quieted down, and Fitz ordered them to fly back over the scene. Approaching with caution, but this time lower, he was able to determine that the museum had begun emergency evacuation procedures and that his back-up state police had jumped into action. They were directing traffic back onto the freeway and away from the area.

A closer look at the construction site revealed a large, fuel tank in the center of the area. Was that a shadow beneath the tank he asked himself? The answer was a second explosion. Not nearly as powerful as the first, the additional blast was accompanied by fire. The flames began to engulf only part of the bare earth below, and a portion of a concrete pour. Emmet was certain that the concrete was the beginnings of an underground parking area. The fuel from the ruptured tank must have puddled in the low spot, which happened to be paved. No place to go but up.

The carnage was fortunately located on the back side of the museum. The occasional window along that wall had been blown out at the original explosion. Only a few patrons were inside, near those windows when the fire started.

There was panic from those inside, struggling to escape, and those outside that heard the noise and now were instinctively running away. The local fire department had a tough time getting through the crowd and traffic. Two engines approached from opposite sides of the museum. One hooked up hoses while the other with ladders was standing by. The helicopter landed a few hundred yards away on a paved section of unfinished road to nowhere. Two local agents that had been posted at a freeway on-ramp joined Fitz. Where was the van? When the pilot had panicked and turned away from the blast Emmet had lost sight of his target. The others admitted to being concerned about the safety of the hundreds of Phoenix citizens. They had stopped looking also.

As the fire died down, Emmet noticed a charred hulk of a vehicle in the debris, beneath the rubble in the underground parking lot. Could it be? He backed out of the way to let a tall, fire department ladder-rig leave the scene, and walked down the ramp.

It was a van, still smoldering beneath a possibly compromised concrete overhang. He had his team call for a tow truck. It took a half an hour, but the truck finally arrived. Danger be damned, he ordered the van pulled out of the wreckage and into the open air.

It was now obvious that the color was white. The vehicle was completely empty. No remains, no remnants. Not a cigarette butt, candy wrapper or registration. For the second time in a decade he had that sinking feeling. He dismissed personnel to return to their bases.

TWENTY – NINE

✳ ✳ ✳ ✳

Tom Lacey had always felt that the diversion at the Musical Instrument Museum was the prime example of the creative thinking that his associates were capable of, a really messy escape, but with no loss of civilian life. The innovative team that worked that mission had all been recalled to Urgent during the past few years.

Also, the training team was relocated after years of service. Specifically, the Fosters and Osburns had chosen to continue working in the service of the cause. Vern Osburn was the oldest within this core group and not in good health. He usually stayed home. Anne and Ellie Foster still helped with education and training of the young.

The community had taken advantage of Anne's years of experience in education. More than teaching various subjects, she had designed schemes that resulted in daily life having an education element. She arranged for shuttle drivers to visit various construction sites while taking children home from school. They would get a tour and get to see blueprints and sketches of the finished product: even handle some of the hand-tools.

Each morning in class one student was asked to tell the class what his/her family had earlier eaten for dinner, or breakfast, and explain what was done in the kitchen to make that meal. Anne knew this lesson at school encouraged dialog and observation at home. She also knew the child was not the only one learning during those exchanges. Jeff Foster had been tasked with planning a more organized fire and rescue system. The growing community could afford to buy whatever equipment it needed. Water distribution was a persistent problem that Jeff continuously studied and remedied with the help of some engineers.

The laboratories placed an ever-increasing demand on water supply, just as hydrants and stand pipes were needed in all buildings for potential emergencies. Tom Lacey knew the importance of these services.

Over the years, through his research team's monitoring and data mining, Lacey was becoming more successful at tracking his opposition. Not that he knew exactly who those individuals were, but he knew his team could ferret them out.

He looked at the chain of events dictated by government protocol: if there had to be a committee meeting before the senate could vote on something of interest to Lacey, his talented researchers would follow the members of that committee.

He was plugged into each member's calendar and appointment book. He knew where they were driving, flying or having lunch. He knew their favorite restaurants. He knew where their wives shopped. It was no secret where the loyalties of each member were. It became no secret how to break a tie and/or control the outcome.

After a few too coincidental accidents, a cadre of federal politicians quietly started talking conspiracy. They weren't sure who was behind such a conspiracy, but it was evident that the big Wyoming project was the beneficiary of too many "coincidences". There had to be a conspiracy.

Tom Lacey wasn't worried, at least not about the politicians. He did worry, though, about the FBI. Very early in the series of unusual events they had assigned a young, talented agent to investigate. With admiration, Lacey had been watching Emmet Fitzpatrick for many years. As creative as the diversion team became, Agent Fitzpatrick came to recognize them.

Once in a while, the team's efforts went unnoticed. Fitzpatrick got close after that desert operation. After the Phoenix chase, Lacey began monitoring the agent's activity and work record. He became more concerned when he learned of the formation of the Odd Case Unit.

Fitzpatrick was awarded a couple of promotions and was put in charge of all investigations at the Los Angeles field office. He turned out for the chase at Phoenix because he recognized the play. Lacey realized Fitz was advancing his investigation as he jumped in the unmarked jet and joined the fray. Lacey wanted him to take one more plane ride.

This particular move took two years of planning and waiting. The research team intercepted a message from Fitzpatrick's secretary to her insurance agent asking how much monthly annuity her policy would buy if she retired soon. She would be 63 and eligible for early Social Security but might want to take it later. To Lacey this meant that Fitzpatrick was being offered a promotion to Washington, DC.

More digging into appointment calendars at FBI headquarters revealed when, and with whom, Fitz was meeting. Lacey called his own meeting.

Fitzpatrick climbed into the back seat of the unmarked car and buckled his seat belt. The vehicle exited the underground parking garage and headed for the freeway. His driver announced, "It's a mess at LAX today, sir. The jet has been diverted to Ontario in order to save you time. We'll have you there in half-an-hour or so."

Fitz opened his briefcase, retrieved some papers and started working. Interview or not, he had some performance reports that were due the day he got back from Washington. The GPS told the driver how to get through the secure perimeter at the airport, and where the jet was standing by. They arrived on schedule.

As Emmet got out of the car his habit was to glance at the tail numbers of the plane. He recognized the registration and climbed the stairs. Still trim and fit, he took them two at a time. He questioned why the engine on the far side was running, but he dismissed it.

As soon as he sat down the other engine started spooling up and the jet slowly rolled onto the taxiway. As only executive jets can do, his accelerated into the turn from the taxiway onto the runway and kept accelerating until airborne. This was really unusual. The tower must have been scrambling to allow that take-off he thought.

The next instant the door behind him opened and out walked a man about his age and nearly as well dressed. Tom Lacey introduced himself to Emmet Fitzpatrick and sat down across from him. Lacey poured Fitz the drink he knew the FBI agent preferred, poured one for himself and proceeded to tell an amazing story.

The plane had been gone for only 30 minutes when, on the ground, Looser and Stretch had finished the packing routine. All planes have visible features used by seasoned passengers as signs that confirm they are boarding the right aircraft. To duplicate the tail numbers, wheel design, number of windows and fuselage decals the Lacey team had created unique camouflage panels. This white material with the painted numbers and images was quickly tugged off the jet as it left the shadows of the hanger. The young men packed the cloth panels into a bag and proceeded to remove any evidence of their presence. The jet would return to pick them up as soon as it delivered its current cargo to Salt Lake City.

In the air, Lacey revealed as much detail about Urgent as he dared. He would not risk exposing people or confidences on the off-chance this federal employee decided to further investigate him. Tom explained that they had one more hour together during this meeting. This flight would end in Salt Lake City where he would pick up the jet owned by the bureau. It had been diverted to that airport at Fitzpatrick's instruction and was waiting for him. Lacey continued with his story.

As intrigued, and confused, as he was, Fitzpatrick chose not to interrupt or bombard this intruder with questions. The creativity and nerve it had taken to kidnap a senior agent of the Federal Bureau of Investigation demanded undivided attention. With about 15 minutes left in the flight, Lacey began his summation.

"Fast forward to today. Your interview in Washington will result in an offer that, if accepted, moves you to Washington, DC. We know you are an honorable, family man, and that your grown children would take kindly to their Dad being a big shot. Your wife would not complain.

"You have certainly thought this through, but your secretary Lucy will not follow you to the nation's capitol. Graham's ego will demand that he take all credit for your heretofore accomplishments. Your friend, the director in DC is only one year away from retirement and you know he will retire to his cabin on Flathead Lake.

"We also know that your time with the civil service entitles you to be able to retire today at full pay. Oh sure, you would get a raise if you took the Washington job, but your monthly pension would only go up a couple hundred dollars or so. You would end your career in Washington, as part of that Washington, call it flexible and immoral circle, with your retirement years consisting of Wednesday lunch with the old farts while the youngsters at the bureau forget who you are or what you did. I can offer you another alternative." Lacy relaxed a bit in his seat: body language read by his guest.

"Urgent does not have much of a law enforcement

entity. We don't need one. There is a community at work that provides such support and encouragement to everyone, of all ages, that crime is not a concern. Sure, never say never, but right now we're OK. One need we do have, however, is an experienced individual to help us navigate outside law enforcement. Even though you are not a practicing lawyer, you speak the language and know the law.

"We have shipments arriving in the United States from foreign ports. They use the rail lines through numerous states and cross an international boundary to get to Urgent. The material in these shipments is all owned by the United States but comes from various ports around the world. Some was shipped under the cover of darkness.

"Within the United States we have holdings in most states and vehicles, such as this aircraft, that must have flexible identities, yet legitimate ones. Good "covers" to use a term you are familiar with. And then there is the matter of industrial espionage.

"We know we will be spied upon, if we aren't already. We have the beginnings of talent to help in that arena, but no leadership and no plan. Just ideas and concerns. Money will be no object. Trust me on that. Position should not be a bother. You will be one of the honored leaders of the entire community. Right at the top and proud to be there.

"Your wife, your children, anyone you care to share with will be proud to know someone who has dedicated the rest of his life to such a worthy cause. Urgent will become better known as our accomplishments grow. Trust me on this too.

"We are about to touch down. This plane will taxi to an area outside the last hanger in line. Your jet is waiting inside that hanger. We don't expect an answer now. We just wanted a place at the table. Here's my card. Have your interview, think about both offers, and please, call me regardless."

Fitz took the card and put it in his pocket. He did not offer his hand. The agent walked down the stairs and through the open hanger door. "These guys are good." He thought, "They know the names of my secretary, my next in command and the location of Director Stevenson's cabin in Montana."

He could think of no description for his current feelings other than bewilderment. He had a lot of thinking to do.

THIRTY

—·· ·— —· —·—· ·

A confluence of timing issues resulted in an upheaval in most of Urgent. It was now referred to as the grand relocation. The population had successfully grown to the point that the South Center could be put on hold. This meant the closing of the Appalachia school (hotel) and the suspension of all recruiting activities. It also meant no more boat trips, no touring of small-town schools, no familiar overnight stops along the rivers and canals.

Over the years, the memory of many people and places had been imprinted onto the minds of the Urgent recruits that followed this path. The individuals in charge had developed ties with those on the outside. The recruiting team decided to invite those capable, of joining the family as it relocated to Urgent. Naturally, there were security issues to deal with, and clearances to obtain. Those were explained up front.

The families transplanted during the grand relocation traveled well-worn routes from the deep South and from Appalachia. The South Center was cleaned up and acted as temporary housing until new accommodations could be built in Urgent. The Osburns were called upon to supervise the revival of the center.

Anne was confident that she could modify the curriculum she created for the Appalachia hotel. Her new students would be of all ages, yet the education she planned on providing was more cultural than anything else. Vern would have the job of keeping the center running.

The town in Wyoming was preparing for population growth by expanding the housing options in the northwest sector, near the airport. There was also an invisible expansion of housing options in the research facilities, below ground.

It was at this point that many businessmen in the South began to notice the decrease in their labor force. It was getting harder to fill those entry level job on the warehouse and factory floor. The frowned upon, often ignored, never appreciated minimum wage workers were not as plentiful - where were they? Any vacancy on the production line, even missing low-paid people, adversely affects profits.

During a regular meeting of some politicians and businessmen the conversation turned to unemployment. Recently released date showed a minimum-wage worker dearth in Southern Alabama. The entry level positions and unskilled labor slots were getting hard to fill. The room was filled with grumbling.

One big city mayor with good connections advised "What did you expect? You guys on the river allowed thousands of your constituents to escape north."

The following hub-bub revealed the denial most were experiencing. They did not know, and could not believe, that life wasn't just beautiful for these citizens. When they were reminded of the unemployment, the education shortfall, the graft, the income inequality, the lack of rural infrastructure, the gerrymandering, the abortion ban etc. that conversation stopped. All knew one thing: to keep going, wages were about to go up dramatically, and profits would drop accordingly. Move to a higher pay scale or move the company out, if you want to stay in business. How did this happen?

Demanding an investigation and demanding satisfaction they agreed to form a committee and get some answers. It was more than wanting to know where these people went. The prime motive was to find out what it would take to get some of the workers to return. Wouldn't money entice the skilled workers back?

One particular businessman was excessively boisterous. His company made small parts for local auto assembly plants and he was not going to raise wages for any of his employees. He was proud of the money he made and "I'll be damned if I'm going to share any of it with those people. Instead, I'll spend it on fighting and ending this fiasco."

Never expecting that they might be watched, the members of the investigation committee started talking to detective agencies, their local law enforcement buddies, and family members.

As soon as these communications began, Tom Lacey was advised. He instructed his researchers to closely determine who was making that noise in the south. He wanted to shut this down in a hurry. Before too long, the players were identified, and Lacey flew to the reservation. In a meeting with Bo Elliott and Edward he detailed the opposition.

Bringing in Ruth to add a creative set of eyes on the problem was a smart move. He followed by consulting with the Osburns and the Fosters. He now had the attention of the recruiting team and their training staff. The brainstorming session that followed lasted over six hours. They set two goals:

First: no invading party would make it across the Ohio River.

Second: he wanted the invaders to know they were being watched.

THIRTY - ONE

Jeff and Ellie helped with education in Urgent for a few years. It had been a peaceful time. The village recruiting system Jeff had established was self-perpetuating. Once in a while he would venture out to have a beer with some of the former firefighters. Normally, though, he stayed close to home, tending to his young fire department. That soon would change.

The threat posed by the fuming businessmen in the South had been detailed by Tom Lacey. Jeff knew his role in putting down that threat was important. He needed to give his recruiters a new task and needed this trip to be solo. Ellie agreed. He loaded up the personal pick-up after having it washed and checked out: it hadn't been on an open road for five years.

His goal was to go south through the center, and along the river, meeting with recruiters at every stop. They knew the neighborhood. They knew the locals and the strangers. He would get a description of the opposing forces from Lacey as they became available. At some point in his southward journey he would encounter the intruder's northward movement.

Jeff's intel revealed conversations confirming that these detectives were not planning on invading Urgent.

It was too obvious and well defended. The hired thugs were going to send their message by targeting loved ones left behind: innocent households along the river route that helped the deserters. Tom Lacey's research team could not find any specific instructions given to these bullies other than to harass. However, to Lacey, the mobilization of this team of investigators was concern enough. If this was the battlefield, so be it he thought. He also thought - big mistake.

Jeff reached the Ohio River at the landing used by the South Center boats. One forty-five-footer was available, as was an experienced pilot. Harry Stone was one of the best teachers on the river, but had doubts about the security clearance requirements in Urgent, so he elected to stay behind while others decided to move.

Harry said that he lived by that old saying that nothing was half-so much fun as "messing about in boats", but there was too much youthful bluster showing. Jeff knew macho and immediately trusted the kid. He helped Jeff unload the truck and they tossed the ignition keys to the South Center security member that had ushered Jeff to the site.

"Cast off that bow line will ya – I've got the stern. Beautiful afternoon. My friends call me Stoney." The boat headed down stream.

Motoring along the slow-moving Ohio River gave them an opportunity to get acquainted. Jeff soon heard the true story about Stoney's brush with the law. Then that was set aside, and the conversation got serious. Harry knew all the overnight stops and most of the residents on the dock at each stop. They set about recruiting those relatives and friends.

Although Stoney was just recently of voting age, his wisdom and conversation with older folks was unmatched. At each overnight spot, Jeff was candid and shared his concern. He quickly sized up which person believed his concern, and which wanted no involvement. If the opportunity presented itself, he isolated the believers and armed them with a Tire Stick. He had brought a hundred with him on the boat and could always send for more.

For this mission, the Urgent leaders had agreed that a harmless message was just as effective as any other. They decided on the Tire Stick as designed and built by Stretch: a battery operated, foot-long device that looked like a stretched flashlight.

It was quite simple to operate: small, rubber fingers on one end tightly slipped over the valve stem cap on a tire. A push of the button unscrewed the cap in a second. Flip the device over and small protrusions fit perfectly into the cavity on either side of the valve stem. Push another button and the valve stem unscrewed over halfway. The Tire Stick was designed to sense the total travel of the valve stem.

The goal was not to remove the stem completely. This would allow all the air to immediately escape the tire. The desired effect was a slow leak that could cause complete deflation of the tire within one-half hour. A leak at this rate could not be heard; plus, it allowed time to negotiate an escape, maybe even strand the driver.

Use of the stick was explained at every stop, as was the suggested approach to the target vehicle. The pros and cons of diversions were discussed. Getaway routes were defined. More often than not, the residents in the port villages and private docks were excited to help. More often than not Jeff and Stoney were also fed.

The route south was serene and lazy as they traveled through Kentucky. As they got deeper into Tennessee the information from Urgent became more definite. Lacey's researchers had picked up chatter about opposition activity crossing the Alabama/Tennessee border and continued harassment along the Tenn-Tom canal.

Their intelligence paid off in the form of a complete description of the boat approaching them from the south. The opposition was using both land and water.

Even before getting on the river Jeff had formulated

a plan designed to avoid confrontation. Remain invisible and travel as far south as possible, was still the goal. Now they were traveling mostly in early morning and late in the evening. At long last they noticed a boat matching the description they had been given.

"That's the boat," observed Stoney.

"Faster than us. Fancy electronics? I see three guys. That's a hide-away color. You gotta boat?"

"Nope – I sold my boat. And what's a hide-away color?"

"Too much like thousands of other boats in all the marinas. Hard to spot if you don't want it spotted. How big was it?"

"Smaller than this one. Now quiet. I'm going below to make a call."

They continued down-stream for one stop and checked on the folks at the dock last visited by the north-bound, fancy boat. Just a little verbal harassment and a lot of questions to which the locals played dumb. The sleuths had left with the understanding that they would be back. Right! They were about to get a surprise.

As Jeff and Harry proceeded behind enemy lines, their reception grew. The positive affect of Urgent recruiting had begun to show itself this far south. They were welcomed by poor parents who had been receiving money from up north. They heard stories of misguided children that had matured and cleaned up their act: some had married and had children of their own.

These grateful friends and relatives were eager to cause trouble, if it was good trouble. More Tire Sticks were distributed. More corrupt politicians were identified.

Within days the distress signals began. Mysterious flat tires. Waiting hours for a tow truck. Water in the gas tank of the boat. Search & Rescue being called out for hours at a time. A message started getting through to the leaders in the south: they had messed with some serious folks. Jeff and Harry continued south.

They were going to bring their forces right to the source of the problem.

As the inconveniences intensified, so did the efforts from the other side. The Urgent team had nothing to fear from the water but crossing the land border into Alabama was a different story. They heard rumors about local law enforcement beefing up watch along the river and setting up roadblocks along the highway.

"You guys from the north don't play with the police. Good folks in the south don't trust 'em. Don't need 'em. You ever done time?"

"Nope. Firefighters and police know and respect each other." replied Jeff.

"In all the years I was working for the city, the police department was about the only department I did trust. At least the guys on the line. Those in the mayor's office are a different story."

"Down here, it's your different story all the way down. Fire guys earn the trust. Police don't. They play games. You play games?"

"Not that kind. Just a little ball."

At each dock they were still welcomed and advised not to worry. The natives knew the law and how to deal with it. That was their history. Sure enough, police cars began getting multiple flats, and the tow trucks were disabled too. When locals called in state reinforcements, the bigger paychecks of the staties did not give them immunity. State police in rural, river areas were also needing tow trucks.

Jeff and Harry had one last mission planned.

Coordinating with friendly folks along the riverbank, they had asked for help in disabling vehicles at one specific time. The decision had been made to deliver the final blow to the labor leaders that had so egregiously discounted their employees.

Ten of the largest and most profitable firms in southern Alabama were targeted. The fancy cars in the parking lots of the manufacturing plants were too visible.

The teams would go after the vehicles of the wives and secretaries, husbands and mistresses if they had one. Tom Lacey had worked overtime and provided quite a list. The helpful locals knew, or knew of, these businesses.

At the last minute, Tom Lacey had asked Ruthie if she was up to helping the boat-people a little. When she had been fully briefed, she told Tom she would take a new crew, plus a well-trained one. It would be like old times if she could invite Courtney, however: "Courtney was pregnant and will deliver any day." Ruth would accept this opportunity for some On the Job Training (OJT), and to keep her hand in.

It took a couple days to drive the pick-ups to Alabama. Along the way, her OJT consisted of stories of past adventures and details of creative ways to get the mission accomplished. Lacey's analysts made all reservations and had allowed the two teams to stay in the same motels while on the road. She insisted that they check in one full hour apart, and not leave together.

When Ruth and her crews got to southern Alabama, they checked into different motels, 20 miles apart, and met at one of the riverbank safe houses to plan the operations. Each team had their own white pick-up with the normal looking camper-top, but those abnormal electronic darkening windows.

Both trucks were capable of the TrakTore. That action would take out a couple roads. She knew she needed a different weapon from her arsenal to close the freeway bridge: an AuTu. In preparation, they had paid cash for both a car hauler and the few scrapped cars this operation required. Her plans for the land action were coming together. The final effort on the river required one mass meeting.

At a convenient location, organized on the quiet, these willing participants met each other for the first time. The size of their support group gave them more resolve than before. Jeff and Stoney enjoyed organizing this resistance. Consuming all the pizza and soft drinks they wanted, the river folks studied maps. The questions they asked of each other shed light on the intricate mission they wanted to join. As a whole the group left more excited than when they arrived.

These ignored citizens in rural Alabama had lived through all the hard times anyone could endure. Crooked politicians were found innocent of sexual misconduct because the crooked judge was guilty of the same misconduct. The mayor was no better, having ties to the industries his brother was appointed to oversee. If the corruption was not so obvious the public might not be so bothered. But the good-ol'boys network was now so full of itself that blatant and unapologetic behavior was flaunted as a badge of honor. In fact, they re-elected state senators that were felons. Rural Alabama wanted these activities to stop.

At 9:00 AM the mayor of Linden, Alabama got to work. His chief clerk advised that his wife wanted him to call her. He had left the house earlier and gone to his weekly morning meeting. What could be so urgent? When he returned the call, she told him that after her visit to the beauty parlor this morning she had a flat tire. He called a tow truck for her.

What a way to start the day, he thought. Just a little earlier, at breakfast, one of his staff mentioned hearing that there was a major traffic jam on the bridge at Jackson, that highway bridge which all the commuters use when heading into Mobile every morning. "Cars backed up for miles. That's the only way across the river."

At the same time, upstream in Demopolis, both bridges that cross the Tombigbee River were closed due to traffic. The police were announcing a petty crime of throwing spikes on the roadway. When the city police tried to respond, the chief could not join them: he had a flat tire.

The morning news opened with a story that Interstate 65 southbound approaching Mobile had been closed. A load of scrapped cars headed for the crusher had broken loose from the car-hauler and crashed onto the freeway. Until further notice the public was advised to detour south to Interstate 10.

That advice lasted for 10 minutes until the I-10 tunnel was closed due to a series of flat tires, actually in the tunnel. It was now problematic if anyone needed to get to work in the city, or at the industrial complex to the south.

The problem got worse when a Mercedes traveling into town on US-90 quit running. That in itself was not news, but the fact that it had stopped in the middle of a stretch of road crossing the delta meant there was no exit.

The disabled luxury car needed to be rescued by a tow-truck driving the wrong way down the four-lane road. Before that truck could hook-up the tow, a similar model car within sight of the first one, quit running. Mobile was in a virtual lock down. Alabama State Police were in a frenzy.

The politicians and labor leaders that had formed the semi-official investigation committee hurriedly met via conference call. One observed, and all agreed, that they were the target of this confusion. It was unanimous that they halt all investigative efforts. This type of traffic activity, regardless of how innocent it looked, was bad for business, and these were mostly business people.

Although it would take months to figure out the financial damage to their campaigns and companies, it would all be silently absorbed. They could not afford to go public any more than they could afford to try another tactic. It had to stop soon.

Shortly after the morning of madness, the river crew met up with Ruthie and her crew at a friendly cabin near the Interstate. She took pride in the accolades bestowed on her for the freeway closure. "You mean the AuTU" she asked – then had to explain the contraction of auto with the military term TU, as in dead, as in tits up."

Stoney was the first to ask for more clarification: "Over the boat radio I heard something about a car-hauler that lost some cars. 'jou do that? Where's the coffee?"

"Wasn't that cool?"

"While at the safe house, we borrowed the dinghy from the riverboat. With an outboard motor to power the vessel, there were no real electronics on board to be bothered by the EMP device we carried. We know it's possible to protect the broadcasting vehicle from the electro-magnetic pulse, but why try if you can rid yourself of those fragile electronic components. It took a bit of timing know how, but what appeared to be a risky accident involved minimum risk.

We started sending signal to disable all vehicles on the bridge from our location on the river. No drivers on the freeway above thought twice about the people fishing in the little boat below.

"The EMP was focused on those that were just behind the car hauler. Then, when those close cars stalled and a significant break in traffic had been created, we blew the scrap cars off the back of the car-hauler. Those driving the crippled vehicles may have noticed the sudden loss of power but were soon so distracted by the chaos created by the scrap cars tumbling down the highway, that they temporarily forgot.

"When questioned later by law enforcement, some might have remembered their cars acting differently, but were not positive it was not a quicker than usual response by their subconscious reacting to the danger.

"It was the disabling of the big-rigs that set things up to get worse. Without power they don't behave normally and caused a few fender-benders. Then folks exited their vehicles to vent at other drivers and the action took place on foot: not behind the wheel.

"The exchange of information involves a lot of time and someone must force all those commuters to get back in their cars and go to work. Just to be safe, we didn't stop the car-hauler.

"Before long one of our friendlies along the river was changing the title on that rig. They wanted to use it to help some neighbors do some logging. We arranged for two tow-trucks to miraculously appear and quickly pick up the scrap and haul it off the bridge. The scrap will be sold for scrap."

The request for clarification was picked up by a resident, "And the mess in downtown Mobile?"

"Yea, one of the challenges had been closing the tunnel. On this OP, we didn't want to get caught on closed circuit TV. Recon revealed the security cameras were pointing down from just above the tunnel entrance. Our solution was to drop the spikes from a drone: released just above the cameras. It was also safest to not retrieve the drones. The team sent them swimming.

"The luxury car roadblock was easy. Some time ago, Tom Lacey, out technical guru, hacked into the satellite communications program that controls signals between US headquarters, and those cars. This is the link that is used by the panic button in the fancy cars. It automatically calls a tow truck, or mother Mercedes, when there is a problem. Not only is there direct cell phone connection into those vehicles, but there is also an electrical connection within those cars that allows them to run.

"When carmakers got fancy, one of the security features they started building into the vehicles was replacing the ignition key with a computer chip. The computer in the car recognizes the chip in the key, and that begins the ignition process. Not too many folks know that the process can be reversed from a satellite, and the car disabled. The push of a button will send a signal to the car's computer to no longer recognize the chip in the key. The car will no longer run."

When the briefing was over Jeff decided to ride with the trucks back to Urgent, and Stoney would ferry one of the newbies to south center. This would allow for quality time on the river for one with no experience, and allow Jeff to get back to Ellie.

They did agree, though, that he could make a few stops to thank some retired firefighters for their service to the cause.

Ruthie decided it would be safest if she drove the first day since Jeff probably would be treated like royalty and "couldn't buy a beer if he wanted to".

THIRTY – TWO

Finding a house in Urgent was not difficult. A new family of elder prestige was given a home, wherever you wanted it. In the length of time it had taken Emmet Fitzpatrick and his wife to pack and wrap up their Los Angeles connections, their new house was ready.

Emmet had never confessed to her, but it took longer than that for him to make this decision. Tom Lacey had been right. The prospect of moving to FBI HQ was the basis of the offer. He was also right in his assessment of what retirement was like in the D.C. area.

Unbeknownst to his superiors, he had arranged for some interviews with former associates that had retired. After the initial joy of sleeping in, and no Mondays, wore off, each spoke of lack of enthusiasm and a sneaking suspicion of mental degradation. No spark and nothing new.

Fitz made the decision, they were moving. Their success at downsizing meant a manageable load within the moving van, and a short unpacking task. He was ready to work within two weeks of being given the keys to the house. What was not known was the fact that he also had keys to a new office in Washington, DC. An FBI facility in Quantico, Virginia housed the Odd Crimes

Unit. At Fitzpatrick's request, they assigned one of the offices to him.

The series of meetings he first attended on the reservation were the most unusual he could remember. One was on horseback and another in a Jeep, both uncomfortable. Then there was the underground gathering, with wireless connections through headphones. This was beneath some warehouse on the east side of the canyon. The headgear was needed to quiet the noise coming from the cacophony created by the generators and other equipment integral to the hydro-electric power producer they were watching.

His impression of the project changed daily, always towards a greater appreciation of the scale. He learned that the power production unit was ahead of schedule. Outside power companies and other interests were already wanting to talk. Then there was his first meeting with Ruthie.

"You can really do that?" asked Emmet.

"Sure can" she said, "or, I used to be able to. I haven't been in the field for about five years now."

"That timing sounds about right' he said. "But some day, I would like to see you handle one of those drones. I remember one of our lab guys in Washington specifically telling me that he could not figure out how that Mylar got draped on the cell tower."

She smiled then continued, "Do you want to hear about some of the other episodes?"

"By all means."

Ruth and Emmet Fitzpatrick had finally found time to have a get acquainted session. When he assumed responsibility for all security duties, Edward had asked Ruth to bring Emmet up to date. This would include a briefing on their gadgets, systems and operations, both past and present. They were using one of the many empty anterooms on the back side of the mill.

The building was windowless on the side away from the canyon, there was nothing to see outside except wind turbines anyway. There were doors along this stretch of wall every 30 or 40 feet. Inside each was a point of entry into the building. There was a door in each of those rooms that went deeper into the mill, but each was locked. The furnished entry ways all had a couple chairs and a table along one wall with an adjoining counter. He interrupted as she was explaining her history and expertise in electronic gaming: "How many moves per minute?"

"1200."

"And that's possible?

"As I said, it used to be."

"One of my toughest foes is also a citizen of Urgent. You will meet Stretch one of these days. Trust me – he's fast too."

"Who else?" He asked.

"Have you met Courtney?" she asked - he shook his head. "Not a big surprise. She and Bo spend most of their time together. Making up for lost time I think. Anyway, she has a gift of recognition and facial identification that won't quit. There is some technical name for it I'm sure, but I can't remember. Let me tell you, she can pick out faces better than a computer."

"She spotted your cars on the freeway outside Dallas at least five minutes before you even suspected our vehicles. We called in the TrakTore based on her input. You probably never even knew you were that close to us."

"We were totally turned around by that move." he confirmed.

"Speaking of the vehicles – let's go." Ruthie stood up and motioned for him to follow her outside. She offered him the passenger seat in the little electric car and drove them along the back of the mile-long complex. Behind the mill was a nondescript building with sets of roll-up double garage doors. They entered through a centrally located regular door into a warehouse filled with white trucks and vans.

Ruth approached the closest pick-up and opened the drivers' door. Fitz went around to the other side and hopped in. She punched a code into the buttons on the radio and red, indicator lights came on. She then gave him a tour of the features of this truck.

Fitz was briefed on the high-intensity laser lights hidden behind the grill and the spike release mechanism behind the rear mud-flaps. He was impressed when she explained the communication system and flabbergasted when she demonstrated the electro-magnetic pulse. To totally disable anything electric (including a car) within ¼ mile was truly astounding.

The rotating license plate brackets were sort of James Bond-like as was the secure satellite communication. The switches to deactivate the tail and brake lights were old school. Before they moved onto the next vehicle, he asked about the tailgate design of the truck.

"Good eyes." she said. "We have had to raise the bed three inches, and chop the tailgate two inches, to make room for all the batteries and electronics."

They walked towards the back of the cavernous garage to a smaller workshop near the corner of the building. Glancing to his right he noticed a fire truck. He paused, and turned towards the truck, observing that there were no markings to identify to which fire department the ladder truck belonged. Ruthie strolled up to his side and whispered, "Now you know how we lost you in Phoenix."

"No way! I want to see this." She opened the driver's door of the truck, reached for the armrest in the door and flipped it open. A series of three switches were neatly arranged in the well inside the armrest. She told him to push the left switch towards the front of the truck. The sound of an electric motor caused him to step back and look towards the rear of the truck. He noticed the rear of the vehicle, bumper and all, gently swing open. He looked inside: it was a large enough cavity to hold a van.

"The other switches raise and lower the floor inside the rig to make loading easier." she said. "Impressive." They closed the back of the fire engine and turned back towards the shop. Emmet thought to himself, "Now I have most of the pieces that went into that death at the airport in Albuquerque". He let that sink in.

The orientation continued in the small workshop, with more coffee and a snack. He knew about the RailOP and asked for clarification on a few points. Fitz did not even have an inkling about Senator Parmenter in California or two other ops that had never made it out of local jurisdiction.

She continued, "Of course the one big thing that brings it all together is Tom Lacey and his computer, rather his research team. When someone can tell you the probable route the senator will take after lunch, you have a good chance of finding that politician. You know Tom and have seen his set-up. Now you know how it all fits together."

He spoke now: "Ruthie, we need to give some serious consideration to who will replace you, and how many there are. When the emergency executive orders issued by Crockett expire, the dogs will howl. It will be really important for us to be at some of these tables and, within reason, let these guys know we are watching. They can't cry conspiracy out loud – they are in too deep. But they will investigate, and they will be applying pressure on the rule makers."

She walked over to a filing cabinet in the corner and pulled out a clipboard. "Just in case, I make paper copies of important documents." she proceeded to read a list of names. About 12 in all. Three complete four-person crews with just as much talent as her crew had.

"All of these young people are good and dedicated. Most of them are full-fledged residents of Urgent, both Native Americans and many with Deep South heritage. We may be letting in outsiders now to fill certain gaps in expertise, but our security detail is all in-house."

215

"The thing I'm really concerned about" she continued, " is being outnumbered. When Tom starts bringing us targets, we need to have assets ready at various locations, so we can act and move on. There is so much to monitor – does he have the manpower? If our personnel can't cut through the mass confusion, then we will miss something; and one day, something really important."

He thought about that for a moment. "Let's go see Lacey."

They hopped back in the electric car and followed a dirt path that extended away from the mill, into the field of turbines and solar panels. The newly acquired valley was not fully outfitted yet, but the plan was obvious.

There was a pattern of three parallel rows of square concrete foundations. On top of the first platform in each row was a tall, imported wind turbine. Between each row of tower foundations was an array of solar panels, high enough above the ground so man and vehicle could travel beneath them. On the far side of each outside row of platforms was a field of panels twice as wide as those areas between the rows. The visual effect of this expanse was striking. At the base of every other concrete square in the center row was a small concrete shed.

One mile into the farm they stopped at one such shed and got out. Ruth made a five-digit entry into a keypad next to the door, and it opened – elevator like. In fact, it was an elevator.

Beyond the narrow space that provided clearance for people to enter, was another pad on the wall. This one took an iris scan. She looked directly at the pad and pushed another code into another keypad. After a brief, almost silent moment, that door opened. They stepped into the actual elevator. Obviously, the only way to go was down. She pushed the lone button.

The descent ended, the door opened, and the pair entered a large work area, filled with rows of workers sitting at desks in front of computer monitors. Walking past one central line of researchers, they approached a glass-enclosed office with more desks inside. Tom Lacey sat at one desk. He motioned them in and tapped once on his monitor to unlock the door they were about to use.

"What brings you down into the dungeon?" he asked.

After Fitzpatrick suggested they needed to talk, Lacey escorted them into a small glassless adjacent room with a forest scene on one wall and a table that would seat eight. They sat around one end of the large wood surface (Fitz wondered how they got it down there) and expressed their concerns. Tom Lacey just listened for a while.

Their fear of being outnumbered had been one he shared. However, he was now confident in his ability to identify potential trouble. There was little doubt that the surveillance being channeled into Urgent was among the most up to date on the planet, due to the new birds.

Urgent had recently acquired five low-earth orbit satellites, launched under the guise of a big tech company. These resources were now producing, but were they getting too much information? Could they be missing real threats in all the confusion of superfluous data? He activated the large monitor that virtually filled one wall and demonstrated his concerns.

Entering mining as a subject, the display responded with a list of sub-headings on mining with a notation as to other key words. These were representative of conversations picked up by their technology, just in the US. The list continued on five more screens at the rate of 250 per screen. And that represented conversation in the past 48 hours alone.

"Now", Lacey said, "magnify this by at least 50 subjects that we are deeply interested in and you see the scope of the data we should be analyzing."

Fitz asked to see the list, then asked to see the names

of the individuals being monitored. Was there a group or affiliation identity for these people? His analytic mind was processing the sources, not the data itself. He stood and approached the wall.

"Bear with me here. It seems like there is an unfathomable number of individual conversations, but not coming from that many individuals. Could we cross reference the source of each entry to a person and see what we have?" It took a while to enter all inquiries into the super-computer and have the searches arranged as requested.

The result was a shorter list – roughly 5000 individuals.

"Tom, do we have, or can we get, a photo of each of these people?"

"Give me some time."

"Ruth, our face recognition wiz, what did you say her name was?"

"Courtney. Oh, if you want to have real people work with a series of photos; I can get you more people. We have identified all Urgent citizens that have this ability. Where are you going with this?"

"It will be a nasty job, but it might solve our problem. Could we get folks that knew these people of concern by sight, to follow some of them via closed-circuit cameras and analyze the threat at that moment?"

Why not was the unanimous answer.

"Then, after working out the unintended consequences, and other bugs, it may be possible to bring in face recognition software."

Again, why not?

Tom Lacey had his researchers begin to amass the photographic data on the thousands of people in question, not only including politicians that usually obstruct democratic ideas, but their aides and office staff. The lobbying organizations used by these congressional members were also of interest. Those lobbyists visited numerous offices when on Capitol Hill. Those offices were tracked.

Then there were the committees – specifically any rules committee. Short lived or continuing, these groups were targets for corruption, masked as lobbying.

Gathering presentable pictures was not initially easy. The researchers combed through group photos to find subjects and extract the data, then enlarge it. They delved into office computers, personal machines and searched hand-held devices carried by whomever they were investigating.

In the course of this expedition, one of Lacey's staffers mentioned that he knew of a former lobbyist that was a resident of Urgent. They found, and began interviewing, Vern Osburn. It had been a while since Vern had been in the field, but he did reveal what he knew about clandestine meetings, those locations, and how surveillance was countered. This was exciting for Osburn, and he helped immensely.

The Osburns had been useful years ago in the founding of the centers and the organization of the schools. Anne was retired for the second time, now with health issues: her knees had been replaced years ago and needed to be changed out again. Vern had become the house husband and welcomed the opportunity to be useful.

During his first visit to Lacey's underground bunker, Osburn had been awestruck.

"Annie." He related later, "He's got this wall sized computer that you can control with a swipe of your hand and it's so fast there's not even time to sit down and look at the display. The office must be 100 feet underground, but you'd never know it. There's pictures of sunny scenes on the walls and it seems like you're looking out windows."

She was getting tired but knew that his enthusiasm would only let up once he told her all he needed to share.

During the days it took to create the photo library, Ruth had begun conversations with Courtney and Bo.

When Courtney was pregnant, husband Bo Elliott rarely left her side. She was pregnant with their second child. Ruth remembered the first child, born during the grand relocation. What a time to have a kid, she thought.

Leaving the photo ID project to the experts, Fitzpatrick spent most of his time on the surface, attending meetings and/or get-acquainted sessions. He decided on his next step during one morning meeting, held in the more conventional tribal headquarters.

It had been a generation since the land swaps and purchases had created this town. The sovereign nation owned it and had subcontracted with various parties and US agencies. A complicated set of regulations and temporary government entities, created under emergency orders, was about to dissolve.

The State of Emergency declared during the Crockett years had allowed his cabinet to suspend many rules and impose others. As was usually the case with rules, they had a limited life. Many were about to expire. There was a temporary life in these matters, and those limits had been, in a few cases, almost reached. If not monitored, there could be an undoing of a lot that had been done. Fitz understood the stakes.

Green power was not new. Generation stations of this size were unsettling to some. Those protesters had been silenced. Melting and researching steel was a time-honored business, which produced CO_2 in the exhaust gas. Capturing the CO_2, as emergency rules required, was an expensive measure. There were those that wanted the old, wasteful days to return. The Federal emergency rules were insurance against reliving those bygone times:

-- At the expense of larger corporate profits, education was funded better.

-- Dirty mining was suspended in National Parks, which were then funded better.

-- Offshore oil exploration was halted due to the

emergency IRS rules that allowed no tax benefits for exploration without tried and true spill prevention plans.

There was a temporary set of corporate tax rules that had analysts crying foul, but those cries fell on deaf ears. There was no way to appeal during the emergency. That was about to change. Fitz was the first to ask if they had access to a team, or any one person, that could help anticipate the consequences they were about to witness. Sean Crockett's name came up.

The past president had been out of office for two terms, but very much in contact. His security was as tight as always. Only a select few could visit him. Urgent had one of the select in house. The group turned to the Chief who, in turn, asked Marina Whitehorse to make the call. In response, Crockett suggested a train ride.

Fitzpatrick and one other were allowed to join the former President for this session. The suggestion of a train ride was his invitation to meet in the crystal mines. Joseph had thought Edward would be the perfect representative for the family, but Junior thought differently.

He asked Ruth to go. Her intuition, observations and all-out curiosity would allow her to take it all in. She had attributes he was only beginning to value.

Marina got the executive jet and flew to Wyoming to pick up the others. During the flight to Tennessee she had more than ample time to introduce the passengers to each other, and allow them to discuss their concerns. Immediately upon touchdown the jet taxied towards the hanger. It was then that a petite, handsome woman exited the cockpit.

Marina introduced her as Lucille, the owner of the plane and the leader of the party. Lucille blushed at the introduction, announced that her intentions were just to listen, and ushered the group down the folding stairs.

Sean Crockett had the same secret service detail as had been assigned to him while he was in office. At least the head of that team: Mark Madison. Both were retired now, but the unmarried Madison had accepted the executive's offer to live, as well as work, on the property. They were virtually inseparable.

When their limousine arrived at the cave entrance, Mark Madison acknowledged Lucille and Marina, introduced himself to the others, and drove them towards the crystal mines.

Not much was said during the awe-inspiring ride deeper into the cavern. The total darkness, the silence, the occasional glitter of a crystal, all wrapped in a humid ethereal atmosphere presented an almost erotic sensual package.

Once aboard the train, Marina finished the introductions and limited the following small talk. As they began serious conversation, early topics had to do with the success at Urgent, accomplishments within the community. The President agreed that the executive orders he issued years ago did have consequences, but strongly agreed that being offered the chance to do so was the highlight of his administration.

"When you have a system so stuck on the wrong track, you need to derail that train for a bit. In the grand scheme of things, we have only been righting ourselves for minutes. Yet, as you suggest, it has been too long for some of our greedy executives. They are indeed, surrounding us as we speak."

Fitzpatrick took this opportunity to start the questioning the former President.

"Where do you see the biggest challenges?"

Continuing his compliments, Crockett was pleased with the trend of increasing the education budget, yet worried Wall Street would go back to its old ways of high-speed trading. Off-shore banking and money transfers would increase with higher dividends and the super-rich's need to play their avoid-tax games. But

Crockett expressed major concern over the return of money into politics.

"We have had a period of growth for most of America and for many reasons. The average citizen has been helped along during this emergency, as have the rest. As I mentioned, there are many reasons, but one in particular resonates with me: that is the lobbying.

"Since the beginning of our nation, there has been lobbying. In its purest form I see it as a valuable tool. A service for the public. In its present form, however, it serves the rich.

"Not that you can that easily buy your Congressman (there are exceptions) but you can now get a lobbyist into the rule-making process. We have representatives of special interest groups writing the rules that govern those groups. That's not right! I foresee a serious challenge there."

Ruth spoke up at this time, "What about the release of environmental reins?"

"That, young lady, is another one to carefully look at. I'm glad you asked. Before I started screwing things up, as they say, I'm quite certain that big money had found its way into the rule-making process of the Environmental Protection Agency.

The EPA does not let outsiders write and administer their laws. But through a back-door approach there have been some strange findings and alternative facts showing up. That back door is the OIRA. How many know of the Office of Information and Regulatory Affairs?"

No hands went up.

"The Office of Management and Budget has a division few have heard about, the OIRA. Prior to, and after, my terms of office, many executive orders have given this office the authority to review rules the experts have written. As you know rules need to be written so those affected by law or rule changes know what to abide by and what goals they need.

"Some of these rules, as written over the years, have handed the agencies monitoring that rule, unlimited power. The thought was that, since the leader of the agency was appointed, there was too much potential abuse of power. Enter the OIRA – review the rules and send them directly to the President. That's a good theory but talk about abuse of power . . ." he continued.

"During the decade preceding my inauguration, a progressive center did a study on the rule changes suggested by OIRA. They operate too much in secret. The researchers could not get minutes or research copies.

"But this group did a "before and after" analysis of rules put before them. For this they studied EPA rules, specifically the OIRA suggested changes of those rules. Since these folks are required to carry their suggestions directly to the White House, most agencies just rubber stamp the changes OIRA wants. That's a fast track to getting the rule you want without discussion, evidence, or even bipartisanship.

"It had gotten to the point that these folks even changed the scientific evidence that agencies used to support their decisions on rules. It has been proven, but buried, that they proposed changes to some science presented to underpin the rule. They also had been accused of altering technical papers, as presented, so they could reason their suggested changes.

"What leads me to worry about the influence of big business, is the presence of lobbyists in discussions with OIRA. They do need to maintain records of meetings with the public: no specifics, just names and dates. Some recently released records reveal that the OIRA has been known to allow 4 to 6 times as many meetings with those affected by the regulations than meetings with the government. They play better with big, outside money than with those whose paycheck is signed by the same person as theirs. Who are these rule changes benefiting?

"They revise the definition of pollutants, of endangered species, of coal ash: why is that? These guys found the science needed to justify changing rules to eliminate formaldehyde from a list of dangerous chemicals, a list prepared by the National Academy of Science: what's the motive?

"I'd like to see the diplomas on the wall of the top 100 PhD holders in OIRA. Do you think there is one that is in science?"

Emmet noticed the President getting louder and more emotional about this subject. He decided not to interrupt at this time.

"This abuse," Crockett said, "has been without challenge for so long that lately a new tactic has been added to their bag-of-tricks: delay. The original law required that the OIRA complete its review of any rule submitted within 90 days. There could be a 30-day extension announced, but only one.

"We know of sensitive subjects with rules in front of OIRA for review that have gathered dust for three years. There is a game played where the OIRA suggests the agency withdraw an old application, wait a while and ask again. No record appears that way – but what does it matter. OIRA operates in secret.

"Concern over this agency became acted upon in 1993. President Clinton signed an executive order that called for more transparency and the exchange of papers between the agency and OIRA be made public. The order has been signed, but not enforced to this day. Again: why and for whose benefit?"

"The Government Accounting Office did a study a decade later and discovered that there had been no change in secrecy patterns. The GAO recommended that all agencies disclose any changes to their rules that were suggested by the OIRA. There has yet to be such a disclosure.

"No – that's wrong. I do remember a follow up report issued by the GAO eight years later that advised one out of eight transparency recommendations had been issued. I can't re-call who complied."

"If it is big money as you suspect" said Emmet "we have a fox guarding the henhouse situation."

"We sure do." was the reply.

"I'm kinda concerned" Ruth emphasized, "about the recent research on drinking-water affected by fracking. Don't I remember the EPA doing some studies to determine whether there was a direct link between the two?"

"Yes." Fitz interjected, "They were igniting drinking water in Pennsylvania and creating earthquakes in Oklahoma. If you have methane gas in your iced tea, that can't be too good for a body."

Sean Crocket suggested that the lack of publicity in that arena only confirmed his position on the subject of the OIRA. "I don't blame them for all ills, but they deserve a lot of credit for gumming up the works."

The Q & A session with the former chief executive was more than four hours. Lunch consisted of cold cuts brought down from the main house by Mark Madison. Soft drinks and water were in the 'fridge. The harder stuff was evident on the side table. The air inside the mine made it almost too cool for a refreshment from the cold machine. Most chose a little wine to have with their nibbles.

During lunch the conversation turned to the duties and responsibilities Sean Crockett had assumed since leaving office. He admitted to liking the money made on the lecture circuit but took seriously his efforts to keeping up relationships with former colleagues.

"While in office, one learns the machinations of big government, that is not only how things get done, but how slowly that is accomplished. The machine cannot be rushed. But it can be greased to prevent it from stalling out. Learning where to put the grease took me all eight years and I decided long ago to keep those contacts active and informed.

"I need to take this opportunity to thank you folks,

along with some of those previously mentioned cronies for helping to change the government's attitude and funding for emergencies, particularly the distribution of what was defense money into FEMA, the Federal Emergency Management Agency. Those slow, but continuous, changes in funding enabled us to get really close to balancing the books in that agency.

"You may remember that when I took office my predecessor had started stripping money from too many federal agencies. Then we had one year when our national, emergency expectations went way over budget. We had three hurricanes, and each was the most expensive on record. California had wildfires that destroyed communities and later record floods. Elsewhere we had serious droughts in one area and serious hailstorms in another. These were messages, and we acted on them.

"A few years earlier I remember a study coming out of Cambridge University that warned the planet about climate change: particularly global warming. The results indicated that a moderate warming of the earth would cause weather related damage to the tune of $400 trillion dollars. We haven't quite saved that much but we did prepare for emergencies and are not in the hole as much as we could be. And, that study was right. The cost of that three-hurricane year was $300 billion dollars. Since then we have exceeded that catastrophic number four times."

At this point Ruthie noticed him look towards Lucille with an inquisitive eye. She nodded back.

"I just got the OK from Lucy to share the whole story with you. That's a relief. I'm tired of carrying this alone. I can't remember the exact date, but years ago in this very cavern I met with a man whose name you don't need to know. He shared this dream with me and told me that he had two associates that also shared this idea. The basis of the idea was that they were willing to spend all their wealth on saving the planet – well really, just humanity.

"Collectively, the three have a large amount of wealth and agreed that it wouldn't be of much value if we humans were doomed. The fact that we are present, in this mine, at this time means we have partially accomplished our goal. Urgent is built and operational.

" The science behind the earth's best generation station has been proven accurate, and credit is due Lucille and her associates. We have inventions at work that we are responsible for. Not that we thought of them. We made room for them. But our behind-the-scenes work is not done. What we have yet to coordinate is just as complex as our success to date, and just as expensive.

"I'll let the elders at Urgent provide you with details of the future. Just rest assured that I am still in the fight along with you. My continuing relationships with numerous Washington decision makers and leaders, both past and present, is even more important now that certain orders will sunset. We have visited the history behind, and reasons for concern about, some of these agencies.

"I am invisibly on the inside of all these issues. I would venture a guess that one day a week at minimum I am in our nation's capital. More often than that I meet associates at out-of-the way places. We play kind of a spy game – having code names for restaurants in various cities. We know the back doors into some of the fanciest kitchens around and which hotels provide security in their basic construction. Mark has more technology at his fingertips than I ever dreamed of. Plus, he can get vehicles and transportation at a moments' notice, completely untraceable.

"I have been doing this with the help of Lucy and her friends, for more than a decade. I have to admit, I love it. The intrigue and concern keep me young. There is a loved one that gets tired of it, but my mental and physical health is more important to her than she'll admit, as is the future of humanity.

"We are here to meet each other and commit to working even more closely in the future. I can't tell you how important your work is. The public may never know, but our efforts may actually succeed in allowing our species to survive.

"When you got on the train, Mark asked each of you to leave your technology on that side table. He has uploaded my contact information into each of them. You'll find me under <miner>. If any of us is in a situation requiring support of any kind, we have each other to rely on.

"When you get back to Urgent, you may share this message and information with whoever you see fit. The fact that you are in this train is security clearance enough for this group. We trust you not to give out sensitive details without good reason.

"When it comes to the working of Washington, the inside of the machine, and back room deals, call me. If I don't know the answers and/or the players I can find out. If you need financial or logistical support while in the field, call Lucille. Actually, get in touch with Marina and she can determine how to accomplish the mission.

"Well, I think our time is done for today. You have a flight back to Wyoming unless you feel the group wants to spend the night. We have more than enough room and there is some lovely wild turkey in the freezer that I know will feed us all."

Marina spoke, "Thanks Mister President, I think we'll fly back to Urgent. There is a bit more we should discuss before we talk to others, and it would benefit us to hold this conversation soon."

Ruthie took in her surroundings one last time. When she took the executives hand in hers, she held it still, rather than shaking it, and looked into his eyes.

Holding this gaze for at least three seconds, he said: "Edward told me to watch you. I'm glad I did."

The flight back to Urgent was smooth and calm. Most of the passengers slept. Emmet Fitzpatrick, however, was deep in thought. These folks had called on the former President of the United States for a consultation – and received an immediate response. The former agent for that former politician could not help but be impressed. He had met Sean Crockett once, at an agency function in D.C. He had been impressed then too.

Fitzpatrick was also amazed at the management structure, or more correctly, the lack of structure. He could not understand the success of a team that appeared to have no central leader.

There were the money people, but they were not hands-on. The technology being operated by Tom Lacey was a single department but did not fit on any org-chart he could imagine. The former college roommates directed above ground and below ground growth separately, with equal success.

Finally, there was the governing structure of the Native Americans, which he never even tried to unwind. It worked but was all too confusing to the man that had lived leadership via chain-of-command. Suddenly he realized: the extreme importance of the mission was the cohesive agent that worked in absence of formal leadership.

President Crockett had only briefly responded to Emmet's question about money in politics. Fitz knew that the issue was more important than was indicated by that short response. With money beginning to appear in politics again, the system was about to repeat its gradual decline into autocracy. The country's democracy would get diluted because the laws, rules, and rule-of-law would morph into a system that favored the upper class.

That change was inevitable, but Fitzpatrick now understood why the president has glossed over the problem: fixing that was not the mission.

THIRTY - THREE

—. .— — .. ——— —.

Junior was out for a ride to look over the site. Being on horseback allowed him to get to any place and also to take in the air and odors. He had always enjoyed the comforting scent of a horse. With the binoculars, he was just able to make out the equipment working the train tracks. They were in sight of the canyon rim now. Things were coming together.

Above the rim of the canyon the big rigs had been lumbering on a dusty road for way too long. Soon a new, hard surface would be laid for those trucks. Large manufacturing buildings had been built with the material the trucks had delivered. In addition, they had erected the basics of a steel mill in one far structure, closest to the river. But the furnaces would not be turned on until the mill was guaranteed enough steel to melt. Once started, steel mills were never shut down.

In order to build these initial structures, he had negotiated an arrangement with the outfit that made most of the area's railroad tracks. There would be business to benefit both the steel supplier and the Nation when the construction plans were a little farther along. Miles of rail spurs would bring hundreds of cars to Urgent. The future power plant could deliver power to both Urgent and the outside steel mill. The negotiations had not been that difficult, and included towers for a few wind turbines.

On this side of the canyon, he could see the town. Urgent was more than a village now. It took at least an hour to cross it on foot. Growth was solid, and the construction was too. Before long there would be sufficient housing to reassign the first wave of workers. Today, everyone was involved in building but as soon as they were ready to turn on the mill, things would change. It takes manpower to operate a manufacturing plant that large, and to start building wind turbines.

The work at Urgent was better organized than at the centers. At least it seemed that way. To most new citizens, the fact that they had a place to call home was a calming factor. Permanent, private dining and real closets were luxuries at first, making work seem less stressful than in the centers.

In reality the demands were about the same. It's just that their physical conditioning and on-going education was making life easier. Evening gatherings were more about what was going on in the real world and less about how to prepare for what might soon happen. Each resident could see the progress made on the roadway up on the plateau instead of studying how to read topography that would affect road building. More satisfaction came from the hands-on endeavors. The former students were now members of a community.

There was the additional reward of advancement. During the initial stages of training, the possibility of taking on more responsibility brought fear to most recruits. Going into the unknown was a big thing. Just the thought of becoming a leader in that unknown led to many a sleepless night.

Once recruits began living in Urgent and became familiar with the culture, those thoughts changed. For the talented and hard-working, titles changed too. Growth in both size and complexity of the project resulted in specialization and the need for leaders in more diversified areas. There were systems within the system. Temporarily, the education received in this environment was weighted towards building more well-rounded citizens.

Higher education was not within the sights of most young people, nor within the budget. Many citizens wondered how an entire country, like Germany and other European countries, could completely eliminate college tuition while this super-rich United States could not. Some day that needed to change.

The approval was given to build the school when population met meeting minimum requirements for a facility large enough to provide all necessities. When the lid on having children was lifted, the commonly expected wave of babies instead was more a gentle tide.

The arrival of Urgent's newest students did not present a challenge to the new school. Early years of formal education were organized and well planned. Young learners went home for lunch and dinner, as did their parents. When the older generation went back out for classes or meetings in the evening the children were either baby-sat or had their own playtime. The family unit was given priority, as was family health.

Hospital facilities were built after the school. For a few years the medical system was comprised of clinics and visiting doctors. Naturally, victims were airlifted wherever they needed to go, but less traumatic needs were addressed in the clinics.

All aspects of routine care were encouraged. Everyone was given schedules for routine dental, vision, physical exams and family planning. Too few residents had experienced a similar health regimen before moving to Urgent.

To recruits from Appalachia and the deep South this was all new. The health issues brought by the newcomers were systematically resolved. Those that arrived with children were immediately looked after. All health care delivery was equal to, or better than, most could have imagined.

Security for the Nation was divided between two teams. Jeff Foster had the responsibility of fire and logistics, of the homes and the structures on the mill side of the canyon as well. His duties took him deep into the underground layers of the research and fluid control facilities. He was one of the few with complete understandings of the hidden complex. He had plotted, and identified, escape routes for all employees that worked and/or lived beneath the surface.

Emmet Fitzpatrick was responsible for the visible, police-type security, although his unit was not referred to as police. Emmet had always wanted a less onerous name for law enforcement agencies; here was his opportunity to fulfill that wish. After conversations with both leaders and other residents, he realized that consideration needed to be given to all interaction between his staff, all citizens, and even the suspected perpetrator. The Nations Office of Considerations (NOC) was formed.

Naturally, there had been glitches in the pacing of residential growth, but that had been expected. With few exceptions, the recruiting had generated enough new bodies to allow construction to continue apace. The South Center had predictably been the more productive of the two, educating the most new citizens.

National Center, as they called the one sited in the Cheyenne Nation, concentrated on bringing in talented Native Americans from all states. Recruiting in various reservations was more difficult because of the generations of substance abuse that started at too young an age. Finding clean kids old enough to make big decisions was hard.

Some had parents that helped, wanting better for their children than they had. Other young folks were virtual orphans. Experienced counselors on all reservations were on the lookout for recruits. However, progress was being made and that was the most that could be hoped for.

As Edward rode a little higher up the knoll, the ditch started to come into view. At least that is what the workers in Urgent called that hole. The dig for the temperature retention tank was massive. Bigger than anybody expected.

The excavation had been started two years ago after the surveying team flew into the area and laid out their plans. The concrete container would hold such a vast amount of liquid at so extreme a temperature that it needed an insulation void built around it. Junior knew that the plans he was looking at were based on calculations by a special computer program. They had considered how the concrete transmits heat, how the earth retains it, how much temperature the plumbing and wiring should be exposed to, and where to put the people that would be working down there. This resulted in a massive hole.

The actual dimension of the temptank (as they called it) would be about the size of a football field. It held millions of gallons of liquid at extreme temperatures. The necessary insulation void around the tank meant they dig a hole over a football field deep, and two more football fields in all directions. The really deep part was the size of nine square city blocks. Then there were the wings.

Edward knew that the ramps for the trucks and trains if need be, could only be sloped about four degrees. So, the ends of this big crater had gently inclined ramps that ran north and south for about one-half mile or more. They were moving an unreal amount of earth to accomplish this feat.

The plans called for the erection of the collection tower on the edge of the hole, away from the canyon. This put it in the middle of the field of turbines and the solar array. The tunnel that was to carry the heat to the tank from the tower was not as deep as the ditch.

It had to be deep enough, though, to meet the tank 40 or 50 feet underground. Someday there might even be a second tower. Beneath that were the temperature reduction tunnels. The plans called for a labyrinth of pipes deep underground which, in case of an emergency, would carry super-hot liquid and dump the heat from that liquid into the earth.

At this depth, the ground temperature was no more than 55F and could absorb all the heat from the temptank since the liquid would be spread out over such a large area. These pipes could hold the entire contents of the tank. Radiating out from the tank in different directions, but slightly towards the river, were the ditches in which the pipes full of river water would flow. That water was currently being used by two new power stations.

The closest one would power the mill. The other would provide power for the town and other needs. Future plans called for the river water to continue through the small plant and on to the temptank. At that point, the water would pick up heat from the tank and carry it out into the vast maze of cooling pipes. After depositing that heat into the earth, the water would flow back through the second, generation station then into the river. In the future they might sell surplus power to the grid but initially they would keep it all.

The earth being removed to make that hole was changing the landscape. The dusty road used by the eighteen-wheelers was getting wider all the time, as was the railroad bed. Both were raised and being compacted through constant use. One day it would be easy to pave them - just pour concrete.

Junior trotted down over the ridge and stopped for a better look at the working area. He consulted the plans that he had stored on his smart phone. They would need to add some warehouses on the far side of the mill, he thought.

He had learned that when the product started arriving the process would extract precious metals from the ordinary steel and stock-pile the different materials in different locations. Product is what they called carloads of steel, or weapons.

He also glanced in the direction of their small emergency runway down near the river. It was still out of the way but there would come a time when a decision would be made to expand and build a terminal for this one or modernize the old one up on the West plateau. "Make a note to look into runway" he said to the phone.

The subsequent thought brought a smile to his face: this was the exact spot he and Harold Knight had first dreamed about this community, fifteen years ago. It hadn't had a name then let alone any neighborhoods or full-scale public services. Hal had planned experiments and Edward had built structures within which to do the research. Neither had envisioned the need to plan for citizen safety.

In the three years since the NOC was announced there had been a marked improvement in traffic patterns around Urgent, for vehicles and pedestrians. Within view he could see three covered walkways that spanned wide, busy roadways. All were on the far side of the canyon and arched through the space between sizeable buildings surrounding, or part of, the steel mill. He knew that the underground researchers had their own paths to these facilities.

One final thought as he nudged the horse towards the corral, "What did we not foresee?"

THIRTY - FOUR

— •—• •• — ••• —

As the growth of Urgent became known, many business and interest groups wanted to know more. Little was done to keep the community a secret; less was done to publicize any specifics.

It became evident, though, that most of the public took sides. There were those that believed the Native Americans had overstepped, and those that understood the lack of trust of the United States government. To know who was on which side could be an advantage. For this reason, Tom Lacey tasked the young Randall James, a less than seasoned investigator, to review the political leanings of a list of people.

Although not a scientist, Randall had been inspired by Harold Knight and actually found Tom Lacey and applied for the job. "How did he find me?" Lacey often asked himself. He headed no formal business and wasn't listed in any database. To find the front door, let alone knock on it, required some connections: or good research. Tom decided to try James in research, and to test the kid's awareness and ambition.

When James had brought Lacey the political research, Tom asked him to memorize the names of those on the liberal side of the ledger and to concentrate on them

238

during his upcoming trip.

"Uh, what trip boss?" James asked

"We are sending you and Harry Stone on a trip out west to negotiate with our friends at the Port of Longview and at the railroad company. Most of the groundwork has been laid, but we want some faces to see other faces, and see the physical set-up. Follow the route."

"Do I know Harry Stone?"

"I guess not. He's doing some facial recognition work with Marina Whitehorse in the lab connected with the schools. However, he has this ability to multi-task: facial recognition, conversation, manual manipulation – it's amazing. We think he will be an attribute to our field activities and would like you to introduce him to the world west of the Rockies."

"Facial recognition?" Randall inquired.

Tom explained, "There is a unique life-long condition most of us inherit, and it's present from birth: the ability to read a face. We now know that babies can distinguish their mother's face from those of other women just days after birth. We look at faces to judge age, gender, racial background, mood, etc. Well, there are those that excel at this and we would like to find them. By the way, people are better at this than computers.

"After the 2011 riots in London they reviewed 200,000 hours of closed-circuit television to try to ID some of the bad guys. The computer identified one human. Some perceptual psychologists were consulted, and they brought in some humans with recognition superiority. They ID'd 190 suspects.

"As it turns out, the Native Americans have a genetic predisposition to be good at this. Thank-you forefathers." said Lacey. "As a matter of general course, we give all our young people the Cambridge Face Memory Test. This scientific device confirms that right now we have three students in the school that excel in face recognition. Whitehorse wants to know these kids and watch them. She calls them her 'supers'. There may be some scientific name for this super-recognition trait, I can't remember. Marina sees opportunities away from Urgent for their futures. Plus, she has development plans."

Once identified, the young people with the facial recognition ability had been groomed to appreciate their gift and trained to work with others in public. Numerous field trips included practice sessions in public places with teachers in disguise briefly appearing at unusual times. They often practiced on vehicles too.

While never picked out of the class as being exceptional or special, these young people had been nurtured in such a way as to benefit the community. They grew into members of teams that ventured into the field for specific missions. These were not secret trips, nor particularly dangerous. All parents had the option of going along if they wanted.

A few did accompany their children, but soon got bored with the waiting, and tired with the basic comfort: or lack thereof. Sleeping in the van brought back some intentionally forgotten memories for most parents. When word got around how slow and uncomfortable this fieldwork was, the adults lost interest. The kids were, after all practically adults anyway.

In that generation the educators had identified five children that were better than average at facial recognition. Two of them were not interested in fine-tuning their talent, but the other three were now a significant asset to the community. All three had helped in their unique way, to smooth the road from village to town.

As the senior member of that team, Courtney had exhibited mentoring skills far ahead of her years. Too young to be their mother, the younger members did treat her as if she were. She had been in the field with all of them and in practice or real scenarios, her observations and street-smarts were unmatched. She deserved all the respect she received. In one incident, she had maintained contact with a suspect even after he had entered the men's room and changed most of his clothes, including shoes.

"She saw through the glasses, fake eyebrows and hat. The small tear on the cuff of his right pant leg was the convincing mark she recognized." Lacey exclaimed. The conversation then turned to the timing, the transportation, and the security of this upcoming trip. Tom Lacey did not want the travels advertised but felt it unnecessary to use maximum security. By the time folks realized these two were not following the usual routine, they would be back. He arranged for the men to meet Ruthie in the toys warehouse, as she called it. She was to brief them in the attributes of the custom vehicles and check them out on the communications devices. They would take one of the vans – the pick-ups were less secure. Randall left the office.

James and Stoney could not have been less alike. James liked quiet while Stoney could carry on three conversations simultaneously. One was portly, the other slender and strong. Between them they weighed 400 pounds, with Stoney being the heftier of the two by 50 pounds. Randall was Native American; his companion more Cajun-like. Yet with different accents they still understood each other.

A few hours into day one of the drive, Stoney commented that he thought they were being followed. The dark SUV way behind them had been closer a few times while they were forced to reduce speed for one reason or another. He had read the license plate the first time and was certain it was still the same car. They decided to call it in to Fitz at the NOC: Nations Office of Consideration.

He advised them to continue on and he would check on their suspect. A while later they received word that the suspect was, indeed, suspicious but to keep driving. They were further told to stop in a few hours at a specific truck stop near Billings, Montana and meet up with Ruthie in the restaurant. In the interim, she had flown in by helicopter and brought Rosita and Sara along to get some experience and help ID and plant the bug on the suspicious car, after which, they left the fuel stop. The drive to Washington State was scenic and enlightening. Stoney had never seen such mountains or played in the snow on the mountain pass. Since his move to Urgent, he had been impressed by the spectacular view of the Rocky Mountains from the east. Even more impressive was the view from the other side, then sighting 14,000-foot Mt. Rainier, followed by Mt. Hood and the entire Cascade range. Stoney also noticed the trees. The thousands of tall evergreens that were the West's national treasures were also treasured by him. Randall enjoyed his companion's youthful energy and amazement at the expanse of the west.

Each did want to learn how the other arrived in Urgent. While on the road, they had plenty of time to share their personal history. All the while remembering to keep track of the traffic behind them.

Stoney's story about running young folks up the canal from the deep south was embellished with tales of alligators and hiding from detectives. He was forced to be creative and self-sufficient at an early age. He was the child of careless parents: "they could care less." Briefly he went into his skirmish with the law over a joy-ride he took on somebody else's fancy boat.

"I brought it back untouched. So I used a few gallons of diesel. What's the problem?"

Randall's description was equally as captivating. He admitted to being wanted for questioning in a northern state. Not by the tribe, or local police, but by some neighboring extremists. As a youth he thought it might be fun to find out what their story was. He left the South Dakota Badlands and allowed himself to be recruited by one Montana cult.

It soon became obvious that their way of thinking was not something he agreed with. It also became evident that he was not allowed to simply quit. These folks were dangerous. To stay alive, he needed to find another place to live. Through a relative of a friend back home he heard about the building of Urgent.

He came to the village uninvited, and spent a month doing surveillance. "Just walking around and looking. I had enough money to eat on and found some great places to sleep within the industrial commotion near the mill. All the workers were really nice, and one guy suggested I meet Harold Knight, who then suggested I get to work. Someday I will need to tell this story to Lacey."

The initial business portion of the trip went smoothly. The staff at the Port of Longview office openly welcomed them, and was quite curious as to what was about to happen. They were even more curious about the rumors dealing with the purpose of Urgent. Stoney learned that too many folks believed the tale that the Native Americans were going to engulf Wyoming and secede from the United States. Also, they were asked about the degree of truth in the reason for the largest power generation station in the country: Was it really to undercut the white man's electricity and put those companies out of business?

Randall observed that the most intelligent conversation was with those folks that were on the list Tom Lacey provided him. They spoke honestly with those people. They met with one retired Port Commissioner that was still active in local politics. This led to a visit to the Longshoremen's Union office and contact information for extra help if it was ever needed.

The offices of the union were surprisingly secure. Randall asked about the main gate and wire fence. He was told that organized labor often drew the ire of various factions. To protect the members, and some assets, the union paid for the security you see and an unseen video system.

"Does that closed-circuit system sweep the fenceline?" he asked.

"Would you like to see?"

Randall's explanation about their being followed was met with an agreement that it was always a good idea to keep an eye on an adversary. The three men visited a locked room at the end of the hall which contained the equipment for the security system. As they entered, the light from the monitor was sufficient to illuminate the space. On the desk was a split-screen view from four different cameras. The union member used a joy-stick control to pan each camera along the property perimeter, and to switch from split to full screen.

There he was. At the far edge of the property, past the main gate, sat the dark SUV. They verified the license plate number and thanked the local for his time and help. Stoney did not know where he heard it but the phrase "keep your enemies closer" came to mind.

The duo took a side trip to Astoria, Oregon so they could get a feel for that port of entry and dip their toes in the Pacific Ocean. The Columbia River meets the Pacific Ocean at Astoria. The unruly and dangerous Columbia River bar is feared in marine circles as a formidable obstacle.

Smaller vessels need to coordinate their crossing of the bar, with the tidal activity. The large ships that were hauling cargo intended for Urgent would not be bothered by the current and eddies. However, they would be concerned about the channel depth at various times. Stoney was armed with a tide chart and some nautical data revealing ships' dimensions. He wanted to study this information on the way home. This was familiar territory for him. His knowledge of the Mississippi delta around New Orleans helped in his understanding of how this river met the sea.

Two-hours upriver, at freeway speed, is Portland, Oregon. While on the south side of the Columbia, the Port of Portland has quite a presence. The team took a few hours to tour the area and analyze the capability of that port in handling Urgent's cargo.

On Tom Lacey's list was the name of an Assistant Port Director whose affiliations were compatible with those of the Native Americans. The travelers invited the Assistant Director to lunch, and they discussed rail cars and freight. At that point along the river, each side had a set of train-tracks. Conversation revolved around the differences between the Washington tracks and the Oregon tracks. Where did they cross the Columbia, how much train traffic, what types of grades, etc.

After lunch they checked in with Urgent. All along the journey, Fitzpatrick's office kept the duo notified of the whereabouts of their fellow traveler. In response, at each sighting of their shadow, they had notified the NOC folks.

Their instructions were to follow a revised route: cut south through Oregon and on into Boise, Idaho; cross the Grand Canyon of the Snake River near Twin Falls and start climbing into the mountains. Stoney asked if he could visit the Great Salt Lake. He received a negative response, but only because the lake had receded so far in recent years that you could not reach the water. As they approached the Rockies, they decided to send a message to their tail.

Emmet had asked Lacey's researchers to dig deeper. Who was so curious that they followed two young men to the Pacific Coast, and back? Lacey determined that an investigative agency had been hired by a large electric conglomerate in Colorado, to gather information on all things Urgent. This made sense to both Fitz and Lacey. With Nebraska having established their electric co-op, and Urgent appearing able to do the same thing, utilities in the Great Plains were in jeopardy.

Many balanced investment portfolios include a position in an electric utility. Some of these investments even get tax-favored treatment. Therefore, utilities and Wall Street have an interest in any movement that eliminates an investment opportunity, particularly if the change in business model is from private to public entity. A major portion of big-company investment analysts abhor anything public.

They honestly feel that their markets and their expertise are the only way:

-- Social Security should not be public.
-- Medicare should be in their portfolio.
-- The Interstate freeway system should consist of toll roads.
-- Our military should be an all-volunteer mercenary force.

Fitzpatrick did not agree, and he did not like his team being followed. At his request Ruth contacted her people and asked for some help. Sara immediately responded. Looser and Stretch were always on-board for any disruption task. They were all deployed. Ruthless wanted a GasCap.

The team determined the distance between gas stations if the travelers got off the interstate and traveled on state and smaller roads for a couple hundred miles. This route took them north, towards the Grand Tetons, and through a one-station town in Wyoming, called Marbleton.

Like a lemming, the private investigator was faithfully following the white van. As planned, both the van and the shadow vehicle were almost out of gas when they arrived in Marbleton. The van driven by Randall at this time, pulled into the gas station and refueled.

As soon as he drove away the intruder's chase vehicle pulled up to the pumps. The driver thought he would catch up to the van since there was no other place to go, except continue along the only road out of town. One minute into the filling process the pump stopped working.

Between them, the station employee and the car driver could not get the apparatus to pump gas. In a phone call to the station supplier they learned that the closest truck was two hours away, and the repair truck farther off than that. Not wanting to use the land line in the gas station, the disturbed P.I. tried his cell phone. No service. No one in Marbleton would be filling up and/or driving anywhere for a while. The next closest fuel stop was too far away.

Later that night, James and Stoney returned the van to the warehouse – mission accomplished. Ruth and the NOC leader visited the building, to welcome them back. The boys asked about the well-being of their nemesis. Ruthie's impression was that he was fine, but a little perplexed.

She knew from her helicopter trip, that they were dealing with a gas-powered vehicle; she needed a Gas-Cap op. To begin the operation, the night before Stoney and Randall were scheduled to fill up, she had sent in a fuel truck and topped off the station's tanks. She then arranged for her flyers to visit the area early the next morning to fly an AmpedOut on the two cell towers in the neighborhood and fly some mylar to the station's tank vent stacks.

The vent cap cover is a little more elaborate than the cell tower set-up because the vent cap needs to be a real seal. Looser has invented a small version of the little robot similar to the device used on the train brake lines. After covering the vent, the bot tightens the line, breaks and drops to the ground. Voila – the GasCap.

Ruth explained. "After you pump enough fuel from a full tank that has no vent, a vacuum is created inside the tank because of the lowering fluid level. Soon, that vacuum overpowers the pump and fuel stops flowing. No one ever looks at the vents. Even if they did, the mirror-like shine of the mylar only reflects the sky. It's almost invisible."

She was sure the station's lead mechanic would have been called to troubleshoot the fuel delivery system hours later. The mechanic would know the pipes had not been accidentally clogged, but would not know why.

Fitzpatrick called for a debriefing with Tom Lacey who took this opportunity to share his concerns. He knew that Urgent had much more growing to do, and many more advances to enjoy. No breakthroughs should be accidentally shared with the public. He wanted complete control of proprietary rights, and the release of information pertaining to those rights.

His vision was to allow no details to be released through electronic or visual means. Security needed to be beefed up. They agreed on the installation of closed-circuit cameras on all roads leading to the area and wanted electronic surveillance of all local lodging. Lacey reminded Fitz that major business forces would soon be concerned about the growth of Urgent, particularly in the power industry and fossil fuel arenas.

Texas, Oklahoma and the Dakotas all had oil wells. Other states had solar arrays, and some were working on wind turbines. These companies were all for profit businesses, and the nonprofit nature of this activity of the Native Americans on non-American land was of concern. It was something over which the big businesses had no control, at least no legal control.

Tom knew his people would stumble upon other individuals hired to investigate Urgent. As the village grew and the industry became more complicated, more outsiders would be more interested. It was the American way. Gone were the days when a business was considered successful if it made money.

Today those profits need to continue to increase or Wall Street will frown upon the endeavor. Companies can't just make money, they must make more money. Without long range planning and research, which normally lead to continued but slow growth, a business today buys a competitor – or steals its idea.

Yes, Urgent would get more visitors. Tom Lacey as the genius in electronic data-mining and Emmet Fitzpatrick as the head of the NOC pledged to be ready.

THIRTY - FIVE

—— —•• •—•• •• — —• •

The manager of the mill approach Hal. All in Urgent knew they were about to turn the heat on and melt some steel, then make some steel. For days the anticipation was palpable. What an uplifting moment. Years of planning, digging, and building had gone into this project. Hal thanked his fellow worker and asked where they were going to start.

"With the trucks, just to get warmed up, then on to the heavy stuff like tanks and guns." He was pointing at the rail yard, across the canyon, and the lines of flatcars that were loaded with similar pieces of armament. It took binoculars to tell the difference between a line of truck bodies and a line of artillery barrels, but Hal knew what was over there. He had spent hours combing every inch of that complex looking for any irregularity that might interfere with this moment.

It had been one year ago this week that the first ship had pulled into the Port of Longview. Few knew of these arrangements, but the US Navy was unloading at Longview, Washington, a port close to the rail line that led to Urgent. On the Longview docks, three of the large container cranes had been reworked in order to lift heavy, irregular shaped objects. Then this cargo had been strapped onto the train cars and long, thunderous trains started rolling.

A few days after Longview opened, Tom Lacey had been invited to witness the slow-moving trains of product. When the chosen day arrived, he took a helicopter up to see the sights with a wider perspective. From his vantage point Lacey could almost take in the entire 100-car train approaching Urgent from the north. He knew there was also a route being followed for material retrieved near the Atlantic Ocean.

That involved getting into the Gulf of Mexico, unloading near Houston, and then north and west through the Great Plains. The first delivery via that system was months away. Much of that product was actually from military bases in the east and south. That closer material was sort of on-call and would be shipped as needed to fill gaps in delivery of the overseas metal.

The aircraft flew in an arc towards the south. He now had a bird's-eye view of lines of train cars sitting near the steel mill, all neatly loaded with similar cargo. The engineers had decided to process like-kind equipment at the same time. Melting a truck body produces a purer steel if the glass is removed first.

Which is why a team was to work the trucks over, separate the various materials and melt the steel parts. Move on to the next item when the trucks are gone. To Tom, the large recycling operation was also visually pleasing; the majority of cast-off parts were hidden inside warehouses. There was no pile of tires; no dumpster of bumpers. This efficiency appealed to him, as did the physical arrangement of Urgent.

Tom had been watching the town change for a few years. The growth in the village itself was evident. The playground behind the school was not there during his last flight across town. The shopping center on the south side of, what was obviously, the main street was a welcome addition. He knew of the condition that all businesses were owned by the employees: "mental note to ask if that is still the case." The even more impressive view was across the canyon.

Beyond the mill, almost growing out of the rail yard, were wind turbines. Although not densely situated, there was two straight, parallel lines of towers. Many did not even have blades yet. Many more were only partially erected. He knew the difference between the filtering turbines (a secret invention) and the clean looking generators.

Between the rows of towers, where the rail lines curved down onto the plateau, was the solar array, acres of small dark platforms that followed the arc of the sun across the sky. Beyond the far ridge, yet visible from the air, was the field of mirrors. The two unique towers centered midway through that field were glowing, yet they were dark in color. That intense reflection meant a lot of sunlight was being directed at them, a lot of heat was being generated. These tall towers were a hazard to low flying aircraft. FAA maps now carried a warning label for Urgent.

The ground around the solar field was clean and had been leveled after the temptank was buried. Lacey knew that deep beneath that perfect surface were miles of pipe and wire. At his mid-west office near Milwaukee, Tom Lacey had examined the plans for this project numerous times over the years. One aspect that always amazed him was the provision that was made to dissipate heat generated by the numerous processes.

The steel mill, the glass plant, solar electric generation, and a few research activities could all require liquid cooling. Yet they did not want to raise the temperature of the river - at all. In fact, he long ago promised the elders, that would be the case. More than the non-natives, the indigenous peoples honored the river.

No-they revered the river. Water is Life is found in teachings and readings. Activists involved in the nation's long-term best interest invariably raised a few banners quoting: "water is life". Therefore, no cooling with river water. Consulting engineers had devised an elaborate system to share the increased liquid temperature with the earth through a long, heat exchanging plumbing system. He could not see one foot of this system, yet he knew it was there. Well beneath those windmills, and solar panels, and roads, and tracks were pipes and the temptank.

The radio idiot light blinked, and Lacey knew the pilot was getting a message. Through his own headphones he heard the tower relay the fact that they might want to land and get to the mill. The helo headed for the helipad at the north side of the mill. They set down.

Lacey walked over and joined Junior at a podium near the main entrance to the administration building. Next to the building, on what usually was a field covered with weeds and grass, was every electric shuttle bus in the Urgent fleet.

This was a serious collection since there was essentially no private vehicles in Urgent. Shuttles were frequent and free, leaving little need for private transportation.

On the grassy area between the building and the fence guarding the canyon, stood the entire population of Urgent. School and businesses had been closed for the afternoon. The launch of this facility would firmly secure their position as manufacturers in the fast-growing alternative energy field. All were invited to celebrate.

Sure, there were other steel mills that made ingredients for other construction. But the mission of this mill was to develop a material that was lighter and stronger than anything else made.

While the initial production was metal of conventional strength, researchers in the lab were developing alloys with better properties. The goal was to produce a one-component tower that could be lifted into place by a helicopter crane.

It would take two adjacent railroad cars to get it near its destination, and it certainly would carry a wide-load badge on the freeway, but the final install was to be one piece done in one lift. That was the objective. That would be a truly unique accomplishment.

The scientists in the research building were also exploring better electrical conductivity. Future power generation in Urgent would result in more electricity than the town and mill can use. The rest of the state could use that power but getting electricity to those users would not be that easy. The farther these electrons travel, the more are lost in transit. The need to develop more efficient power delivery was always the goal.

Junior stepped up to the podium and tapped on the microphone. There was no resounding sound.

Towards the front of the crowd were Bo Elliott and his younger wife Courtney. How Urgent had changed since they arrived. The growing group had taken a while to recognize Bo's organizational skills. Once he was appreciated and moved from south center to the village, he single-handedly impacted the rate of construction.

Soon after this transfer, some innate sense of inventory and rate of use of components had Bo in the accounting office almost every day. He was concerned about orders and deliveries and confirmed when such items had been delivered. The answer was to put him in charge of the entire process. Thereafter, rarely did he visit the office because construction rarely slowed down.

His marriage to Courtney was one of the first high profile Urgent romances. She had been out on assignment for a few years, and he was building a village. There was a 20-year age difference, but as each matured, so did their relationship. A rumor swirled that Courtney had a fling or two while out west. Nothing serious – nothing lasting. When she decided to stay with Bo in Urgent, she found a job she liked and found she was near the man she loved. They got married.

Also, towards the front of the tangle of people was Harold Knight with Brittany Odom on his arm. There had been more rumors that Hal *knew* his brother's assistant. The two were a shiny, sophisticated looking couple. The younger brother beamed and smiled that affecionate grin.

Junior tapped on the mic again. It worked.

"OK folks. I'm going to get started with a few words before it gets too hot out here. It seems in our design of this place we forgot to plan for shade during our outdoor picnics."

There was a cheerful chuckle among the crowd.

"I think it is very important to acknowledge the effort and dedication every one of you has put into this operation. There are young ones in arms: the future. There are a few seasoned veterans, like myself; even charter members.

"Almost one generation has passed since we started working towards this goal. To thank each of you individually would be one long, boring, sun-burning talk. However, we all know that I won't go any farther without singling out Chief Joseph, my Dad.

"That man had the vision and wisdom and the guts to spend years fighting for this dream. His nation is better off for his leadership. The whole planet is better off too. Behind me is the largest single producer of green power in this country, possibly the world. When this mill starts producing the components needed to build more power generation stations faster, we will also be the most self-contained manufacturing facility around.

"I'm not going to get into some lengthy discussion about the need to address climate change. I'm looking at a sea of intelligence and you all know what we are fighting. If nothing changes, those babes in arms will not be leaving their grandchildren a living breathing ecosystem.

"All this is to save our species." His arms waved around in a complete circle. "My sense of pride in you and for this town is bottomless. There is a core of our citizenry that was born in another country/state. I did not look it up, but thousands of you left the comfort and safety or your birthplace to travel this journey with us. When you took your first step, we were most likely redskins. Now we are brothers.

"Look at what you have accomplished together. This clean, productive, efficient and attractive landscape mirrors your soul.

"There is a tradition out there", he said, pointing way beyond the horizon," to celebrate man's major achievements by inviting famous politicians to come for a visit and speech, and cut a ribbon. You may have noticed we lack heavy duty governors and such today.

"This is your day, not anybody else's. I'm the only one talking and the only one scheduled to address this gathering. We do have some figures in attendance that you might like to chat with, or not. In a few minutes you will find my dad, Tom Lacey and Marina Whitehorse under that white awning. We have given them chairs so they can stay until they have greeted everyone that wanders by and have answered every last question. I'll probably sit over there too.

"Bo Elliott, he's right here in plain sight for a change, was asked by the Chief to do the honor of throwing the switch that will start this mill working. He had a better idea. The first child born in the Urgent medical facility is now seven years old. Bo asked if she could work the switch. We modified it, so she could. Most of you know Bo's family and will agree that Leah is the perfect person for the job. She is the new future. The Urgent first-generation from deep-South immigrants.

"Leah, please." Junior requested.

After the young Leah pushed the big, red button, everyone heard a motor start to whir. Then the emergency plant whistle gave off a series of five short one-second bursts. The whir got louder, and some waves of distortion could soon be seen around the top of the smokestack.

The mill at Urgent was powering up.

THIRTY - SIX

As his reputation grew, Harold Knight visited the major laboratories on all continents. He became welcome in all of them and continued to learn whatever was out there. He was well read in the field, but never wrote. When Urgent made the news as a thriving community, the engineers of the world knew what his team had accomplished. All the scientists knew his research. But the researchers did not know all his science.

A few years into the Urgent project, Hal and Junior had decided to subdivide this mammoth task. The needs on the business side of the canyon with all that technology and all those sub-contracts required constant attention. Hal took on that responsibility.

Junior was in town dealing with housing and schools and airports, as much as Hal was out-of-town. There had been a tradition of meeting every Sunday evening to exchange stories and debrief each other. Each knew what the other's area of responsibility was, but neither got into specifics or personnel.

Edward worked closely with construction workers, architects and those responsible for growing the village. Harold seemed to work with those underground: literally and figuratively. Hal's team of thinkers was getting larger, yet it did not appear larger because they were seldom seen.

When asked about this, he offered that their research kept them in the lab for such long hours that they returned home after others had closed their doors. Junior and the inquiring public accepted this explanation. The truth was, there was under-ground lodging for those that wanted it. A handful of researchers, in fact, had chosen to live in those units and not be housed in town.

One of the many challenges in establishing such an impressive scientific community was integrating them into the residential community. Not that the citizens of Urgent did not welcome newcomers, they did so graciously. Security, however, was the concern of the scientists. To confide in the locals about your job and area of expertise, was to invite misinterpretation at minimum.

Less likely but more troublesome was the rumor mill. Work in the research facility was too sensitive to allow nontruths to become public legend. The risk of a security breach was too great if the scientists socialized too much with the mill workers.

Although the quarters were cramped, there always was a bed in this ever-growing underground community. Those that required full-sized, above-ground housing could end up on a waiting list for a few months. It was normal, though, for a single researcher to give up his house in the village to a couple and move below ground.

Even within the facility itself, there were unique areas blocked off from prying eyes, and ears. Security doors and corridors separated parts of the building. Not everyone knew what everyone else was involved in. All the researchers were aware of that and appreciated this anonymity.

Shortly after the first large modification of the facility, some employees expressed a need for lodgings within the buildings. Two underground dormitories were built: male and female scientists too busy to go home could stay at work. Soon this area proved to be too small and was enlarged. More sophisticated food service was installed: a real kitchen rather than pre-packaged meals. Eventually this resulted in even fewer scientists spending time above ground. The neighbors knew why and honored the absence of these valuable citizens.

The shuttles that ran the neighborhood-to-lab route unloaded below ground on the lab end, and at more than one location. The bus stops were named for the lab supervisor resulting in confusion about the number of stops. As personnel was rotated a newly promoted researcher might have a bus stop named in his or her honor. Those in other areas paid no heed: they just needed to know which stop was theirs.

Emmet Fitzpatrick as boss of the Nation's Office of Consideration (NOC) had added another layer of security: the bus route was periodically changed, and more than one shuttle serviced the facility. This one change in transportation resulted in Emmet's being the only individual in Urgent that knew where everybody worked, and how they got there; and he knew that fact. He had a perfect mental map of the research facilities.

Try as they might, though, it was impossible to mask the growth of the facility. Old timers complained about the length of the shuttle ride, and the dearth of parking on those rare days when they wanted to drive. The constant construction was also a nuisance. Large trucks seemed to always be moving dirt around and interfering with normal traffic patterns. Veteran workers would refer to the area as "big dig two", in honor of the generation that Boston was under construction. It would be nice to have a little quiet.

As the man in charge of security, Emmet Fitzpatrick had become accustomed to quiet days and peaceful nights. He may have only been on the job four years, but there was nothing wrong with slowing down at his age. A vibrating wrist-phone interrupted that peace: Tom Lacey had a story.

On one of the now-few peaceful mornings the bright, young researcher Randall James had knocked on Lacey's door.

"Boss," the youngsters all called him that, "I'm a little concerned about some conversation I have coming out of Chicago." Tom had closed the door and motioned towards the chair in the corner. Randall sat down while Lacey used the matching chair on the other side of the small, corner table.

He listened as the eager under-study shared his thinking. The cell receivers in the downtown waterfront section of Chicago had been on the receiving end of heavy traffic out of the reservation. The computer program had identified key words that could only mean that Urgent was the topic of conversation. Further investigation indicated that rental car availability in Cheyenne has been heavier than usual.

"Just for fun, I have cross-checked the activity at other agencies and locations for this time of year. Casper also has rental car issues."

"Your point being?" Lacey had asked.

"I think we have been getting visitors, and it's continuing."

Urgent was a public place, so visitors were not unusual. Visitors that had been enjoying the sun and outdoors usually arrived by mini-van or motor-home, wanting to see the massive steel mill. There were signs directing them to the road through the wind-farm and past the solar field. Some signs had data, some had diagrams and plans. There were pullout areas for parking.

Only recently had two families pooled their resources and started a fuel/convenience store on the highway intersection. Tom knew they had fought hard with an oil company to get that firm to spin-off an employee owned partnership. There would be no profits paid to big oil, but it did get an exclusive, stating that theirs was the only fuel product delivered to, and with signage on, the reservation for ten years.

The business was in its second year. Therefore the partners did not yet know the true profit picture. However, vehicles with out-of-state plates were constantly stopping for one reason or another. Yes, visitors were welcomed. Visitors in rental cars were unusual. A number of them renting multiple cars at the same time led to questions that needed answers. Tom thought Fitz should know this.

Fitzpatrick knew that Lacey had the technology to track down the individuals listed as the drivers of the rental cars. He also knew that this could take time. All Fitz required was a well-placed inquiry and the local investigators were at work.

Early in its growth, Urgent had been a self-contained community. Little was known about the village, outside the village. That naturally changed as evolution dictated that exchanges with the outside world educated all involved about the ways of the other side. Particularly affected were local shops that wanted a share of Urgent's business: they had to be employee owned to be accepted by the Urgent citizens.

Many national firms spun-off employee-owned branches in order to do business with the Nation. Everyone that worked/owned those firms knew who to thank for this type of business entity. They were thankful and cooperative.

Within 24 hours of placing a few phone calls, Fitzpatrick called Randall James with a list of names to look into. The cooperative clerks at the rental car locations had provided both names and home addresses. Reviewing this list reminded James of the list Tom Lacey gave him when they visited Longview, Washington a few years ago.

In response to today's request, Randall took 24 hours to investigate the rental car transactions and made an appointment with Tom Lacey. "They all come from Wall Street," he confirmed to his boss.

"They took four different flights to get here and rented

four different cars. FYI- they are all booked on flights back to New York and Chicago within the next two days. It looks like some quick, but thorough, research operation. If they are all going home, I'd guess they're done with their investigation."

"It's the bank," his boss said. "The Wyoming Nation bank we recently chartered. Let them investigate all they want. We have nothing to hide and they have a lot to learn – and fear."

"What's the big deal?" asked Randall.

"For us – nothing. For them – a lot.

"When we first established business in the village, we insisted that employee owned businesses got preferential treatment. In order to truly pull that off, we needed to build a bank. While that sounds like some simple operation, it isn't. You need to realize how big the big players are, and how rough they play."

Lacey continued, "The big banks do not want any more competition: particularly from a type of entity that actually returns the profits to citizens rather than shareholders. Our state bank was only the second in the country at the time of its formation. South Dakota was first. What makes our financial workings troublesome to Wall Street is that state banks are owned and operated by depositor/citizens.

"We make the rules, we decide on the operations and transactions, we keep the profit: if any. We are more like a credit union than a full bank but have a for-profit registration. Imagine what would happen on Wall Street if every state in the union had one of us?

"So, in establishing our bank we ran into some trouble. Nothing we couldn't handle but we needed to get tough in order to get this done. I'm sure the big boys thought one little fight would scare us into submission. We have not submitted, and in fact have grown. Have you paid any attention to our financial statements?"

"Uh – not really."

"Well, go look it up." Lacey ordered.

"We have grown every year we have been in business. In fact, a large part of our growth is from outside the Nation. Good people in Sheridan, Cheyenne, Casper have opened accounts with us. The computer makes this easy. We have a reputation, now, of being the place to consult if a business wants to make the transition to employee-owned and everyone knows we strongly encourage that type of business entity. I can't imagine what an impact this has had on the total revenue stream in those cities.

"Not that we have all the money, but I suspect that our growth outpaces the population growth in Wyoming. That means financial dealings in the state are treading water if you do not count our bank. They must have noticed that."

"But we're talking Wyoming," young Randall said, " And only part of it at that."

"That's true, but we are that important. You need to understand the change in banking. Originally, banks were invented to make money and get it into the system. Everyone went to a bank to borrow money.

You wanted a horse 'n buggy, you borrowed some cash from the bank and gave it to the seller in one lump sum. Then you started making regular payments to the bank, with something extra called interest. The bank made money off that loan to you. The bank made money off each of the thousands of loans like yours. That money the bank made was real money. The rest of the cash flow went round and round, from hand to hand. The interest was the money made by the bank. The only new money.

"Fast forward to today. Banks charge fees for a whole bunch of services they provide. Some you and I never use, some we never even heard of. Bounce a check and they charge you a fee. Rent a safe deposit box, get a signature notarized, ask for a paper statement, on and on. Banks make more money from fees than they do from loans. Granted there might be exceptions, but they make more in fees from the under-educated and under-employed.

"If you closely examine their fee structures, they appear to prey on folks in trouble, or close to trouble. So, while our Nation is a small player in the banking community, we have taken a lot of their target customers away from them. Those guys are here to figure out why, and if they can do anything about it. I'm guessing that they need to interview local business owners, citizens and other bankers to determine if they can disrupt our operation in some way."

While Tom Lacey and Randall were deciding that the foreigners were no threat, Emmet Fitzpatrick was on-line with Ruth. The opportunity for some training in fieldwork was just too good to pass up. He asked her to assemble both a seasoned team, and a young one, and meet him at tribal HQ. This old, seldom used building would not be obvious to the visitors. There was parking in back.

Ruth really didn't want to help, but it was an in-town gig and she did owe Fitz some cooperation. She assembled her teams and they met late that night. Since time was tight, she wanted one team member in each hotel to monitor activities in the morning. The complimentary breakfast usually appealed to the visitors and friendly front desk staff would help identify the subjects of the operation. She wanted them observed all day, without any contact being made. Quiet and invisible she ordered.

They piled in her van and drove to the warehouse to get the other vehicles. A pair was assigned to watch the hotel in Cheyenne where the visitors had registered. The other team sent two members to the lodgings in Casper. The less seasoned went to Casper, as it was a less luxurious hotel. Ruth went home for the night.

The teams began reporting activity from both locations by eight the next morning. The Cheyenne suspects had fired up their two rental cars and were heading towards Urgent with two occupants in each car. The team had their pick-up following one while the team van followed the other. Something odd was happening in Casper, though.

At breakfast there were five people at the same table. When advised of this, Ruth decided to join the team and hurriedly took a helicopter ride to Casper to join the team. She caught up with them as the visitors were just finishing breakfast. Two pairs of men jumped into the two rental cars, while the fifth man walked towards a third car, a dark sedan with New York plates. Where did he come from?

Quickly, Ruthie identified herself and told the front desk clerk that she needed a car. Confirming that no rental car agency had a counter, much less cars, at the hotel, the clerk offered her personal vehicle. After getting the key and car identity, Ruth dropped a fifty on the counter and started out the door. "Just in case you need to take a cab." she declared as the automatic door closed behind her.

Carefully pulling into traffic a few cars behind her subject, she allowed herself time to get acquainted with the new ride and to assess her situation. All normal operation assets were in other vehicles – she only had her grab bag/purse. Part of that package had always been a scarf and some sunglasses. She wrapped the scarf around her head, pulled her collar up around her neck, and put on the sunglasses.

At the next traffic-light she pulled up next to the car she was following and looked, not into his car, but into the mirror she had just aligned. His window was down in the early morning temperatures, and she could clearly see all features.

Pretending to talk on the phone, she took his picture. When the light changed, Ruthie turned left, away from the suspect's direction of travel. He was on the road out of town, heading towards Urgent. She knew how to intercept him and continue the surveillance. Ten minutes later she was three cars behind him and on the state highway.

On the outskirts of Urgent, two of those three cars turned off the highway in the direction of the town. Where was this guy going? With only one car between them, she had to back way off. At the bridge leading towards the airport he activated his turn indicator. He's going to the airport she reasoned. There's nothing there of any interest. No scheduled flights, no charter planes in hangers that she knew of. It was time for help.

Emmet answered the phone when the caller ID advised it was Ruth. It was voice activated and always in his ear. "Yeah Sherlock." he kidded.

"I've got an unusual follow going on here. We have an unannounced visitor that I glommed onto at the breakfast meeting in Casper this morning. His car we didn't know about, so I decided to track him from the hotel.

We are on the road heading to our airport and I'm in danger of getting too close. Nothing now between me and him except some room that I'm letting get greater all the time. Can you come out and help?"

"I'll jump in the Jeep and pick him up just before he enters the plateau." Fitz advised. "What's he in?" On the way out of the building he grabbed his high-powered binoculars, a pair of two-way radios and a second pistol. Ruth did not carry a weapon, but she knew how to use one, just in case.

To reach the airport from his office, Fitzpatrick needed to cross the canyon and skirt the north side of the city. The roads were all paved now, so little dust was evident as he topped the ridge south of the airport. Stopping along the side of the road he trained the field glasses on the other road and saw the approach of the dark sedan she had described.

Activating his phone, he told Ruthie to back off and Fitzpatrick proceeded to drive and close the distance between himself and the subject. The airport at Urgent was a minimum-sized, light-security facility. They had

265

filled and graded an ancient erosion channel. It was now wide enough for an access road on each side, plus the runway and one taxiway.

There were no large fences along either road or the taxiway. Knowing he could cross it at numerous places, Emmet kept pace with the dark sedan, but on the other side of the runway. The sedan slowed and turned in at the hanger closest to the two-story airport tower. Keeping the building between himself and personnel in the ground floor office, the driver got out of the car and quickly opened the trunk. Withdrawing a large cardboard box, he carried the box through the back door of the building that, Fitz knew, led to a storage room. Soon the man emerged, jumped into the dark sedan, and drove away: he was empty-handed.

Fitzpatrick fought the urge to immediately find out where that carton had been placed, and what was in it. Instead he calmed himself and slowly began moving in the same direction as, but far from, the suspect. His instincts were spot-on. At the first intersection beyond the airport the dark sedan turned right and headed up the hill above the plateau.

One mile later, still within sight of the airport, the car stopped. The distant stranger got out. This time carrying a small object and a short, collapsible shovel. With this military style tool, he dug a hole and buried the object. Then, he returned to the vehicle and made a U-turn. Emmet got on his phone again to inform Ruthie of these recent activities.

It was not a great surprise when she advised that her other teams had reported similar activity. Objects had been buried that morning in eight different locations, on the other side of the canyon: all around the mill and out into the field.

"I need to meet with everyone ASAP, but not before we know for sure where these folks are spending the night. Tail all of 'em to their beds." He ordered.

"No problem. I've got to get this car back anyway."

266

Driving back to Casper gave her plenty of time to think. She concluded that a few more expert minds needed to be involved. She contacted Stretch and Courtney and asked that they meet her that evening. Coincidentally, Fitzpatrick's de-briefing was being scheduled for the same time. They decided to combine the meetings. After each of the teams gave a quick report, it sounded like all the buried items were identical. Only the cardboard box had not been buried and was significantly larger than the other items. They agreed they should unearth the closest item and proceed from there.

The buried item was an electronic device of some kind. About the size of a large, human fist, it had a short, stout antenna protruding from the top. When buried, this had been the only part visible. Ruth had suspected electronics: hence the invitation to Stretch to attend this meeting.

Top priority now was to investigate the box. They sent Stretch out to the airport along with a member of Jeff Foster's security team. A density and magnetic scan of the box revealed nothing to fear. They brought it back to the group after Stretch insisted they visit the site above the airport that contained one other device.

It was slow, painstaking work, they had to be extremely careful when removing the covering from these mysterious metal marvels. Stretch determined that there was a communication-gathering network that had been planted – literally.

The little bulbs that had been placed in the area could sweep the airwaves around the mill and field. All data was broadcast to the box, which then relayed the content to the device on top of the hill. This broadcast skyward. But to whom, and where?

Stretch said he could find those answers, but they needed to allow the system to be activated first. As of now – nothing was listening or talking to anything. They took detailed notes and hundreds of photos, then proceeded to put it all back.

At the end of the meeting, Ruth took Courtney aside and confided in her. "The odd man out at breakfast, looked vaguely familiar. Would you please look at this photo?" She retrieved her phone and powered up the photo gallery.

"Sure Ruthie." Ruth enlarged the face within the frame and showed the screen to her friend. "That's the guy in the unmarked car that went by us in Texas." Courtney said emphatically.

"WHAT?"

"Remember on my first OP when we were leaving Texas and you needed to call in that TrakTore in Dallas 'cause those blue cars that I called black were driving all around us? The first time one car traveling in our direction went by us I saw the passenger. This guy was in that seat."

"Courtney, I think that could be a guy that worked with Emmet." They looked at each other. Their mutual concern fell aside gradually. Emmet Fitzpatrick had been such an asset in the growth and security of Urgent. He certainly could be trusted.

He was with Ruth when they visited the President in Tennessee. That was a high-security meeting. Crockett trusted him. No option – he needed to be brought into this conversation immediately. As they turned towards Fitz, he was just finishing a conversation of his own.

"Tom was disturbed to hear about our visitors. He told me his first instinct that they were bankers looking for secrets was obviously not right, at least not the bankers part. But the secrets idea still holds.

We need to know!"

THIRTY - SEVEN

— • — • •• — — ••••

Emmet Fitzpatrick said nothing for, what seemed to Courtney like, five minutes. He was obviously in deep thought – looking blankly at the photo on her phone. "I wondered where he had gone." he finally whispered. "Sit down, please. This is going to take some time. I don't know how much has filtered down through the Urgent grapevine, so stop me if you have heard some of this. When I decided to retire from the bureau, there was a promotion opportunity I had been considering. The FBI, just like most large organizations, moves people all around the board. My move, though, was a little more confusing than normal.

"My new job would have been in Washington, DC. Naturally, there were a few agents in line for that job if I chose not to take it. Also, there were some folks that would have advanced when I left the previous position in L.A. This guy, my former assistant, was one of those people. His name is Willard Graham.

"When I turned down the promotion Willy was really upset. He wanted my job a lot. Then, when I retired, he thought his ship had come in. He was on a high for a couple weeks, until Washington announced they were moving an up-n-comer in from bureau HQ.

Our superiors had decided Graham would not be advanced. He quit.

"There was a lot of experience there, and he was a few years too young for early retirement, but he quit anyway. Put all the benefits on hold, forfeited an early retirement package, and just left. He never did stay in touch with me and I didn't try to find him. It all was for the best, really.

"Graham had a personality that was just a bit too rough for leading a large office like L.A. Too gung-ho, as they say. He saw his work more as spy in the field type stuff, than desk work. In fact, he used to write for *Studies in Intelligence*. They even printed his papers a couple times."

"What?" Ruth asked.

"Oh, it's a publication of the CIA that shares ideas, and tales, and book reviews with the intelligence community. Willy liked the spy stuff and would embellish on an idea he had during one of our missions and submit it to *Studies*. When he got carried away it was obviously a few hundred words of fabrication and they would reject that article.

He was able to revise two escapades to the extent that the good guys might have performed as described, and the bad guys might have been that stupid. Those papers were published, and he made sure everyone in the office got a copy."

"But enough history – we need to find out what he's doing here, and on whose behalf. A couple years ago I heard he had set up shop as a PI, but lots of private investigators don't make it that long. I guess he is in it big-time."

Courtney, Ruth and Emmet began the in-depth discussion needed to trace a driver of a rental car back to where that trip started. This would involve Stretch and his electronic expertise, all info they could borrow from the rental car and hotel desks and no small share of Tom Lacey's computer expertise. For his part, Stretch had to wait until the monitoring system was turned on. Willy and his associates had yet to activate the sending device, but they would. To zero in on who was listening to this broadcast would involve a lot of work and a little luck. Stretch began preparations.

Simultaneously, Courtney and Ruth got on the computer and started gathering information from the merchants in various cities. With the names, credit card numbers and state driver license data; they began deciphering a profile of the nine visitors. They added the initial information picked up through Randall James careful eavesdropping.

The overheard conversation surrounding their travels had originated near Chicago. The addresses listed on the rental car documents included homes also near New York City. Employment info was a little sketchy since all indicated they were self-employed: including Willard Graham. "What was a self-employed former FBI agent employed at?" thought Courtney.

Lacey called a meeting, to include Emmet Fitzpatrick and Jeff Foster. He wanted serious minds in on this – he was worried. It was obvious that someone was investigating Urgent - who and why? Equally as obvious was the expense that was involved in sending nine people into the field for a few days. The "someone" had money. Graham did not have those kinds of funds. Who had the money?

Emmet asked that Lacey's computer dig up the names of any registered security or investigative firms with offices near both Chicago and New York. Three names were displayed on the screen. All had more offices than the two specified. It was Jeff that spoke up, "We need to monitor the activities of all three, at all offices. Can we do that Tom?"

Looking over the entire list, Lacey realized that, at most, six major metropolitan areas were represented. The first impression was confusing due to the numerous names of suburbs and smaller, local cities.

However, all large cities have a number of suburbs. Lacey's knowledge of metropolitan geography revealed only a handful of different locales. He could pull together a team to dig into these locations, at least during the day. Any around-the-clock activity would be impossible. From morning until after dinner, though, he could devise a surveillance schedule with his staff and other help.

Before he could answer, Jeff Foster continued, "I know this is a lot of watching, and I have an idea that might help. When we ran that interference operation in Alabama, I had a river pilot named Harry Stone – Stoney to his friends.

This guy can carry on two, at minimum, conversations at the same time. I'm wondering if he can even track more than that? If you want, I can try to locate him via my contacts in the area of the South Center. Although, our retired river "rat" might know all his haunts. Want to give it a try Courtney?"

She knew she would be brought into this assignment. Spending a bunch of time on a boat didn't appeal to her any longer. Before she could gracefully decline, Lacey interjected, "He's here in Urgent. You will find him in Marina's education lab."

"OK." said Fitz, "Let's see if we can assemble a team to figure this out ASAP. I'm thinking we also better get Brian and his technology on this. It has been a while since he and Brittany got personally involved in one of our OP's, but I know she really enjoyed it.

Brian is still a super-techie and attends all the conferences and seminars. Most of the time Brittany plays R.A. and stays in the shadows, even though she is his sister-in-law. We all know, though, that she is as up-to-date as he: not a bad Research Assistant."

"Great idea." Lacey enthusiastically replied: "Besides, I haven't seen either one of them for a couple years."

Lacey formed for a team of actors and coaches that would work this problem to its conclusion. Who, why and where? The complexity of a search of this type would require many meetings at various places. Knowing that all normal methods of communicating could be compromised, they began using code words for locations and meeting briefly in person to pass information. He asked that translations of typical conversations be broadcast in native tongue. Lacey issued each an old-fashioned Citizen's Band radio. These walkie-talkie type units operate on frequencies not monitored by the electronic gadgets buried around Urgent. All conversation in and out of the research labs were to be via landline. The group's behavior was much like a clandestine espionage operation, only in its own hometown.

Brian used his west coast office, albeit carefully. They flew both private and commercial into Seattle and other airports. Rental cars were handled with cash and other-than-real ID. The vehicles belonging to the distraction teams were dusted off and tuned up.

None of the original team members, however, were driving long distances. That chore was left to the younger, less experienced Urgent security personnel. Although now just a vacant warehouse, Tom Lacey's Milwaukee location would also be used. Great pains were taken to undetectably locate, identify and watch the watchers.

After weeks of studying computer screens and listening to chatter over the air, the team was getting an idea of who was monitoring their activity. Lacey then called a meeting of the senior players in this endeavor, to gather at an unusual location: Sean Crockett's summer home on Mount Desert Isle in Maine. Arrivals were coordinated to take a few days and occur, poetically, by land and sea.

THIRTY – EIGHT

···· ··— —— ·· ·—·· ·· — —·——

Emmet Fitzpatrick decided that an offensive operation was in order: directed at Willard Graham. Knowing him as he did, Fitz remembered the ego and the compulsions. His adversary was an intelligent man, but with a couple human weak spots. A plan was forming.

His perfect team would involve getting Courtney Elliott (nee Jones) out of retirement to travel but her two children would not allow that. He remembered that young Sara, from Ruth's team, had energy and intelligence: street smarts. Fitz decided to bring in the confusing personality known as Stoney: Harry Stone.

During one of their infrequent encounters, Bo Elliot had expressed an interest in getting away from the mill. He had performed at the highest level in that mammoth task. Why not, thought Emmet?

They put young Randall James on standby. He was a bit of a geek but Stoney spoke highly of his traits as a traveling companion: "... really observant and analytical." The team retired to the warehouse to gather the necessary supplies and vehicles. Fitz began heating up the computer. He wanted to go too but thought it unwise.

Willard Graham had invested in waterfront property

in Saratoga, New York. He had always enjoyed horse racing, and further enjoyed mingling with beautiful people. It was obvious that his investigative work had been with wealthy clients, for Graham was amassing wealth himself.

Beyond watching horses run, he was obsessive about fast, foreign cars. He had a four-car garage at his Saratoga address, and a storage facility in Watkins Glen, New York, the home of the nation's first, big-league sports car track.

Graham liked to drive in the local races and considered himself better than average. He didn't have lightning reflexes or a fearless driving style. His edge was that he saw everything on or near the track.

He had uncanny visual capabilities and that kept him out of trouble. He always finished a race, albeit not always first. In addition, he lived life that way. Those that knew him said that multi-tasking was an understatement when it came to Willard Graham.

During his normal morning perusal of the headlines of four newspapers and the classifieds in three web-sites he noticed an entry offering an unusual auto for sale in his part of the planet. The listing was for a 1973 Ferrari Dino, a particularly rare automobile. Lately they had been increasing in value at an impressive rate. But beyond the cost, the prestige of owning this car would immediately affect Graham.

The Dino was listed by a private party and scheduled to be available for viewing over the upcoming weekend. A link to a website made for the car confirmed that it would be at a car show on Saturday.

Also, there was a preview on Friday night at the lot of a local car dealer – at Lake Chautauqua – in New York. Graham's wheels started turning.

He had a meeting scheduled for early afternoon on Saturday. His largest client ever had hired him to compile a complete report of the workings of that rogue Indian research facility in Wyoming.

The money people would be in an attorney's office to receive his report for their boss.

Willard knew the machinery he installed was gathering data now and would have more in the next few days. He knew that information was being transferred to his computer in Saratoga. He could pick up the computer and memory stick, then dictate the report while flying into the city. It would be tight getting to that meeting in Manhattan on time, but not impossible. At his disposal were cars, an airplane and a helicopter. If needed he could get clearance to land on the roof of their offices and make a grand entrance. Then fly home much richer, and with a Dino in the garage.

The cost of the car would not be an issue. He began to arrange to have it moved to his warehouse and have himself moved back across the state from Chautauqua to Saratoga, and then to downtown New York City. This would involve a few changes in transport, but the Dino was worth the inconvenience. Of primary importance was that the Ferrari be on the trailer Friday night, and locked up in Watkins Glen by Saturday morning. He wondered if he could speed the process up a bit.

His attempts to e-mail the owner were unsuccessful. No phone number was shown in the listing. He would just need to keep trying. His assumption was that the car was on-route from another location and he would be contacted once they settled down. He decided to finalize a deal for an enclosed trailer car-hauler to meet him Friday afternoon. The actual location of the car-show was Maple Springs, which was only a few minutes' drive from the county airport.

Not knowing the most convenient place to load the Dino, he chose to have the car-hauler wait out-of-sight and out of the way. His computer had the schedule of everything that regularly flew out of Albany County airport, the closest airport to Saratoga and his point of departure for this trip. There was nothing that would fit his tight schedule. He chartered a plane to get to

Lake Chautauqua. The return trip would be from the Elmira-Corning airport. He planned to ride with the Dino to Watkins Glen. From there ELM was the closest place to find a runway.

He chartered another plane for the next morning to get him back home. That Elmira-Saratoga charter flight could not depart until the tower opened at 7:00 AM. In a twin-engine plane he would be in Saratoga in two hours. A car would pick him up, take him home to get the disc with the Wyoming information, and whisk him back to the airport.

The same chartered craft would proceed to New York while he was dictating the report at 15,000 feet. His mind was working at normal speed in arranging all details such as: chauffer, clean clothes, printer on the plane, food in the car, sleep in Manhattan, and bank the money.

Willard's first bit of concern surfaced when he arrived at the car dealer's lot only to find no Ferrari Dino. Unable to get confirmation to the owner that he really was interested, Graham had taken the liberty of arriving unannounced. He was at the dealer's lot, but the car wasn't.

At first, Willard Graham was in doubt as to the instructions he had received. The website for the car dealer had cautioned that the warehouse containing the car collection had no signage. That small, barely readable "Exotic Cars" sign in the window confirmed the no-advertising ethos. Upon closer inspection he did find a live person to speak with and did enter a warehouse loaded with cars. None as exotic as the Dino, but all were far from the average rural, New York ride.

When confronted, the dealer explained that he had just gotten off the phone with the truck driver delivering the Dino. Due to a mechanical issue, they were way behind schedule and would not arrive until midnight. Graham did have the rental car he picked up at the Jamestown-Chautauqua County airport and decided to have a real meal for a change. He followed directions into Jamestown and ate a late dinner. He arrived back at the car lot long before the Dino did. As soon as he saw the car, he knew he would buy it.

At midnight, though, the issue became how to pay for it and safely protect all parties. All obvious options were discussed and, for various reasons, eliminated. An agreement was reached: to have the treasurer of the Chautauqua Institution (a personal friend of the auto dealer) handle the transaction first thing in the morning. In fact, Graham called her, woke her, and received assurance that she would be in the office at 7:00AM.

The driver of the car-hauler was a large, good ol'-boy from the south. He advised he had instructions not to leave the car. He would sleep in the cab of the truck, parked in front of the car lot, under the lights. Graham asked the truck-driver to haul it on into Watkins Glen the next day as soon as the paperwork was finished.

"Nope" he advised. "Gotta head for Cleveland for a noon pick-up, and that'll be tight. Plus, I need to talk with the mechanic in the morning and fix this air-brake issue. Damn car-hauler."

Not a problem, Graham thought to himself, his original arrangements would still stand. He would use the car-hauler standing by at the local airport.

Transportation for the next morning was getting a little confusing. The car dealer advised that they had recently started overdue, all-night road construction on the other side of the lake, near the institution. The crew wrapped up at 8:00 AM, but it usually took them a few minutes to put the equipment away.

The subsequent traffic had been nasty the past couple mornings. There was no telling what would happen on Saturday, but he suggested that the water taxi could get them across the lake, and back to this eastern shore.

It runs every 45 minutes at that hour of the day and stops across the street from his destination.

It was about 20 minutes from this east-side pick-up point to the dock at the institution.

"What institution?" Graham asked.

"Man, you are from outta town." Replied the dealer. "The Chautauqua Institution is the cultural mecca in these parts. Sort of a faith-based, artsy Disneyland. Famous people from all over give lectures and classes and performances to audiences that also come from all over. World class speakers and artists find their way here."

Willard wasn't impressed. This back and forth across the lake sounded like a two- hour round-trip, but it would be productive. By the time he returned the rental car he would have closed the deal on the Ferrari and could direct his airport car-hauler where to pick up the new car. Then they could quickly drive to Watkins Glen. He made a few inquiries, found a motel, and bedded down for the night. Not the Ritz!!

At 6:45, Willard Graham was standing at the dock watching the water taxi putt-putt across the lake. No wonder this short crossing took so long. He had confirmed that the car dealer was up and on the way to the institution. Willard would be there shortly after seven. He was the only passenger, which made for a quick turnaround at that eastern pick-up point.

"Morning" the taxi driver said. "The folks at the institution said this trip's all paid for. They also said to bring you straight across. Got no others waiting at the Mayville stop. I'll drive us right there. You ever drive a boat?"

"What? 'er, nothing this small." replied Graham.

"I usually drive bigger, faster ones. You like to go fast?"

"Yes, but in my race cars. I'm a lot more secure than on the water."

"Race cars? Oh boy. How big is the engine? How do you like Chautauqua?" the driver asked.

Graham did not know how to respond. At about the time he was taking a breath in the midst of his story of getting the Dino, the boat's engine sputtered and quit. The driver tried to restart the engine, but to no avail. He proceeded to look into the fuel tank and announced that they were: "Outta gas. Local kids and their siphons. I'll call the dock."

After a brief conversation on the old-fashioned Citizens Band, all-weather radio, the passenger was told that another boat was on the way. They could see it leaving the institution dock and heading their way. As the rescue boat got closer, Willard could see a beautiful, dark skinned woman at the helm. What an unusual sight in this white, protestant corner of New York. He also could see that she was not looking where she was going, but rather behind her. A closer inspection revealed the object of her focus: the boat was low in the stern.

It had either taken, or was taking, on water. Was it sinking? He called out to her. She shouted back that she was not going to make it. Quick thinking resulted in her tossing a life jacket, and paddle overboard. She swam towards the powerless, but still floating, taxi and was helped on board. The only visible portion of their rescue vessel was a few feet of the pointy end, pointing skyward.

"We are going to salvage that dump and find out what happened to the transom." she shouted.

"It had better not be that plug. I preach that plug to every skipper on the lake."

"Oh," she sheepishly said, "permission to come aboard? No time to waste." she continued "I'm already wet so I'll see if I can grab the bow-line and secure that wreck. Then there's a chance I can salvage the full fuel tank and we can use that to get us all to dry land." Then she dove back into the chilly lake.

"You gotta cell phone?" the taxi driver asked Graham. When he nodded, he was handed a card containing the number of the taxi company and told to call them for a ride when he got to shore. The cell phone did not work.

"Oh, good." The driver said. "Another week-end fix-it project by the local cell company. They scramble to keep up as the tourists come to town. Keep trying. I bet you gotta cell company where you come from."

Saturday morning on Lake Chautauqua is usually peaceful. Young people and their water toys, as well as young adults with expensive watercraft, sleep in and respect lake quiet time. Before 9AM not much attention is paid to the water. This day was no exception. It was close to nine when they were finally able to flag down a boy on a jet ski.

He did not have room for a passenger, so they gave him a message. He scooted off towards Bemus Point, back on the eastern shore: the location of the closest fuel dock. Willard Graham had given him some money to buy gas, and a gas can if necessary. Just get back quickly.

While the youngster was away, the attempts to retrieve the fuel tank from the sunken boat were bearing fruit. The taxi driver had a folding, multi-tool in his craft, which included a screw-driver blade. He had given his fellow driver the tool to use underwater.

The young diver was having difficulty with the underwater visibility, but soon announced she had removed two of the six screws holding one tank onto the side of the boat. Soon, raising her hands in triumph, she broke the surface with a smile on her face.

"Throw me a line."

The men on the boat were pulling the fuel tank up from the depths when they heard the returning jet ski. The young man also had a smile on his face, and a gas can in his lap. Now the stranded travelers had all fuel they needed. It was easier to empty the gas can into the fuel tanks of the floating taxi than to contend with the severed, ragged fuel line from the wreck.

As the taxi driver was filling the tank, the jet ski driver offered: "I'll try to help you tow if you have an extra line."

"What do you mean tow?" asked Graham.

"Well, the guy at the gas dock told me to remind you that you can't leave that hazard floating in the middle of the lake. He said, 'explain to them that they will remove it immediately'."

"Where do we take it?" Willard complained.

"There's no place to haul it at the institution, or on that side of the lake. I'm guessing we go back to the Bemus Point dock and haul it there."

"But that's ...". "Yea, I know." the taxi driver interrupted. "The wind's come up and is blowing us away from Bemus Point. We'd better get started."

They did. With the drag from the partially sunken vessel, and the head-wind fighting them, progress was slow. It was soon obvious that they were at least an hour from their destination.

"We have to figure out a faster way for me to get to shore." Willard complained. He knew there was no more room on the jet ski. The obvious answer was to go get a faster boat that could carry at least two people. To accommodate his wishes the jet ski was dispatched again.

They watched the youngster diminish in size as he approached the far shore. On the return trip he was piloting a small, aluminum rowboat, outfitted with a 25-horsepower outboard motor on the stern. Willard confirmed to the taxi driver that he was going to hold the taxi service to their word in that he would not pay anything for the exciting ride halfway across the lake.

"Get me to the institution ASAP." he barked. The young man mocked a salute and they were off.

All eyes were concentrated on the far shore, the dock at the institution. There was no reason to look back. They did not see the odd taxi driver (Stoney) and the woman rescue-boat pilot (Sara) salvage the partially sunken boat and speed up the tow. The taxi had been carrying a small air pump hidden in the forward locker. The pump was fitted with a hose that neatly slipped into a concealed hole in the bow of the underwater boat. It didn't take much air to correct the almost vertical position of the submerged vessel, since it had a custom-made, air bladder hidden beneath the transom: the back end of the boat. That bow compartment also contained some clean, dry clothes for Sara.

Once pointing a little flatter, the towing got easier and the boat being towed began to self-bail its water back into the lake. That boating group was around the interstate bridge that crosses the lake just south of Bemus Point before the group signing the Dino title had left the treasurer's office at the institution.

After signing, the car dealer had suggested they jump in his car, which was parked in front of the institution offices. He would get them back to the Ferrari and the car-hauler. Willard never looked back towards where the lake group should be.

Earlier in the morning, Graham had driven as close to the dock as he could and carelessly parked just off the dirt road leading to the water's edge. He had seen the signs announcing the big car show scheduled for that day but there was no sign of activity and he knew he would soon return. When he finally did return, his car was nowhere to be seen among the hundreds of vehicles that had gathered for the big, annual car show.

He knew where he left the rented vehicle and saw evidence of the dirt path leading towards the lake. But there was no direct, line of sight along that route. Just a knot of different colored cars. The two men walked among the various shapes of iron and rubber until they found the car that belonged to Willard for the day. He retrieved his luggage and asked the dealer to play chauffeur a little longer.

"No problem."

As they were driving back up the lake to the spot where the Ferrari was waiting, he phoned the car-hauler at the airport and told that driver where to pick up his load for that morning. Willard then contacted the chartered aircraft to ask for a change in itinerary.

"Pick me up at JHW (Jamestown-Chautauqua Airport) ASAP. File a flight plan for ALB (Albany County) as the destination." The charter service advised that more fuel would be needed for that length a flight. Considering refueling time, the plane would not be able to meet him for at least an hour. It was approaching 11:00 when he finished that conversation.

The two car-haulers met, and the Dino was moved from one to the other. He gave the truck driver detailed directions on how to find the garage in Watkins Glen. The auto dealer dropped Graham at the airport. Once there, he explained to the agent where they could retrieve the rental car. He paid the charges related to that service.

While Graham was waiting for his flight, the car dealer (Jeff Foster) returned to his lot and helped the car-hauler driver (Bo Elliot) load and return the unusual cars they had rented from the exhibitors at the car show. They then returned to a company van and met Marina Whitehorse at the restaurant across the highway from the Chautauqua Institution. She expressed pride in her performance as the treasurer of that institution.

At 12:25 the chartered plane touched down and taxied to the waiting passenger. The pilot briefly turned off one engine to load his fare, and they were off. The state of New York is about 350 miles wide. Willard Graham needed to cover 300 of those. After a brief stop, he then needed to fly south, to the city. The afternoon meeting would be late afternoon. Wheels-up to touchdown took over two hours of flying. Graham had left his car at the Albany airport. He broke records getting to his house on the river.

His computer equipment was in his office. As he was in the process of retrieving the drive with the recordings, he noticed the readout indicated only thirteen hours of data. This, he thought to himself, will be plenty of material for his report. The portable printer was loaded into a small suitcase along with the laptop and paper.

He jumped back into the car and sped to the airport. Clearance for this leg of the chartered flight was given to the pilot at 3:45. Estimates were about an hour to touchdown at LaGuardia, depending on traffic. Saturday afternoon traffic was as heavy as usual at this international airport.

Using his personal phone, he made some calls and got a helicopter to meet him at about 4:45. It would be just enough time to conjure up his report. Making sure the security measures of his computer were off, he inserted his ear-piece and activated the machine. After three minutes of meaningless noise he listened to a section that was unique symphony of steel mill mingled with an exercise in texting on a portable device. He began skipping forward in the recording.

He was searching for anything meaningful in the English language but was hearing a foreign language. At the half-way point in the eaves-dropping he jumped to the end. Still nothing. All he had been able to hear, except machinery, he could not understand. The language on the recording was nothing he could translate.

Graham knew the upcoming meeting was a bust. Obviously, there would be no money to take to the bank. Beyond the embarrassment and destruction of his credibility, there was the matter of how financially deep into this effort he was.

The thousands he spent on hiring help to survey the Wyoming location and additional thousands to plant the electronic devices were gone. Furthermore, the manufacturing on those custom listening stations had a price tag of tens of thousands. They were of his design, secretly fabricated to his specifications.

Plus, the cost of the Dino. He was guessing that he was maybe a million dollars backwards in this escapade. Each time he drove that Ferrari, he might not enjoy it so much.

THIRTY - NINE

• •— •—• — •••• •—•• —•—— —

The residents of the island and surrounding community were used to watching black limos drive through the village and onto the island. They knew who owned most of the large, residential compounds, and knew those folks took their privacy seriously. Taxing the rich guys was what maintained the infrastructure on the island. The not-so wealthy benefited from this symbiotic relationship and were willing to stay quiet about the island's social activity.

It was also not unusual to have a couple of seaplanes taxi up to the dock on the lee side of the island. The property was on a sheltered stretch of coastline, partially protected by an island to the west of the main island. After unloading, the aircraft departed to spend some time waiting in more protected surroundings than in the exposed, choppy saltwater of Western Bay.

One by one, the party grew until all guest rooms in the nine-bedroom house were occupied. This was the first time this group of individuals had been in the same location at the same time. Mark Madison, the former President's aide, had been on location when the first guest arrived. All had been asked to bring some provisions. They did not want to alert the island merchants by buying a large supply of groceries. Also, they were all instructed to place any electronic device into the special vault built to shield all signal.

Mark acknowledged the arrival of Ruthie by stating that it was good to see her again. "Quite different surroundings than in some dark mine, isn't it?" He helped her with her luggage and groceries.

She remembered him from the trip to the President's Tennessee home and continued the small talk while he escorted her to her room. She hung up her clothes, unpacked and accepted his invitation to meet him in the kitchen for lunch. She was not surprised when she encountered Crockett and Lucy at the kitchen table beside a short, stocky, well-dressed man. Being introduced to Eduardo confirmed her guess that he was of South American descent. She detected very little accent and noticed how well-spoken he was.

Ruth joined them and listened in on their conversation. She did not feel confident in discussing world affairs with world leaders. Soon, though, they asked her opinion of things more local, and within her sphere of knowledge. She didn't notice when the conversation became more important than her appetite.

"To answer your questions," she offered, "Yes, we did have a mop up operation in the south. As you both know, we primarily staffed Urgent with unwanted citizens from the South and Appalachia. I should say under-valued, not unwanted? These folks were severely exploited for their muscles and lied to when they were about to approach the voting booth.

It took over a generation, but it grew to become an exodus of a few thousand citizens. Finally, some businessmen down there noticed a change in the labor pool, which resulted in an increase in their labor costs. They sent out some spies to find out where their workers had gone. Our response is well known, but only to them and us. The public thinks they had a bad, multiple coincidence traffic day."

"Oh yes. I remember," said Lucille. "You brought Mobile and surrounds to their knees."

"Wasn't that cool?" Ruth cheerfully replied.

"We even went so far as to gently suggest some civic projects, but that was more to tell the locals we appreciate their work than to punish those greedy businessmen. We all know we don't have time for punishment, or even lessons. All these firms will want to do business with Urgent eventually. It will be on our terms and at our prices."

"That's some sophisticated thinking you have there." said President Crockett.

"Thank you, sir. I don't know about the sophistication compliment. I just know that is how I have been taught and how we live life in Urgent. We constantly hear that we don't have time to waste."

"It might interest you to know," Crockett started, "that you are standing in a state that has a history of reinventing itself. Maine has been helping its small businesses through collaboration with community colleges. We have increased the incomes of our poorest workers by nearly 30% in a couple decades. There is also an effort to help employee owned stores, a lot like the emphasis Urgent places in these organizations.

In fact, I think we stole some ideas from Urgent. There is an Independent Retailers Shared Services Cooperative that works with the independent business. There have been no big tax break giveaways to entice big moves into the state."

At this point, Edward entered the room, apologizing for sleeping so long.

"It must be the time zone thing." he said.

Ruth introduced her husband to Lucille and Crockett. He acknowledged that he knew the President by sight, and Lucille by reputation. "When Ruthie returned from your gathering in the crystal mine, she gave me a complete briefing."

"She was just giving us a briefing too." said Lucille

"The creativity your people use to accomplish their missions is enjoyable to share."

"If I may," Ruth interjected, "but we have never been out in the field to have fun and do goofy things. Our missions were well defined and planned. These operations were based on intelligence as good as the agencies have, thanks to your generosity. And I know that the equipment we invented was also thanks to your generosity. But our sole intent has always been to smooth the way for Urgent to grow as needed."

Lucille apologized for her poor choice of words, but Ruth interrupted her mid-sentence. "I know what you meant and I'm not correcting any mis-interpretation. It's just that I look back on the people I hurt and the havoc we created and would like, no <u>need</u>, to go on record saying that it had to be done.

"We did not form that group to resist those people. We don't have time to resist. Our future depends on our ability to get on with saving the species. My beautiful husband has shared stories of the past. The weather, nature, the ground we walk on: all are changing. All are responding to our neglect. You have known this for some time.

"I'm assuming that's why we are all here. I have just begun to connect all the dots and really need to see some results of our efforts other than slowing some stupid senator down."

"You are absolutely right, Ruth." Crockett interjected. "That is precisely why we are here. The latest science reveals that warming in the Arctic is proceeding at a faster pace than previously thought. When we lose all the sea-ice up there we will have a change in ocean temperatures and currents.

Every continent and all marine life will be affected. As I understand it, there is some magic number that our carbon dioxide content should not exceed. Some think we're there: beyond a tipping point to fix problems that are caused by too much CO_2 in our atmosphere. I expect more definitive input from a guest arriving later today. You all know Harold Knight?"

All nodded. The conversation ceased for a few minutes while the guests helped themselves to more coffee and breakfast items. "That's Maine Lobster on the benedict." commented Mark Madison. After breakfast, the table was abandoned and cleared. The guests excused themselves and the kitchen went quiet. They regrouped in the library. The contents of the bookshelves and the decorations on the walls were demanding attention. Obviously, mementos from world travels, or gifts from world leaders.

The arrival of a black limousine attracted the guests to the windows. Steven, the philanthropist, emerged from one side while Harold Knight exited the back door on the other side. Mark Madison greeted the travelers and ushered them into the library.

The President suggested that they return to the library after they unpacked. The vehicle disappeared into a partially hidden outbuilding 200 yards down the gravel driveway from the main house. The driver would be Madison's guest at the cottage he maintained on the campus.

Ruth, again, fell silent. She now stood in the same room with two of the country's richest people. After more small talk, Harold comforted her with the advice that Brittany, his wife, would be arriving later that day: "Probably by boat."

On the other side of the library, Edward broke free from a conversation with Steven and crossed the room to greet his old college friend. Hal and Eddie uncharacteristically hugged each other. The growth of Urgent had kept them so busy they rarely saw each other. Their subsequent catching up took the group into lunchtime.

The ever-growing party fit nicely around the large table. Between a seafood bisque and a never-ending supply of lobster rolls there was little in-depth talking. After the post meal coffee, the more serious topics returned. Hal was asked by the President about the CO_2 numbers and what science revealed about a further increase in that element. He replied:

"Yes, there is a level of carbon dioxide content in our atmosphere that we do not want to exceed. Yes, we are at (and above in some parts of the planet) that level. What excessive greenhouse gas means is that a lot of irreparable harm is being done. Warming the air is one thing. We get storms and heat and unusual weather patterns. Those you have all seen and even experienced. Remember that first five-year drought in California?

"That was publicized as a "one off". Then we had another, worse one. It's not over. The snow pack in the mountains had dwindled and they are making water, using the ocean as a source. They are lucky. When South Africa went dry, they had not even started on any desalinization plants. Remember that crisis?

"On the other side of the world we have the Alps. They too, have a smaller snow pack. That results in less potable water in that part of the planet, but also less snow. Think about the winter sports. Millions have been invested in ski facilities in the Alps.

"It used to be that half of all the world's skiing was done there. At one point that was a multi-billion-dollar industry. Jobs for young people. Training Olympic champions. Imagine what it used to be vs. what it is now. Skiing was a world-wide $44 B dollar industry a generation ago. Look at it today. But the big scare is the food chain. Beginning with the oceans.

"This concerns us not because of the financial impact, although that is tremendous, but because of marine life. Starting in the north, since we need to start somewhere, researchers have looked at ocean temperatures, melting sea ice, and the impact on life within those waters. There is an expected series of events that occur when those cold waters warm.

"We all have heard about some species being forced out of the warming waters while other move in. When the food that supports those transient species doesn't move too, we get starvation and extinctions.

"More troublesome than that is the change in currents. The earth has a couple main systems for moving water. The recirculating of ocean waters is important to replenish nourishment and maintain temperatures. One system is the Atlantic Meridional Overturning Circulation – referred to as the AMOC. This system moves north Atlantic cold water, which is denser, towards the equator and brings the warmer tropical water to the north. Understand that these ocean temperatures drive the weather.

"Without this circulation system, we might encounter really nasty winters in Europe and longer droughts in their summer. Currently the Gulf Stream prevents these drastic weather events in Northern Europe. But without such a current, this part of the northern hemisphere is downstream on the atmospheric jet stream and could really get hammered, consistently, year after year. We have already had a few really bad years in that European corner of the planet.

"There are many bright minds studying this problem today. The earth experienced these conditions thousands of years ago and scientists are trying to determine what happened then. But rest assured, if AMOC totally collapses we will not want to live in that part of the northern hemisphere. It sounds a little too basic, but this system of currents is controlled by sea ice in the Arctic. If all that ice melts we could be in for a weather disaster, in addition to changes in the food chain.

"While we are on the subject of ice melting, we all know that sea-level has risen five inches since we started this project. What you need to know is that science has just confirmed that the rate of rise will be accelerating, since the rate of melt is accelerating.

"Earlier projections were somewhat fundamental, and necessarily optimistic. Yet there comes a point where urgency dictates that we take a closer look at the truth.

We are at that point. Today we have examined how much heat the ocean is storing, and its potential for faster warming. We get satellite measurements on the density of sea ice and glaciers revealing the rate of melt from beneath. We see the movement of atmospheric moisture and its effect on the warming of the planet – particularly the huge deserts and vast drylands.

It's not looking good!"

The group in the dining room all gathered around Hal's laptop as he pulled up a computer simulation of this scenario. They marveled at a few more examples of catastrophic weather possibilities and discussed each at length. Ruth was feeling more welcome now, since none of them (even the super-rich) was not overwhelmed by the art and science in Hal's machine.

Common wisdom was that government response was inadequate and too slow, while big business couldn't seem to take it seriously enough to spend any money on any type of fix. The scientific community had delivered proof of the catastrophic losses resulting from sea-level rise. Yet today, after years of watching the deterioration of weather and life on some parts of the planet, mankind was not united on what to do.

"That's why we're here," said Hal. "We acted on this threat 20 years ago and it looks like we are the only ones ready to act on it today. Let's move to the library and get comfortable. I know others are on the way, but we can bring each other up to speed on the success of our venture."

The intense concentration was disturbed by the entrance of Brittany and Brian Knight. They had indeed been traveling as a research team. The two had arrived by boat and had been met at the dock, and escorted into the house, by Mark Madison. Still wearing their foul-weather gear they exchanged pleasantries and hugs all around the library. Then they excused themselves to stow their suitcases. They joined the party in the library for drinks, snacks and more in-depth conversation about climate change and the known response to these conditions.

The next hour was rapidly spent through the telling of stories and modern history. Sean Crockett shared some of his Washington tales and Hal told the group of his recruiting efforts in the scientific community. Edward was the historian with the data and facts about Urgent. Only the philanthropists remained quiet.

When the conversation turned to goals, Hal had the floor. Science had provided Urgent with the foundation and means to become self-sustaining. He was the one in the room that knew the progress on all fronts, the only one that knew it all. Edward listened as his close friend began to explain the scientific progress. Brian Knight interrupted.

"Before my brother shares his report with you, I want to say something that, actually, is the reason we are in this room. You will find this subject to be germane to Hal's findings, but I think you need these facts first. Most of you know that the grounds near the mill at Urgent were bugged. It was a truly impressive installation, with a repeater/broadcast unit picking up from a dozen or so buried listening devices. We spent over a month figuring it all out, and it is serious enough to call for this gathering.

"We believe Hal's successful recruiting of top, young scientific minds over the past years has raised the curiosity of some powerful people. All indications are that these people have donated to and tried to control the results of the scientific research in many top universities.

"Over the years the brothers have painstakingly donated to engineering and scientific colleges to the extent that their name appears on too many buildings and labs. They have vetted some upper management and influenced hiring and firings at these institutions. In fact, they are part of a growing group that controls a lot of science by dictating what a grant applicant may research.

"In addition, many young graduates interpret those large donations as support for the university. The newly minted scientists willingly go to work in the labs owned by the brothers, often at less than going rate. Most of you know who these people are. We believe their suspicions have caused them to retain a serious big-time investigating firm with instructions to find out where these missing young minds went and what they are doing. The brothers undoubtedly think they paid for these researchers. They feel they own them.

"Let me assure you that this was not an easy project to unmask. Tom Lacey (he'll arrive soon) and his staff have done an incredible job at pulling aside the curtains on numerous stages to get to the true actors. Emmet Fitzpatrick and his crew at NOC have been filling the airwaves with hours of Native American speakers, confusing the issue. To avoid raising more suspicions, we have left the bugging system in place and are taking appropriate measures to make it sound like it is business as usual at the mill, or no business at all.

"Our best take is that their intent is fact-finding at the moment. There was a hint in one conversation about a specific university also wanting to know the route its graduates took. The questions started when these bright minds were not available to the alumni association, nor to the philanthropy staff. We do know that this group can play dirty if they want to, so we're being careful. They have invested loads of money in loads of PhD students, only to have the graduates drop out of the scientific labor pool. They want to know how many we employ.

"In keeping with his cautious instincts, Tom arranged for the slightly humorous timing and modes of our travel to get here. I'm not convinced that we really needed to revert to true spy tactics, but I'm no expert at this. He is."

With the floor opened for questions, the noise level in the room increased and too many voices made for a childlike cacophony. Edward and Ruth retired to a couch on the window side of the room and knowingly watched. The big news was about to be shared.

She had kept the secret since Eddie, as she called him, had told her about a year ago. It could wait a few more minutes. Plus, she had promised Joseph.

FORTY

•—• • •—•• •• •— —••• •—•• •

Progress at Urgent was stable, constant and usually uneventful. Ruth remembered her father-daughter conversation, but not the exact date for that very reason; it was uneventful at the time.

One afternoon, while Edward was tending to the growth of his town, Joseph had dropped in for a chat with Ruth. His intent was to welcome her to the family. Once she shared the news of her pregnancy, he became more intimate. He spoke of the pride in his son's work and leadership. He shared some family history, including his wife's death when Edward's was born, because "...he wanted her to personally share the story with his grandchild – when it was time."

He spoke of the value of the schools in town that his grandchild would get to attend. His admiration of Marina Whitehorse as coordinator of local education was boundless. He told Ruth that he took great pride in the members of the Nation in building the structures, in hiring the teachers and in watching the new students enter the buildings.

"Many mornings over the past years I have purposefully wandered over to the school and watched the students play."

He shared his observation that, at first the school was quite fundamental and the teachers a little green. But the students and faculty grew to know and trust each other. Then the school grew. It soon was necessary to have two schools for different aged students. That allowed for teaching to get more specialized as well.

The work force was specialized. Joseph spoke of the intimate conversation he had when his son confided that the workers under Edward's supervision would be startled to see the maze of labs, offices and sleeping quarters that were below ground. Subterranean needs in Hal's world were as complicated as those in the sunlit streets of Urgent: maybe more so. The rapid increase in population resulted in an accommodating infrastructure that operated outside the norm. These residents did everything a little differently. Even the mail delivery was odd. There were no street addresses.

As he understood, in the world of science, most discoveries and/or serious breakthroughs result in a scientific paper. That written announcement appears in honorable journals and is read by the author's peers. Science tradition dictates that fellow researchers then try to replicate the work described in the paper. It is this way that ideas become experiments and theories become facts.

Individuals that were attracted to Hal's lab, though, just disappeared. Not that they were out of touch or contact. It's just that their research never was made public. The "black hole" of Harold Knight's world became a closely held secret in the materials science community. Everyone knew, but no one talked about, this mystery. The research lab grew over the years. Both above ground and below, there was constant activity indicating the installation of new equipment and the structures needed to house it.

The need to leave the lab to test physical properties was the first to go. Stress tests could be made in-house as could pressure testing. Then the lab progressed to cryogenic testing: cold metal experiments. Hal had explained that the chemical components of the concrete in the temptank offered the curious team the need to get deeper into chemical metallurgy. Chemical properties, and chemical transformations of metals became of interest. And, what happens when this chemistry is placed under extreme pressure, extreme heat, extreme cold?

The alloy field brought an entire team with questions all their own. When a bit of one metal is combined with another metal, what are the resulting properties? Considering that there are over 90 metals in the periodic table of elements, there is an unlimited number of products that might result from combining two or more of these elements, a lifetime of testing for most humans.

"But it will be the next generation's lifetime." They never spoke of the exact number of years Joseph had been alive. Only that his life was much closer to the end than any other point along the timeline.

"Most members of the nation, and citizens of Urgent, have become accustomed to visits by distinguished individuals. Many of these visits have been made by Tom Lacey. He and I have spent hours at various locations discussing history, growing pains, and the future. That man has a unique mind and because of that, my total respect. He has exhibited an honor and trustworthiness befitting a leader of any peoples.

I share this because, if I live long enough, Tom has said he will arrange for the finest send-off any member of this Nation (or any nation) can ever hope for. My son is busy and must raise your family, that is our future. When my time comes, I want you to tell Edward not to worry and/or grieve for me."

Ruthie was brought back to the present because the room got a little quieter. As questions were answered, the noise level returned to a murmur and Harold was able to speak. He explained that the public goal of manufacturing a lightweight, super-strong alloy had been almost reached. The scientists working to make a material substantially lighter than titanium, but less brittle, were done.

"It's a bit technical, but some cross-link nano-technology has enabled us to accomplish just that. The metal we have invented is a lot stronger than aluminum with less flex, so it has better memory. It is stronger than what we thought we could get: easily able to withstand being lifted and set into place as a one-piece tower.

"The workers at the mill are trying to take it one step further. They would like to make an optional component for the tower that is sort of an electricity booster. The goal here is to allow this tower mounted module to increase the speed of electricity as it flows into, then out of the tower. Researchers are having some good fortune blasting an advance hole in the electrical wires and then sending a faster signal through that hole, along the same wire. Never before tried with electricity, the concept is like drafting the car ahead of you.

The leading vehicle is configured to push the wind out of the path of the next vehicle. That second vehicle is more efficient, by a measurable amount, So far, the super high-speed electrons that are paving the way, do lose some of their organizational tracking. We experience data loss. The trade-off is that the signal that follows can carry more data than that which is lost when the original blast was set off. The net signal is not even yet, but our researchers have faith that the next experiment will produce a net gain in signal."

We haven't hit the market with this knowledge. In fact, the whole discovery is under wraps. Our friends in the industry know we are working on an idea to improve electrical transmission but are unaware of our progress. I'm wondering if the announcement of this breakthrough will placate the folks spying on us?" he asked aloud.

"Don't count on it." said Tom Lacey as he entered the room. All had been so intrigued with the progress report that they failed to see another limo pull up in front of the house. "I'll find the room later." said Lacey, "I don't want to miss the good part."

Hal continued, "Well, if Tom's right – we have a decision to make. First, though, I want to remind all of you that you are in this room because you have been, or will be, an important asset to Urgent's mission. We started this project because of the dreams and deep pockets of some enlightened individuals in this room. The mission was simple: do what we could to help mankind survive its mistake in ignoring climate change for so long.

"Throughout the world there are countries that are working quite hard to reduce greenhouse gas emissions. It may be too little, too late but they are doing the best they can. Those small players, and others with no money for technology, are looking to the larger and wealthier nations to act on this crisis. But the United States, as the largest culprit, has not acted as it should. Without our help we believe the entire effort, and mankind, are doomed.

"So, we set a goal, built a city, moved and hired thousands of people. Urgent is appropriately named and has behaved as expected. Our scientists have done what we asked of them. The citizens have adopted their new way of life and adapted to their new surroundings. The earth still has an atmosphere.

There are undoubtedly those that feel our proclamation of making better transmission towers falls short of what a big player should do in this situation. You are absolutely right. The towers and materials science are only a small part of the real plan. Deeper in our thoughts and deep in the mill is a primary goal: we are going to manufacture, build and install a shield for the earth."

The room went silent!

FORTY - ONE

Tom Lacey was the first to speak. "I gotta sit down."

"Hal didn't have time to give me specifics." said Brian, "Please tell us more."

"I need to bring you all up to speed." replied Harold Knight "We have had some developments recently that I have not shared with any of you. I'll try to sum up our activities and progress.

"The idea is quite simple. Since we have man screwing up the planet even though man is trying to fix it – it's a sure bet that we will not solve this climate change problem before it's too late. To put it simply, there is a decade that passes between the cause and effect. So, by the time we think we have fixed it, we will not have. This group has decided to act on its own.

"In this room we have some of the richest folks on earth. They are behind this goal, are funding it, and are helping in ways we can't imagine. In fact, we don't need to. The success of Urgent as a growing community is sufficient evidence of their dedication. As is the rain forest activity, but I'll come back to that.

"At this point I might ask them if they think the money will hold out. We have spent a lot and only recently have started generating income through our generation of steel and power."

Lucille spoke, "We had a conference call on that very subject as we were travelling to this meeting. The answer is yes. Based on the potential of Urgent supporting itself a little better as time goes on, our assets will see us through. We have been told that the next phase will not take as long as this first phase, and that money will be spent at a faster rate. That's still within our budget and allowance for this endeavor. After all, it's a make or break proposition, and we don't like the alternatives if we don't make it."

Harold started: "You all hear Lucille, now listen to this. Under the cover of our research on metals for sale to power companies, we have been working on a strong alloy from which we can construct a large shield. The scientists have two possibles that in testing right now. The manufacturing process will be cutting edge, and totally owned by our people. No material like this has even been publicly hypothesized.

"Through a combination of heat, pressure and amazing metallurgy, we have a lightweight film that can withstand severe tension. We want to be able to pull it and not have it tear. One unusual feature must be if it is penetrated, it will not rip apart. There are proprietary designs at work here, using nano-technology. That's a brief description of the shield material.

"In a lab beneath one wing of the mill is a brilliant group working on the structure to support this material. We have prototypes of frames that can withstand severe hot and cold yet remain flexible. An important aspect of this frame is its strength relative to thickness in one dimension.

"We have a design that involves an accordion fold of this shield to modular dimensions that allow it to fit in a spacecraft. Once released from confinement, though, we need the largest area possible when unfolded. Need I say how elaborate this structure will be? One fact

I can share is that our scientists will be using a material lighter, and stronger, than that which we have announced to the world. No one outside of Urgent even knows we are working on this.

"Our structure will easily snap together with a similar frame, and be able to carry a small, electric current. We are working on materials that allow the current to flow only in one direction. We don't want the system to self-destruct if it's plugged in backwards.

"Deeper under the mill, towards the north end, is an area none of you have ever visited. We are well into the design and build of a launch vehicle. Reusable rockets have been around for some time now. You all know the US companies that contract with the government. Ours will be wholly-owned and for a specific purpose: daily scheduled launches to grow the shield. We figure we will need eight rockets initially.

"Our craft will be smaller, and more nimble than the usual televised version, because we will be carrying a lighter cargo. It's referred to as payload and ours will only haul about as much as an average person. Yet the shield of that weight, when unfolded, will amount to about a mile of area. So, in four launches we cover two miles square, that's two miles on each side of the square. Undoubtedly, these sizes will change as our technology is revised.

"For the sake of our conversation, though, assume we can launch one a day. In 36 missions (one month plus) we have covered six miles square, again – that is six miles in each direction. That equates to almost 20 miles square a year. Do some math, carry that out for a generation, and we will have more than a dot in the sky. That's the objective.

"We know we can't control all the light and heat that is aimed at the planet. Our goal is to shade the poles a bit. If we can prevent even, slow down, the inevitable total loss of sea ice and cold at the poles, mankind might stand a chance.

"Our only hope is to allow those waters to cool down, to allow the jet-stream winds to return to paths and intensity that were usual at the beginning of the century. This should cause the glaciers and ices to stop retreating, hopefully even grow some. I know you have thousands of questions but let me continue with what we have accomplished. When I'm done you will have thousands more.

"Deeper beneath the mill, at the far end of the north runway, we are digging a really deep hole. When we finally pierce the concrete surface, the residents will be aghast at the size and design of our launch channel. Research has revealed that when we contain the launch within a tube for as long as possible, it takes less thrust to get the rocket to altitude.

"In addition, there is less fuel consumed, so less pollution, although, we're really not too worried about that part. The reason we're not worried is that our propellant is not a pollutant. The only thing the atmosphere will absorb is a whole lot of the CO_2 we took out of it earlier. Our final push to get the rockets into space will be compressed CO_2.

"You all know that some of our wind turbines are not generating power but are cleaning the air in the area. These tall bladeless towers, the ones scattered around the solar array and turbine field, have been removing airborne pollutants for some time now. Soon it will be time to put the extracted pollutants to good use by helping power the rockets. The smelting process has produced gasses which we have captured.

"I mentioned that this gas will be used as the final stage push to achieve altitude. The first stage, and majority of thrust, might not be considered thrust at all. We will use a magnetic field to launch the birds."

At this, the guests redirected their gaze to each other, some then raised an eyebrow.

"This is the part that most of you do not know about. We have recently had a breakthrough in our efforts to harness fusion as a source of power for Urgent. Fusion energy is created in a hot and high-pressure environment. There are different ways to contain and control the thermonuclear reaction: one is with a magnetic field designed to hold the hot plasma in place and allow it to burn. We have just run tests on our magnetic field and are good to go.

"Our design calls for a series of magnetic events to launch the rockets. The first will be an electric charge delivered to a magnet at the base of the chamber that repels to start the rocket moving. At the appropriate time, another magnetic field is activated, and directed to an array of three towers erected directly above and surrounding the rocket. This magnetic field then, grabs the rocket and pulls it upward.

"It is equally balanced between three magnetic rails, and the ever-faster chain of magnetic impulses pulls the rocket faster. When the top of the tall tower is reached by the bottom part of the space vehicle, the final magnetic push is powered by the full delivery of our thermonuclear capability. The rocket will have reached escape velocity and will coast through earth's atmosphere. However, it is carrying a large tank of compressed CO_2 that can provide additional thrust for maneuvering or stability nudges.

"I have to admit, we're a little concerned about the noise all this might make. Those studies are going on now. I thought we had the launch chambers far enough away from the residents, but the town has grown towards them. We may need to erect sound barriers along the edge of the canyon. We'll see.

"One final chapter to this story, and that's the cots. The imaginative team involved in this project couldn't continue to call them carbon dioxide powered robots, so the acronym for CO_2 – COT- is now used. They will be robots, and they will be powered by compressed carbon dioxide. Now you know why each launch will have a tank aboard.

"In outer space, propulsion systems are particularly tricky. There is some old law about one action having an equal and opposite reaction. Imagine those reactions when there is no gravity or friction. The need we have is for something to be able to carefully fly around the shield and snap the pieces together. Our solution is a robot. Actually, a team of robots waiting in space.

"Obviously, this will be quite complicated and intricate, but I can simplify the activities a bit. When the payload is unloaded, we need helping hands to move it into position and unfold it. Any self-furling (if you will) shield section would dedicate too much room to the equipment needed to make it unfold. Let's have the COTs do that. The section needs to be snapped into place. The COTs again. And finally, the entire shield needs to be yanked around space in order to keep our orbiting planet on the dark side of the shield.

"We have a team of robotic engineers doing the design work in one of our labs. They have built sophisticated dexterity into these small devices and are currently fine-tuning the communications between the COTs and all other parties, even contact with the man in central command while he's up there.

"Yep, we will need to start this building process with some human at the controls and in the neighborhood for a while. Our small space station will be the nucleus of the shield and the hotel for man or woman.

"Oops, I think I misspoke. That wasn't the last subject – the space station is. We have a great, efficient design on the drawing board. This involves our buying a launch from one of the US companies. We will need to include a human in this trip too. We will be able to add to the capabilities and services later without man, but the first trip to set it up, turn it on and program the computer will require a human. No idea who – yet."

The questions came fast and furious. Even the philanthropists were unusually inquisitive.

How could they have that much research going on

below ground?

How long until we can relax security and secrecy?

Where will the rockets land?

Tom Lacey brought the group back to reality with an observation pertaining to the reason for this meeting: the bugging of the mill.

"If you will follow a thought with me, I think I see where our opponents concern is grounded. Hal just outlined a collection of research projects that, by their nature, are top heavy with scientists.

"Metallurgy, rocketry, hydraulics, nuclear physics, aviation, environmental engineering, computer science, chemistry, electronics, systems engineering, and atmospheric science to name a few. We have picked the brightest graduates in these fields that seem psychologically fit for the secrecy and working ethos of Urgent. That's a hell of a lotta talent.

"We have some really rich friends that want to know what we're doing. I doubt if our light-weight tower story is going to calm them down. So how much do we allow them to discover? Or how much do we tell the public which will negate the need for a portion of the espionage. Please give these questions some thought.

"While you are deliberating these issues, I need to add one more to your plate: deforestation. And, Marina needs to take over here."

"Nine or ten years ago" she started "we realized that in spite of Urgent's rapid growth, it wasn't enough. Our three philanthropists again met to discuss their main concerns. Deforestation surfaced as number one, with water issues being a close second. While it may be possible to combine these in specific locations, they agreed to concentrate on the forests, and also agreed they needed some help. Allow me to introduce Eduardo, our fourth philanthropist. His area of concern will be forests of South America, to begin with.

"During the next few days, each of you will have an opportunity to discuss hot topics with Eduardo, or any other person here. For now, I just wanted you to know that we have jump-started a massive reforestation effort in and around the Amazon.

"Eduardo and Harold have found the brains, the manpower and the initiative to build a HQ campus in Brazil. Through connections with the government, he has delivered manpower in the form of high-school and college students getting credit for working in the Amazon. I know he will want to speak with some of you about your education programs and methods of rewards. In the interim, we need to think about the information release of this program also.

"Have no doubts, as soon as we announce our plans and goals, we will get visits from cities, states, even nations. The bundle of new technology we just discussed will pique the interest of both business and government. We need a game plan to coordinate our response to the profit-making industry and the other ones."

"Hell." Brian interjected, "We need a game plan for our citizens. For years the grapevine in Urgent has been ripe with speculation on what was happening in the areas that are off limits. What accomplishments and truths can we share with our workers and families?"

They finally returned to the dining room to eat, but the questions never ceased. Even Mark Madison entered the conversation, asking what the drivers under his care could be told. The answer: nothing yet.

After dessert, the questions died down. The long-term thinking began. The brightest minds engaged in this project were on the same wave length. The scientific, moral and legal concerns were brought to the table and, one by one, put to rest. The group now had a mantra, second to "we don't have time":

"Prepare to launch."

URGENT STATE